THE ENEMY WITHIN

THE ENEMY WITHIN

A Chief Inspector Woodend Mystery

Sally Spencer

Severn House Large Print
London & New York

This first large print edition published in Great Britain 2004 by
SEVERN HOUSE LARGE PRINT BOOKS LTD of
9-15 High Street, Sutton, Surrey, SM1 1DF.
First world regular print edition published 2003 by
Severn House Publishers, London and New York.
This first large print edition published in the USA 2004 by
SEVERN HOUSE PUBLISHERS INC., of
595 Madison Avenue, New York, NY 10022.

British Library Cataloguing in Publication Data

Spencer, Sally, 1949 -
    The enemy within. - Large print ed. - (A Chief Inspector Woodend mystery)
    1. Woodend, Charlie (Fictitious character) - Fiction
    2. Police - England - Fiction
    3. Detective and mystery stories
    4. Large type books
    I. Title
    823.9'14 [F]

    ISBN 0-7278-7363-6

Printed and bound in Great Britain by
MPG Books Ltd, Bodmin, Cornwall.

For Luis de Avendaño –
good friend and webmaster extraordinaire

A Note on Bonfire Night

Though in these safety-conscious days Bonfire Night is no longer quite the important event it used to be, in my childhood it was still regarded as a pretty big thing. What made it so special was that it stood out from Christmas and Easter in one hugely significant way. The latter two events were *supposed* to be for children, but were *in fact* organized by adults. Bonfire Night was ours. It would not have happened without us – and we knew it even then.

Preparations for the night began some weeks before. Once the site had been selected – and most sites, as evidenced by the charcoal circles permanently burnt into the ground, were used year after year – the kids began to collect the material they needed for their bonfire. Some of it was cut down from nearby woods (conservation was not such a big deal back then!); some of it collected from friends and family. The resulting structure, which could be anything up to thirty feet high, was a mishmash of things. Tree branches would protrude out of tea chests; doors from old garden sheds would balance precariously on top of discarded armchairs. And crowning the whole improbable structure would be the guy – a dummy dressed in old clothes, stuffed with balled-up newspaper and wearing a hideous cardboard mask.

But, to misquote a famous phrase from *Butch Cassidy and the Sundance Kid*, who was this guy? His name was Guido (Guy) Fawkes, and in the ten years preceding 1605, he had served as a mercenary in the King of Spain's army in the Netherlands. He returned to England to find the old place much changed. When he had left, the throne had been occupied by Elizabeth I, a monarch who, in the interests of domestic peace, had been willing to turn a partially blind eye to the practice of Roman Catholicism. The new king, James I, a dour Scot, was much less inclined to tolerate what he regarded as the Papal heresy, and for the first time in over a decade, Fawkes found himself unable to follow his religion openly.

He was not alone in his dismay, and was soon recruited into a conspiracy of like-minded Catholics. The main problem, they decided, was the king himself. If he could be assassinated, a more amenable monarch might take his place.

Once the plot had been articulated, the means of carrying it out became obvious.

The king intended to open the new session of the Houses of Parliament on November 5th. It would be an ideal opportunity to kill him.

This would not be as difficult as it might at first appear. As incredible as this may seem to the modern reader, it was then possible to rent cellars under Parliament. This the conspirators did, packing it with enough barrels of gunpowder to blow the building sky high. Since there was virtually no security in those days, the plot would have stood a good chance of succeeding, had not one of the conspirators written to a friend to advise him not to attend Parliament that day. The friend became suspicious and handed the letter over to the authorities. The cellars were searched, and Guy Fawkes arrested.

He was tortured until he revealed the names of his fellow conspirators, then sentenced to death. Since his crime was treason, he was hung, drawn and quartered – a particularly barbarous form of execution in which he was cut from the gallows alive, had his intestines and genitals removed (a process he was made to watch) and then was sliced into four roughly equal parts. Several of his fellow conspirators suffered the same fate – and to the delight of countless generations of children to follow, Bonfire Night was born.

November the First

The means may be bloody
But where is our choice?
We must do what's needed
To silence the voice.

One

It had all seemed so easy when they'd watched it played out on the screen at the Saturday morning pictures. Sitting on the edge of their seats, the ice-lollies in their hands largely ignored, they had thrilled as the blackened-faced commandos reached the edge of the clearing and dropped to the ground. They'd gawped – wide-eyed and hardly daring to breathe – as their heroes wriggled rapidly on their bellies across the stretch of land which separated them from the barbed-wire fence guarded by the jack-booted men with the duelling scars.

'Don't get caught!' they'd mouthed silently. 'Don't get caught!'

The suspense had been intolerable but – thankfully – short-lived. Even before the first sticky stream of melted ice-lolly had begun to run down the boys' hands, the commandos on the screen had risen to their feet again, and the Germans who might have raised the alarm lay dead.

What a thrill! What an adventure!

Real life, it was now becoming clear to

13

them, was not like that at all. The black boot polish they had daubed liberally on their faces was starting to itch. The tea cosies they had borrowed from home did not fit as tightly as the soldiers' woollen caps had done, and so kept falling off their heads. But far worse than either of these things was the discovery that crawling along like a commando could hurt – could *really* hurt!

The ground, already hardened by the early winter frosts, scraped mercilessly against their bare knees. Their progress, unlike that of commandos, was slow. Their lungs afire, they looked up, convinced they must have almost reached their target. Instead they saw that the wigwam shape, looming up against the dark early winter sky, seemed to be even further away from them than when they had started. And if all that were not enough, the petrol cans were not only difficult to drag along with them, but noisy, too.

Though neither was prepared to admit that he was the weaker of the pair, both suddenly found that they needed to stop crawling.

'Why don't we just stand up, an' *walk* across to the bonfire?' the older of the two gasped.

'What if it's guarded?' replied the younger, in a panic.

The elder rubbed his right knee, convinced that it was bleeding. 'There won't be no guards at this time of night.'

'But you said there would be,' the younger one protested.

'I know, but—'

'That's what you told the others. You said it'd be dangerous.'

'I didn't really mean—'

'An' that was why we should be the ones to do it – 'cos we're the bravest members of the gang.'

'I know what I said,' the older one growled.

And he'd meant it – in the camp!

Back there, surrounded by broken furniture and old tyres, it had been perfectly reasonable to see the pair of them as Gregory Peck and Anthony Quinn – scaling the cliffs of Navarone, planting the explosives to destroy all the enemy cannons. Out here, however – on this piece of cold, hard waste ground – he was finding it harder to sustain the illusion.

'So what are we goin' to do?' the younger one asked. 'Have we to call it off?'

The older one gave the prospect his very serious consideration.

No! he decided.

It was tempting, but it wasn't possible. He'd bragged to the others – perhaps a little too much, now he considered it – about what they were going to do. To call it off would mean a tremendous loss of face, and might even cost him his position as chief of the gang. Besides, if they retreated along the same route by which they'd arrived, that would involve more crawling. And he was *tired* of crawling.

'There won't be no guards,' he said firmly. 'They'll be at home – havin' their tea or watchin' the telly.'

'You can't be sure of that,' his partner hissed hysterically.

'I will be in a minute,' the older one said, rising stiffly – and apprehensively – to his feet.

He glanced quickly and nervously around him, half expecting that bigger boys – thirteen- or maybe even *fourteen*-year-olds – would suddenly appear from behind the huge stack of wood.

Nothing! Had it not been for the distant hum of traffic, and sound of the London express clanking into Whitebridge railway station, they could almost have convinced themselves they were all alone in the world.

'I told you they wouldn't be here,' the older boy said, his tone suggesting just a little contempt for his companion's earlier fear.

The younger boy stood up. 'So what do we do now?' he asked.

'We do what we come here to do in the first place,' his leader said impatiently.

Crouched low, they quickly made their way towards their target. They were almost there when the younger boy stumbled forward, lost his grip on his petrol can, and landed heavily on the ground.

'What the bloody hell do you think you're doin'?' the older one demanded.

His friend groaned. 'I think I've broken me leg,' he sobbed. 'I can feel the bone pokin' through.'

The older boy knelt down and ran his hand up and down the leg.

'You big cry-baby,' he said when he had finished his tactile inspection. 'Get up! There's nothin' wrong with you.'

'I've broken me leg!'

'Do you want me to go back an' tell the rest of the gang you're a sissy?'

'No, but—'

'Then get up.'

The younger boy climbed slowly to his feet. The pain, he discovered, was not as bad as he'd first thought, but even so, he was buggered if he was going to admit that now.

'What made you fall over, anyway?' the older boy asked.

The younger boy bent down and picked up something from the ground. 'A shoe!' he said. 'A lady's shoe. It looks nearly new.'

'Throw it away.'

'But it might be worth somethin'.'

'Only if you happen to know some one-legged woman who you could sell it to.'

The younger boy flipped the shoe over his shoulder and retrieved his petrol can.

Now that they were no longer pretending

to be commandos, it took them only seconds to reach their target. The older boy uncapped his jerrycan, and began to slurp petrol over the side of the bonfire. The younger boy did not follow his example. He had other ideas. Anybody who knew anything about bonfire building was well aware that however big the particular bonfire grew, there was always a hollow section at its core – a hollow section packed with the stuff which would actually start the fire. And what *kind* of stuff was it, usually? Old clothes, cardboard boxes, newspaper – and comics!

And comics!

It was more than possible, he reasoned, that there were already comics in there. Comics he'd never read. It would be a shame to burn them with the rest of the bonfire.

He reached into his pocket, and pulled out the flashlight his granddad had given him for his birthday.

'What the bloody hell are you doin' now?' the older boy demanded.

'Nothin'.'

'Pour your bloody petrol over the bonfire, like you're supposed to!'

Ignoring his friend, the younger boy squatted down and shone the flashlight into the hollow. 'I've found the other shoe,' he said.

'You what?'

'Remember that lady's shoe I fell over? Well, I've found the other one. An' ... an' ...

I think I'm goin' to be sick.'

'What's the matter?'

'The ... the shoe...' the younger boy gasped. 'It's still got the lady's foot inside it!'

Two

A virgin copy of the Shostokovich Jazz Suites lay submissively on the record player turntable, ready for its first encounter with the gramophone needle. A box of expensive Belgian chocolates sat on the coffee table in expectation of a frenzied attack. In the fridge, a bottle of Polish vodka was chilling nicely. And judging by the sound coming from the bathroom, the tub was already half full of steaming water. It was the perfect recipe for the quiet night at home which Monika Paniatowski had been promising herself for some time.

And then the phone rang.

Paniatowski made a grab for the receiver, and listened intently while the duty sergeant on the other end of the line fed her the details of the report which had just come in.

'So the body was found under the bonfire on Mad Jack's Field,' she said, when the

19

sergeant had finished. 'Is foul play suspected?'

'It's a pretty odd place to die of *natural* causes,' the sergeant pointed out.

Indeed it was, Paniatowski agreed silently. 'You've dispatched all available patrol units to the scene, have you?' she asked.

'First thing I did. There should be quite a crowd already there by the time you arrive.'

'And Mr Woodend?'

'He's been contacted. But since he lives in the back of beyond, there's no tellin' when he might get there.'

Paniatowski tried to summon up the healthy outrage which the disruption of her plans seemed to call for.

It wouldn't come.

And why should it have, she asked herself?

After all, who in their right mind would savour a night of solitary self-indulgence, when the alternative was to drive out into the dark night and share what would probably turn out to be a particularly grisly murder?

Paniatowski remembered Mad Jack's Field from her childhood. Back then it had been surrounded by houses on all four sides. Now, though there were still houses on three sides, a new industrial estate had grown up on the fourth, and it was along the feeder road built for the estate that she made her approach to the scene of the crime.

Strictly speaking, Mad Jack's was not really a field at all, she thought as she pulled her six-year-old MGA round one of the new road islands. True, in defence of its status, it could be pointed out that there was indeed grass growing on Mad Jack's Field – but given the amount of rain with which God punished Lancashire, grass would grow on anything which was not actually continually on the move. Besides, as well as its grass and nettles it also boasted an abundant crop of half-buried house bricks, glass bottles and discarded cobblestones. So it was not so much in a state of *being* anything, but should rather be regarded as once having *been* (the site of an old brewery) and as eventually to *become* (an extension of the new industrial estate).

'Did I really just think that?' she wondered aloud, as she used her free hand to pull a cigarette from the packet on her dashboard. 'Did I actually let that thought pass through my mind?'

Being, been – and eventually to become!

Christ, she was sounding just like Charlie Woodend in one of his more philosophical moments. In fact, now she considered it, the longer she worked with Cloggin'-it Charlie, the more she was starting to sound like him in all sorts of ways. Which was not necessarily a bad thing, she supposed – as long

21

you were also willing to accept that promotion wasn't important to you, and that pissing off superiors was a natural function of any decent working bobby.

She reached a second roundabout on the new road, and saw Mad Jack's Field up ahead of her. A number of official vehicles had already arrived on the scene, and instead of parking parallel to the pavement – as they would normally have done – were positioned at ninety degrees to it, so that their backsides stuck out into the road almost as far as the white centre line.

Paniatowski nodded her approval at this clumsy arrangement. Mobile floodlights would have been better, of course, but since such modern equipment was considered a frivolity by the quill-pushers who controlled expenditure in the Mid Lancs Constabulary, car headlights shining on to the field would serve almost as well – until, of course, their batteries went flat.

Paniatowski parked in a free slot. For a moment her hand hesitated over the dashboard, then she switched off both the engine and the lights. Enough car batteries were already being sacrificed in the interests of justice, she decided. The MGA, on this occasion, could be spared the humiliation.

A young constable, standing on guard duty, watched Paniatowski climb out of the car.

Nice legs on the sergeant, he thought. Very nice legs. Nice face too. Her blonde hair was lovely, and so were her green eyes. Her Slavic nose was perhaps a little too large for Lancashire tastes, but he'd have tolerated it – if he'd ever been given the chance.

'Evening, Clive,' Paniatowski said. 'Mr Woodend here?'

The eyes were blue, not green, the constable corrected himself. Piercing blue. Somehow, they managed to both allure him and to scare him off.

'I asked you if Mr Woodend was here,' Paniatowski repeated.

The constable coughed awkwardly. 'Sorry. I was miles away for a minute. No, he's not turned up yet, Sarge.'

Paniatowski stepped off the pavement and started to cross the field. The constable continued to follow her with his eyes. Nice narrow waist, he thought. Breasts which, without being over-large, would give you something to hang on to. True, she was much older than he was – possibly even pushing thirty – but that was no reason why she shouldn't feature in his guilty fantasies the next time he locked the bathroom door securely behind him.

Two more uniformed constables were standing on guard in front of the bonfire, one of them two feet to the left of the central hollow, the other two feet to the right.

23

Sticking out of the hollow itself was a rounded female bottom wrapped in a brightly coloured sari.

'Who the hell's that?' Paniatowski demanded.

'Dr Shastri, Sarge,' one of the constables replied.

'Dr Shastri? The new police surgeon? Are you sure?'

'That's what her credentials say.'

Now there was a real turn up for the books! Paniatowski thought. It had seemed incredible enough when the brass had appointed an Asian to the post. That the Asian in question was also a woman was little short of a miracle.

The doctor seemed absorbed in her work. Paniatowski lit up a cigarette, then turned her attention back to the constable.

'Who found the body, Walter?' she asked.

The constable pointed. A little way away from the bonfire was a small group made up of a fourth constable, a man and a woman, and two boys of ten or eleven. The couple had chosen to position themselves some distance from the boys. They held their bodies as stiff as statues, but their eyes were taking in the scene with all the interest of keen television viewers who had unexpectedly found themselves dropped into the middle of an episode of *Z Cars*. The boys, in contrast, looked more worried than intrigued.

24

They were finding it hard to stay on one spot, and but for the presence of so many uniformed policemen they would undoubtedly have legged it long ago.

Paniatowski drew on her cigarette, and walked over to the group.

The man was wearing a thick duffel coat with the hood up, and had a prominent Adam's apple. The eyes behind his thick glasses glared at Paniatowski, as if he resented the fact that she had freedom of movement while he was confined to one spot.

'What happened?' Paniatowski asked.

'If you don't mind, I'd prefer to keep that to myself until a detective finally deigns to turn up,' the man said.

Paniatowski produced her warrant card again. 'I am a detective.'

'Are you sure?' the man asked.

'Can you read?' Paniatowski countered.

The man examined the warrant card in exaggerated detail. He was probably some kind of clerk, Paniatowski decided – the kind who wore a blue blazer with the top pocket stuffed with ballpoint pens.

'Well, I never,' the man said, having completed his examination.

Paniatowski sighed audibly. 'You were going to tell me what happened,' she reminded the man in the duffel coat.

'Oh aye. So I was. Well, we were takin' a short cut across the field, the missus an' me.

Weren't we, love?'

The woman, her hair in curlers under her headscarf, nodded.

'Anyway, we come across these two nippers,' the man continued. 'Screamin' their heads off, they were. Well, we calmed them down a bit, and then they told us about the body. Once we were sure they weren't just taking the mickey, I told my missus to go and ring the police. I thought I'd better stay here myself – sort of on guard, like.'

'You seem to have behaved quite properly and responsibly, sir,' Paniatowski said, not at all surprised when a beam of complacent pride came to the man's face. 'Have you already given your name and address to this officer?'

'Yes, I have.'

'Then you might as well go home.'

'Just like that?' the man asked.

What was he expecting? Paniatowski wondered.

A medal?

Or did he perhaps think that his initial involvement entitled him to a grandstand view of the rest of the case?

'We really don't need you any more, sir,' she said.

'Humph, it's a wonder anybody bothers to do their duty,' the man said. 'Come on, Mabel, let's be gettin' home.'

Paniatowski waited until the couple had

26

gone – the man storming off, the woman following meekly in his wake – then she knelt down so that her eyes were at the same level as those of the two boys.

Two frightened, blackened faces stared back at her. She ran her index finger down the larger boy's cheek, and some of the blacking came off on it.

'I didn't know we had any commandos in Whitebridge,' she said, looking at the tip of her finger. 'Would you like to tell me what you were doing here? On some kind of mission, were you?'

'We ... we was just cuttin' across the field, like that man was,' the older boy said.

'No, you weren't,' Paniatowski contradicted him. 'If you were just taking a shortcut, you wouldn't have gone right up to the bonfire and found the body. Is the bonfire yours?'

'No.'

'Then whose is it?'

'The Stott Street Gang's.'

'It stinks of petrol,' Paniatowski said. 'Did you notice that?'

'No,' both boys said quickly.

'Funny, it was the first thing that struck me. *Why* do you suppose it smells of petrol?'

'Don't know,' the older boy said.

'You don't like the Stott Street Gang very much, do you?' Paniatowski asked, gently.

'They always make fun of our bonfire,' the

younger boy said in a rush. 'An' that's not fair. Theirs is bigger, but that's only 'cos they're older.'

Paniatowski gave him the sort of smile that one underdog reserves for another. 'And you thought that if theirs just happened to burn down, so close to Bonfire Night, they'd never be able to rebuild it in time. Is that right?'

'No ... we...'

'Where did you get the petrol from?'

'My dad's garage,' the younger one mumbled.

'You could have killed yourselves,' Paniatowski said. She turned to the constable. 'Make sure their parents find out about what they'd be doing, will you, Ted?'

The constable nodded. 'Oh, I will, Sarge. You can bank on that. I've got two holy terrors of my own at home, an' if they'd been up to anythin' like this, I'd tan their arses so they couldn't sit down for a week.'

Paniatowski wheeled round and walked back towards the bonfire. It was a crazy thing the boys had being planning to do, she thought – and she hadn't been joking when she'd said they could have been killed. She hoped that the parents would give the kids such a bollocking that they'd never hear the word 'petrol' again without wetting themselves.

That said, she felt a grudging admiration for the kids' spirit.

The police surgeon had apparently completed her initial examination, and was standing beside the bonfire waiting to be questioned. She was younger than Paniatowski had expected, and – in the sergeant's opinion – far prettier than any woman outside Hollywood had the right to be.

They shook hands, then Paniatowski said, 'What can you tell me?'

'The victim's probably in her late forties,' Dr Shastri said. 'I'd guess that she's been dead for less than two hours, though I'll have a clearer idea when I've got her on the slab.'

'Cause of death?'

'Her throat's been cut. It's a very neat slash, inflicted from behind. I'd say that the knife was extremely sharp, and the killer certainly seemed to know what he was doing.'

'So you'd guess he's killed before?'

'I would not be prepared to go that far. He could just have been lucky. Or perhaps he's been practising on dummies.'

'But you don't really believe either of those things, do you?

'You are quite right, of course. It looks like the work of a professional.' Dr Shastri smiled, to reveal a set of small, regular, pearl-white teeth. 'As my old professor of anatomy in Bombay would have said, in this business you can't really call yourself a proper butcher until you've had the experience of working with some real meat.'

29

'By the cringe, but it's a rare thing in these days of everybody standin' on their dignity to hear a sawbones like you bein' poetical,' said a deep voice just behind them. 'I think we're goin' to enjoy workin' together.'

Three

The police surgeon and the detective sergeant turned their heads. Standing just behind was a man dressed in a hairy sports jacket. He was a big man in every way. His head was large; his facial features looked as if they might have been blasted out of a mountainside. His heavy torso was supported by trunk-like legs and feet clad in size ten boots. He was the sort of man who caused little old ladies to take a tighter grip on their handbags, until, that was, they noticed his benign expression.

Paniatowski positioned herself between the doctor and the new arrival. 'Dr Shastri, I'd like you to meet Chief Inspector Woodend,' she said. 'Chief Inspector Woodend, this is Dr Shastri.'

'A very nice introduction, Monika,' Woodend told her. 'The court chamberlain could not have done it better.'

'Thank you, sir,'

'Call me Charlie,' he told the doctor as he shook her small delicate hand in his large paw.

'Charlie it will be,' Dr Shastri replied, smiling. 'And you must call me—'

'I'll call you "Doc",' Woodend interrupted her. 'We always call the police surgeon "Doc". So you think our killer knows his onions, do you?'

'I beg your pardon?'

'Sorry, lass, that's probably not a term they use much in medical school. What I meant was, you think that he's – at the very least – a gifted amateur?'

Dr Shastri nodded. 'Yes, I would have to say that he was.'

From somewhere close by came the unexpected sound of a tinny mechanical bell.

'What the hell was that?' Woodend asked.

'Sounded to me like an alarm clock,' Paniatowski replied.

'An' where is it?'

'Inside the bonfire?'

There had been the smell of smoke in the air before the clock went off – smoke from the countless cigarettes which were being puffed at all over Mad Jack's Field; smoke which the wind carried from the shift-work factories on the edge of town and the rows of terraced houses whose owners still stuck stubbornly to using solid fuel. But this

31

smoke had an entirely different taste to it.

It was *wood* smoke! Woodend thought. More than that – it was the kind of wood smoke which is thrown out as the flames lick persuasively around branches which have, as yet, refused to co-operate with the conflagration.

The Chief Inspector had only just completed his analysis when there was a loud 'whoosh', and one side of the bonfire burst into bright, dazzling flame.

The sudden heat – cutting through the chill November air – pricked against the skin of everyone close enough to feel the effect. The roar of the flames – and already it *was* a roar – filled their ears like the warning of an angry lion.

The flames spread rapidly, greedily devouring the petrol that the older of the boys had thrown on the bonfire earlier. Twigs inside the inferno crackled. Thicker timbers groaned their resistance. Bright red sparks were already dancing above the apex of the bonfire to form a glowing halo.

In the distance, a woman screamed. Somewhat closer, a panicked man shouted that someone should call the fire brigade. No one had expected this. No one knew what was really going on.

Dr Shastri was still close to the blaze, Woodend noted – far too close for a woman who was dressed from head to foot in the kind of loose, flammable material that flames thrive on.

The Chief Inspector took a step nearer the doctor, grabbed her arms in his powerful hands, and swung her clear of the fire as if she weighed no more than a doll. Once he'd placed her on the ground again, Woodend turned quickly back to the bonfire. The flames had spread rapidly, so that now they formed a fiery canopy over the hollowed-out middle. It could only be a few seconds – at the very most – before bits of flaming wood began falling on the corpse which was still lying there.

Paniatowski had seen the same danger as he had, and was kneeling down in order to do something about it.

Woodend pulled her back from the flames. 'Leave the body to me!' he shouted.

'But, sir...!'

'Get all these other silly buggers safely out of the way!'

Woodend moved closer to the fire, and sank down on to one knee. He tried to see straight ahead, but the intense heat and smoke made normal vision impossible. His hands groped blindly in front of him, and the right one brushed against what could only be the dead woman's ankle.

He knew that, to make the cleanest job possible of pulling the dead woman clear, he should probably locate her other ankle with his free hand, but his brain – which was registering the fact that his eyeballs felt as if they were frying – counselled speed over elegance.

Wrapping his thick fingers firmly around the ankle he already had hold of, he took a step backward.

The dead body wouldn't move! The bloody thing was snagging against something!

He was tempted to take a deep breath before trying again, but the only effect of that would be to draw even more of the sodding smoke straight into his bloodstream.

His cheeks felt on fire now, and he could smell cooking meat which he hoped wasn't him. Behind him he could hear a distorted voice – it sounded like Paniatowski's – screaming that he should come away. He ignored it. One more pull, he told himself – one last big effort on his part – and he would have the corpse free of the inferno.

It came away with such ease this time that, for a moment, he almost lost his balance. He swayed, and in the second or so it took him to readjust his weight, the fiery arch collapsed into the hollow.

The bonfire swayed dangerously, then a part of it began to topple forwards. Woodend dragged the corpse clear of this new danger – but not before the blonde, curly hair which topped the victim's head had caught on fire.

Paniatowski was suddenly by his side, her jacket in her hands. As a coughing fit coursed through Woodend's body and forced him to double up, he saw his sergeant drop to her knees and use her jacket to smother the victim's head.

Woodend's lungs began exacting their full revenge for what he had put them through. His chest heaved. His head swam. All the noises around him melded into a single, unpleasant cacophony, and he began to doubt that he would ever breathe normally again.

The attack passed, and Woodend cautiously straightened up.

Paniatowski was barking instructions into her police radio. 'Get a fire engine here, Bob! Quick as you can! Get a bloody fire engine!'

'Who were you talkin' to?' Woodend asked, coughing again – though not as badly this time. 'Was it Rutter?'

Paniatowski nodded. 'Yes. How are you feeling, sir? Up to carrying on for a while longer?'

'Just about. As long as I don't make any sudden moves.'

'Then you'd better see this.'

Paniatowski bent down and picked something off the ground. Straightening again, she held it for her boss to inspect.

Woodend did his best to focus his still-streaming eyes on the object. Part of it was black and frizzled, the rest yellow and curly.

35

In other circumstances, he thought, he would probably have recognized it immediately for what it was. But these weren't other circumstances. His brain was still too fuddled, his body still complaining about being poisoned. He hadn't been sick yet, but he was in absolutely no doubt that he soon would be.

He made another attempt to identify just what it was that his sergeant was showing him.

A cap of some kind?

No, that wasn't it!

Yet from its shape, it seemed as if it had been specifically designed to be moulded to the shape of the human head.

He was now probably steady enough on his feet to run the risk of looking down again, he decided. He turned his eyes from Paniatowski's hand and cautiously tilted his head so they were fixed on the ground.

The woman's body was still where he had left it when the coughing fit had struck him, but it no longer looked quite the same. She'd had blonde hair before, he remembered. Blonde hair which had caught fire as he'd pulled her free. Now, though, there was no sign of burning on her head: she was completely bald.

And suddenly he understood exactly what it was that Paniatowski was holding in her hand.

Four

Jamie Clegg sat at his desk in the Mid Lancs *Evening Courier* office, reflecting on the unexpected twists and turns that life could suddenly come up with.

Take this office as a case in point, he told himself. Though it was almost nine o'clock at night, there were at least half a dozen people still working there. Yet only a year earlier not a single desk would still have been occupied – even by a keen young reporter like him.

Of course, it had to be said in all fairness to himself that there wouldn't have been much point putting in the extra hours back then. The *Courier* had been quite happy, in what now seemed like those far-off days, to continue to occupy the same boring niche which it had occupied so comfortably for the previous sixty or seventy years.

All that had changed when the Editor died. After his funeral – splendidly covered in a six-page spread by the *Courier* – the paper's ownership had passed into the hands of his niece. And it was her husband, Dexter

Bryant, who had taken over as Editor.

Dexter Bryant!

Just the name had brought a shudder of anticipation to Jamie's thin, but eager, frame.

Dexter Bryant – possibly the most successful crime reporter that Fleet Street had ever known! Dexter Bryant – who was so good at pointing the police in the right direction that many people felt he should have held a high rank in the Force himself. It was Bryant who had speculated about the motives behind the Dulwich Public Convenience Murders – and been proved triumphantly right. It was Bryant whose stories filled the front pages of the national newspapers day after day.

He had hit the office like a whirlwind.

'Local news doesn't have to mean *boring* news,' he'd told the staff. 'Human interest is the same everywhere, and there are stories every bit as interesting in Whitebridge as there are in New York. All we have to do is get off our backsides and find them.'

'The paper's doing all right as it is, Mr Bryant,' one of the older reporters had grumbled.

'Is it?' Bryant had countered. 'Is it really? Then why is it only the *Mid* Lancashire *Courier*? Why aren't we selling it in places as far away as Warrington and Lancaster?'

'They're a funny lot of folk in Warrington and Lancaster. They wouldn't be interested.'

'Yes they would – if we gave them something to be interested *in*! Why are all our advertisements for second-hand cars and ironmongers? Why can't we attract adverts from national companies? I'll tell you why! Because we don't work hard enough to please them. But that's all about to change.'

And change it had. In the first few months of Bryant's editorship, a number of the older reporters had resigned. There'd been no point in staying on, they'd told anyone who'd listen to them. Bryant was heading for disaster. He'd taken over a perfectly manageable tramp steamer of a newspaper and was trying to turn it into an ocean liner. Well, he'd soon learn. The *Titanic* had gone down, and so would the *Courier*.

But the *Courier* hadn't sunk, taking with it all remaining hands. Instead, it had sailed from triumph to triumph. Circulation was rising. The paper was being talked about, instead of merely skimmed and forgotten. And best of all – from Jamie's point of view – the national dailies, always on the lookout for fresh talent, were starting to take a real interest in the men who put the *Courier* together.

Jamie was vaguely aware of the phone ringing in his boss's office, but since the Editor seemed to get calls at all hours of the day and night, he paid no particular attention to it. So it was not until Dexter Bryant flung open his office door and looked around expectantly that the young reporter felt the hairs on the back of his neck start to rise.

'Can you come in here for a second, Jamie?' Bryant asked.

Of course he could, Jamie Clegg thought. He would follow this Editor through fire and water.

By the time Clegg entered the office, Bryant was already back behind his desk. 'Ever heard of a place called Mad Jack's Field?' he asked.

'Yes, sir.'

'Then get over there as sharp as you can. With any luck, we might be the first paper on the story.'

'What story?' Jamie asked, almost choking with excitement.

'I'm not quite sure, to be honest,' Bryant admitted. 'But my contact at the fire station's just told me that two tenders have set out – going hell for leather – for this field of yours.'

How casually Bryant used the words 'my contact', Jamie thought.

If *he'd* had 'contacts' he'd have put real weight behind the words.

'*My contact* says there's a big scandal brewing in the town hall,' he'd have told his mates in the pub.

'*My contact* says they're going to build a new by-pass on the north edge of town,' he'd have announced to his mother as she made his supper.

Yet it was plain from the way he used the words that 'my contact' held no magic for Bryant – that he regarded his contact as no more than a tool of his trade.

A sudden thought floated into Jamie's mind like a black cloud, and he felt his burning enthusiasm begin to dim.

'Mad Jack's is one of the fields that the kids use on Bonfire Night,' he said, disappointedly.

'So?' Bryant countered.

'So the brigade's probably been called out for no other reason than that somebody's set that particular bonfire alight.'

A look which Jamie had begun to think of as Bryant's 'teaching smile' came to the Editor's face. 'Who do you think would have been likely to call the fire brigade out?' he asked.

'Somebody who lives near the field?' Jamie hazarded, and when that seemed to fail to satisfy Bryant, he added, 'A passer-by? A policeman?'

'Say it was a policeman. What kind of policeman would it be?'

'A constable. Or the desk sergeant.'

'Not a detective inspector?'

'No.'

'The call to the fire station was made by a Detective Inspector Rutter. Now why would

41

that be?'

'I don't know,' Jamie Clegg confessed.

Bryant quickly dialled a number, then indicated that Jamie should pick up the other phone on his desk in order to be able to listen in on the conversation.

'Whitebridge Police Headquarters,' said the voice on the other end of the line.

'Who am I speaking to, please?'

'Constable Danby.'

'Well, Constable Danby, this is the Mid Lancs *Courier*,' Bryant said. He covered the mouthpiece with his hand. 'We're in luck,' he told Jamie Clegg.

'Are we?'

'Almost certainly. From the sound of his voice, I'd say Constable Danby sounds just the kind of man we can have jumping through hoops if we handle him properly.'

'Are you still there?' the policeman asked.

Bryant took his hand off the mouthpiece. 'Yes, I'm still here,' he confirmed. 'Tell me, Constable Danby, is Detective Inspector Rutter in the building?'

'Yes, he is.'

'Then I wonder if I might speak to him.'

There was a pause from the other end. 'What's this about, exactly?' Danby asked.

'It's a matter of a somewhat delicate nature which I am only willing to discuss with Mr Rutter,' Bryant said, winking broadly at Jamie Clegg.

'Is it urgent?'

'Does it matter to you whether it is or not?'

Another pause. 'The thing is, Inspector Rutter's left instructions he's not to be disturbed unless it's urgent.'

'Why is that? Is he working on an important case?'

'I'm afraid I couldn't say, sir.'

'Well, never mind then, I'll catch him in the morning,' Bryant said. 'Sorry to have bothered you.'

'That's quite all right, sir,' the policeman assured him. 'That's what we're here for.'

Bryant spread his hands like a conjurer who has just completed a successful trick. 'There you are,' he said.

'Am I?' Jamie Clegg asked.

'Of course. Let's consider the evidence. One: Inspector Rutter is working on an important case, which, since we know nothing about it, could only recently have come to light. Two: despite the fact that he's too busy to come to the phone to talk to me, he does find time to ring the fire brigade. But how did he even know there *was* a fire?'

'Somebody rang him up and told him about it?' Jamie Clegg said, feeling incredibly stupid.

'Why didn't this *somebody* call the fire brigade first?'

Jamie Clegg pursed his brow. 'I don't know.'

'Because the person who called him didn't have access to a phone. He was using his *police radio*. That's why it was left to DI Rutter to actually call the fire brigade.'

'Of course.'

'Next question. Why contact Rutter at all? Why not leave it to the duty officer?'

'Because the fire has something to do with the important case that Rutter's been called in to investigate!' Jamie Clegg said excitedly.

Bryant positively beamed at his young protégé.

'I knew you'd get there in the end,' he said. 'Well? Don't just stand there. Go and cover your story.'

'Yes, sir! Right away, sir!' Jamie said. 'Thank you for giving me the chance, sir.'

'There's no need to thank me,' Dexter Bryant said. 'You've done me the odd favour in the past, and that's all the thanks I need. We're a team, Jamie. Now take yourself off to Mad Jack's Field while the story's still hot!'

'Yes, sir. I'm on it, sir,' Jamie Clegg said, thinking – as he rushed towards the door – that you couldn't *buy* the kind of training he was getting for free from his new boss.

Five

There had not been that much of the conflagration left when the fire engines arrived,
but the crews had, nonetheless, dutifully
drenched what there was before winding up
their hoses again and returning to their
station. The next emergency service unit to
arrive was the ambulance. The driver and his
mate handled the corpse in much the same
way as they would probably, had they been
in a different line of work, have handled a
particularly delicate piece of furniture – with
a great deal of care and absolutely no emo-
tion.

Woodend waited until the ambulance had
set off for the morgue, then turned to the
uniformed sergeant who was standing next
to him.

'How many lads have you got on this job,
Wally?' the Chief Inspector asked.

'Fourteen, sir.'

'Which is probably what we would need if
we were guardin' the Bank of England. But
since we aren't, we can probably make do
with a lot less, don't you think?'

45

'Shouldn't take more than three to patrol the perimeter, if that's all you want doin',' the sergeant said.

'That's all I want,' Woodend agreed. 'Pick me out a reliable trio, then send the rest back to their regular duties. What about yourself? Are you still on duty?'

The sergeant shook his head. 'I was just on my way home when the call came through.'

'Then bugger off before somethin' else turns up,' Woodend advised him. 'An' make sure your Elaine knows that it's only through my kindness an' consideration that you've been returned to the bosom of your family before they've all gone to bed.'

The sergeant grinned. 'I'll do that, sir.'

As the patrol cars pulled away, the field grew darker and darker. For perhaps an hour, the formerly undistinguished strip of wasteland had basked in the glow of a dozen sets of headlights. Now its moment of glory was gone.

Woodend looked through the increasing gloom at the sodden pile of wood and paper which had once been a bonfire, and wondered just how much valuable evidence had either been burned up or washed away.

'The Chief Constable will want my balls on a plate for this, Monika,' he said to Paniatowski.

'I suppose he will – since misery seeks company,' his sergeant replied. 'But it really wasn't your fault, you know, sir.'

Woodend shrugged. 'Maybe it wasn't, but lack of culpability's never been much of a barrier to Mr Marlowe havin' a go at me in the past.' He laughed. 'Still, I suppose I should be grateful.'

'Grateful?'

'Aye. The only alternative to his tryin' to roast me over a slow spit is to have him bein' nice to me – and I don't think I could stand that.' Woodend paused to light up a Capstan. 'What's the thing that most strikes you about this case, Monika? The way he killed her?'

'No,' Paniatowski said. 'The way he decided to dispose of the body.'

'Aye, that is odd,' Woodend agreed. 'He could have buried her somewhere out on the moors. We'd have searched there, of course, once she was reported missin'. That's standard procedure, and everybody in White-bridge knows it. But that would have at least bought him time. It could have been weeks – perhaps even months – before we found the body.'

'We might *never* have found it,' Paniatowski pointed out.

'But he *didn't* bury her on the moors, did he? Instead, he plumped for stickin' her in the middle of a bonfire. Why? Because it's only four days away from Bonfire Night, an' he was hopin' that the kids would burn the evidence?'

47

'No,' Paniatowski said with conviction.

'Why not?'

'Firstly, because he didn't bother to hide her properly. Those two little kids found her easily enough – and they weren't even looking.'

'An' secondly? There is a secondly, isn't there?'

'Yes. Secondly, there's the alarm clock we heard ringing just before the fire broke out.'

'What about it?'

'I'm willing to bet that it was the timer on some kind of home-made incendiary device.'

Woodend nodded. 'So am I. You think he wanted his victim cremated, then, do you?'

'Not necessarily. If that had been his intention, he'd have soaked the bonfire with petrol, like the kids did.'

'So what *did* he want?'

Paniatowski hesitated. 'I've got a theory,' she admitted. 'But it's based on the belief that this isn't a domestic murder. So before we go any further, can we rule domestic murders out?'

'We can never rule out *anythin'* in this game,' Woodend reminded her. 'But I have to say, it doesn't bear any of the hallmarks of a family killin'. An' it's not just the way the murderer chose to dispose of the body that makes me think that. When husbands kill their wives, they usually do it with their bare hands, or with a blunt instrument like a hammer. Knives are very uncommon, an' even if they are used, they're used messily. I've seen a couple of murdered wives with dozens of stab wounds on their bodies. I've never seen one who's had her throat slit. Does that answer your question?'

'Yes.'

'Then let's get back to the one I asked you. You don't think he wanted to cremate his victim, so why did he light the bonfire?'

'I think he did it because he wanted to create a stir.'

Woodend nodded again. 'He'd have managed that, all right. A burnin' bonfire would have brought people runnin' from streets away.'

'Exactly. So by the time someone discovered the body, there'd have been quite a crowd gathered around the fire.'

'An' you think that's what he *wanted* to happen?'

'I can't come up with any other explanation for his actions. The way I see it, he probably thinks of himself as something of an artist. That makes the victim his canvas, and her murder the act of creation. And in order to feel that his handiwork is fully appreciated, he needs to be sure he has an audience.'

Woodend shook his head dolefully. 'I wish you'd never said that.'

'Why? Because you think it's completely

off the wall?'

'Far from it, I've been havin' similar thoughts myself – an' I was rather hopin' that you'd be able to talk me out of them. I don't *want* it to be that kind of case, Monika. It's hard enough work catchin' honest, straightforward murderers, without comin' up against one who likes to turn the whole bloody thing into some kind of sick game.'

When the headlights of his Ford Pop picked out the blue uniformed figure patrolling the edge of Mad Jack's Field, Jamie Clegg felt his stomach perform the minor somersault it always did when he spotted an officer of the law.

'You're an idiot!' he told himself aloud.

A prize idiot, in fact. Because he wasn't a little boy any more. He no longer need fear that the bobby would ask him if he'd scrumped the crab apples which were bulging in his pocket from somebody's orchard. Nor was it necessary to worry that the constable might have heard that he'd asked Lizzie Dibble to show him her knickers. He was a grown-up now – a hardboiled reporter out on an assignment which had been personally handed to him by the great Dexter Bryant. If anything, the presence of the bobby should have reassured him – because that presence proved that something serious *had* actually happened on or around the field.

Jamie parked the car close to the kerb, and began to walk towards what was left of the bonfire. He had not gone more than a few yards before a gruff voice said, 'An' where do you think you're goin'?'

Jamie swung round. For a moment he was disconcerted by the fact that the voice sounded old enough to be his father's – but that wouldn't have deterred Dexter Bryant, and he was buggered if was going to let it bother 'Scoop' Clegg.

He reached into his pocket for his press card, and held it out for the other man to examine under his flashlight.

'Reporter!' he said, unnecessarily.

'That's as maybe,' responded the constable, who didn't like the duty he'd been assigned in the first place, and certainly didn't like having to deal with jumped-up kids who would probably be earning more than *he* was in two or three years' time. 'Yes, you may indeed be a reporter, as it says on your card. But I'm still goin' to have to tell you to move on.'

'I work for the *Courier*!' Jamie Clegg said, close to outrage.

'An' I *read* the *Courier*,' the constable responded. 'Have done for years an' years – probably since long before you were born. But what's that got to do with the price of fish?'

Jamie Clegg swallowed hard and pulled his notepad out of his pocket. 'If you could just answer a few questions...' he began tentatively.

The constable shook his head. 'The only feller around here who's entitled to answer questions about the murder is Mr Woodend...'

The murder! Jamie repeated silently in his head. So there'd been a *murder*!

'...an' it was Mr Woodend himself who told me that nobody's allowed near the crime scene – not even a reporter from the Mid Lancs *Courier*. So, all things considered, you'd best get back on your bike, son.'

Get back on your bike!

Jamie Clegg felt a wave of humiliation wash over him. What did this bobby take him for? A paper boy? A butcher's delivery lad?

'I didn't come by bike,' he said. 'I came by *car*! *My* car!'

The constable chuckled. 'Then climb back in it, an' get your little legs working the pedals,' he said.

'It's a Ford Popular, not a kiddie car!' Jamie said, but – having suffered enough blows to his self-esteem already – he did not stay to hear the constable's response.

His heart was beating furiously against his ribcage, and his cheeks burned as if they were on fire. He opened the driver's door of his Ford Pop and slid behind the wheel.

'You'd best get back on your bike, son!' he repeated bitterly.

Well, he could certainly do that – metaphorically, if not literally.

But should he?

What would Dexter Bryant do if he were faced with a situation like this one, he wondered?

Six

It was still possible that there might be a mundane solution to this murder, Woodend thought as he gazed down at the extinguished fire which might yet turn out to be the ashes of his own career. It was still possible that, come the morning, some dishevelled man would present himself at police headquarters and confess that – in a bout of temper – he had killed his wife and stuffed her in the bonfire.

But while it just *might* be possible, it was far from likely. Because Monika was right. This killer did not see death as a conclusion. For him, it was only part of a process.

'DI Rutter's just arrived, sir,' Paniatowski said, from somewhere behind his left shoulder.

Woodend turned around. Someone was certainly approaching, and even though the distant street lights did not provide enough illumination to see him clearly, there was no doubt that it was Bob.

It had something to do with the way Rutter walked which made him so identifiable, Woodend decided: the broad strides which carried with them the suggestion that he was a very important business executive rushing – but with dignity – from one vital meeting to another.

From the very start – from the time they'd worked together on the murders in Salton – Bob had always looked more like a businessman than a policeman. And that was far from a disadvantage in a force which seemed increasingly to assign more value to appearance and cost-efficiency than to good police work. In fact, if Bob could only bring himself to give up his annoying habits of honesty, loyalty and straightforwardness, Woodend thought, there was absolutely nothing to stop him going right to the top of his chosen profession.

Rutter drew level with them, and came to a smart halt.

'You took your time gettin' here,' Woodend said, acting instinctively on the principle that while he might love the inspector like the son he'd never had, there was never any harm in taking a high-flier like Rutter down a peg or two.

'Took my time?' Rutter repeated, unconcerned. 'I didn't know there was any rush. Besides, I thought it might be useful to drop in at headquarters and see if there was anything to be learned from there.'

'An' was there?'

Rutter shook his head. 'No one's reported that a woman of the right age has failed to turn up at home when she was expected.'

'Maybe she's *not* expected – at least, until later,' Woodend suggested. 'She could be a factory shift-worker. Or a nurse on night duty. She might even be a barmaid or pub entertainer.'

'I had already thought that possibility through,' Rutter told him. 'I've had the lads back at the station ringing all the local hospitals, factories and pubs. If one of their employees has failed to turn up, we should hear about it within the hour.'

'Anythin' else?' Woodend asked.

'I've alerted all motor and foot patrols – especially in this area – to keep an eye open for any suspicious characters. There's always the chance that the murderer's still hanging around near the scene of the crime.'

'Aye, there is always a chance,' Woodend agreed. 'But not much of one. Not with this feller.'

Rutter took out his cigarettes, gave one to Paniatowski and placed a second in his own mouth. He didn't offer the packet to Woodend. He already knew that if had have done, the offer would been refused. The Chief Inspector, though he rarely put his thoughts on the matter into words, considered corktipped coffin nails to be far too safe and unmanly to ever consider smoking them himself.

'So what do we do next?' Rutter asked.

'There's not much we *can* do,' Woodend replied. 'This area needs searchin' – there may still be some clues that haven't *quite* been destroyed by the Mongol hordes who were here earlier – but it'd be stupid to attempt a job like that until it's light again. So, all in all, I think we could do worse than adjourn to the nearest pub an' await further developments.'

'Can we clear up one point before we go?' Rutter asked.

'Course we can, lad.'

'You said it was highly unlikely the killer was still in the immediate area. Why is that?'

'Monika an' me think he's too clever to do anythin' so obvious.'

'Do you?' Rutter asked, sounding unconvinced. 'Based on what?'

Woodend grinned. 'Based on the fact that we're both highly trained professionals who have been proved to be right *almost* as many times as we've been proved to be wrong. Isn't that true, Monika?'

56

Paniatowski said nothing.

'Are you with us, lass?' Woodend asked.

Still no reply. Woodend turned to look at his sergeant, and was surprised to see that she had slipped out of her high-heeled shoes and was beginning to edge away from the remains of the bonfire.

'Is something the matter, Monika?' Rutter asked.

'Shut up and keep talking!' Paniatowski whispered.

It was a confusingly worded request, but both Woodend and Rutter knew exactly what she meant.

'Don't suppose it matters what we actually *say*, as long we keep our voices at just about the same tone an' level,' Woodend guessed.

'She's seen something, hasn't she?' Rutter replied conversationally.

'That's the only explanation I can think of.'

Suddenly Paniatowski was gone – sprinting towards the edge of the field, chasing a dark figure who had risen from the ground like a zombie rising from its grave.

'Shall I—?' Rutter asked.

'Monika can look after herself,' Woodend told him. 'Anyway, as fit as you think you are, you'd never catch up with her now.'

Paniatowski's quarry was running awkwardly towards the boundary of the field. It was the petrol can he was carrying which was causing him problems, Woodend thought. It wasn't particularly large or heavy, but it still had the effect of throwing him off balance and slowing him down. Paniatowski, without his disadvantages, was closing the gap between them. Barring mishaps, she would catch up with him before he even had time to reach the road.

A mishap occurred!

Something – a tin or a brick, or maybe a root – caused Paniatowski to lose her footing, and she flew through the air like an acrobat stretching out for an invisible trapeze. The man whom she was chasing stopped for a moment – perhaps to catch his breath, perhaps to assure himself that Paniatowski no longer presented a threat – then belatedly dropped the petrol can and, with a fresh burst of energy, sprinted towards the road.

One of the constables patrolling the perimeter had seen what was happening, but though he set off in pursuit, it must already have been clear to him that he had started from too far away to have any real hope of catching his man.

The fugitive crossed the road and disappeared down a back alley which led to a maze of other back alleys. Though the constable continued to follow, he knew his man was lost.

By the time Woodend and Rutter had reached her, Paniatowski had rolled herself over into a sitting position, and was massaging her left knee.

'How bad is it?' Woodend asked worriedly.

'Laddered my bloody nylons,' the sergeant said through gritted teeth. 'And they were fresh on today.'

Woodend found himself examining the ladder. It was a cracker – a champion among ladders – running all the way from her calf to the middle of her thigh. Then he felt a sudden wave of self-consciousness. Though his interest in Monika had been concern rather than prurience, he could see how it might be misinterpreted. He quickly turned away, expecting Rutter to do the same automatically.

But Rutter didn't!

Worse yet, there was nothing at all self-conscious in the way the inspector was looking at Paniatowski. This was no explorer getting his first exciting glimpse of a hitherto unknown territory. Rather there was an ease about the whole encounter which suggested that Paniatowski's body was as familiar to him as his own back yard.

Which was not good! Woodend thought. Not good at all!

'If I give you some support, do you think you'll be able to stand up?' Rutter asked Paniatowski.

'I'll give it a try,' the sergeant answered.

Rutter bent down and grabbed Paniatowski under the armpits. It was a perfectly normal, natural thing to do. It was not even slightly sexual. But watching the scene, Woodend couldn't help wishing that the inspector had taken hold of the sergeant a *little* more gingerly, and could have seemed at least *a mite* uncomfortable with the contact.

'You want to tell us what's just happened, Monika?' Woodend asked, the words coming out more gruffly than he'd intended.

Paniatowski, now upright and still being supported by Rutter, pressed her left foot tentatively on the ground. It caused some pain, but she looked as if she could live with it.

'I heard a noise,' she said. 'I was convinced that someone was watching us. Then I spotted him. And that's about all there is to it.'

'So perhaps the killer did return to the scene of his crime, after all,' Rutter suggested.

'Not a chance!' Woodend told him.

'How can you be so sure of that?'

'Because of what the man tried to take away with him.'

'The petrol can?'

'That's right.'

'I'm not sure I'm following you,' Rutter admitted.

'The petrol can didn't appear on the scene

until those kids brought it, long after the body had been dumped,' Woodend explained. 'The killer would have known that – or at least would have known it had nothing to do with the murder. On the other hand, the man who tried to take it away *didn't* know. He thought it might be a clue. Hence, he couldn't have anything to do with the crime.'

'I suppose you're right,' Rutter conceded.

'I *am* right,' Woodend said. He turned to Paniatowski. 'Think you can walk to the car?'

'Probably.'

'Then we'd better get that knee of yours some medical attention.'

'I don't need it,' Paniatowski protested. 'The knee's all right.'

'It'll be even better after the application of a little embrocation,' Woodend insisted.

'I'm not having horse liniment rubbed into *my* knee,' Paniatowski said firmly.

'Of course you're not,' Woodend agreed. 'We'll use vodka embrocation – an' we'll apply it from the *inside*.'

Seven

He knew he was in his bedroom. His mind and his memory both told him that it was so, and his fingers – running along the edge of the familiar mattress – only reinforced the belief. Had he opened his eyes – which he wouldn't, because he didn't *choose* to – he would have seen the bedside light he had not bothered to turn off, and the ticking alarm clock which was standing next to it. Yes, there was no doubt at all about where he was.

Why then, did his sense of smell keep telling him he was somewhere else entirely? Why, even though such a thing was impossible, did his nose insist that that it was inhaling the sticky cloying smell of decaying vegetation which belonged to a place thousands of miles away from Whitebridge?

There had been four them in the jungle that day – himself (LH), Jacko, Socks and the new sergeant. It had been meant to be no more than a routine patrol. Out just before dawn, back in time for tea. In theory they were looking for communists, but they did not expect to find any, because everybody knew there were no commies in this particular sector.

Like hell, there weren't!

Right from the start, the sergeant had tried to stamp his authority on the patrol. He had seen more active service than they could ever imagine, he'd told them. Had any of them ever killed a man? No? Well, he bloody had. And not just the one man, either.

'Ever been in the jungle, though, Sarge?' Jacko had asked.

What was that supposed to mean, the sergeant demanded.

Nothing, Jacko replied. No offence meant. He just wondered if the sarge had ever been in the jungle, that was all.

'I've fought on the burning sands, and up to my waist in water,' the sergeant replied. 'I shouldn't think a few trees will bother me.'

But the jungle was not 'a few trees'. The jungle was a tangled mass of roots, branches and creepers. It sweated and it groaned. It drained the strength out of a man after only a few minutes. It was deceptive – creating false trails which seemed to lead the walker in the direction he wished to go, yet in reality doing no more than lead him round in circles.

Spend more than an hour under its sweltering canopy and it was no longer possible to believe that any other world existed. Memories became dreams, the jungle was the only reality. The three young commandos already knew this. They could only hope and pray that their new sergeant would soon come to realize it too.

Despite his men's protest that they should stick to familiar trails, the new sergeant led them further into the jungle than they had ever ventured before. By noon – though the sergeant would not admit it, even to himself – they were lost. Prickly heat made their backs itch unbearably. Countless insects, ignoring the creams the men had applied to their whole bodies, were slowly and patiently devouring their legs and arms. Their tongues were swelling with thirst, but they had drunk too much of their valuable water already, and so forced themselves to conserve what little was left. When they finally managed to persuade the sergeant to call base camp for assistance, they discovered that their radio had stopped working.

It was perhaps half an hour before dusk when, still wandering aimlessly, they heard the sound of machetes cutting their way through the vines, and the tramp of heavy boots on the ground. As quietly as was possible, they retreated into the undergrowth and crouched down. A minute or so later they saw what had been making the noise – a column of perhaps twenty-five heavily armed members of the Malayan Communist Party.

There was a clearing no more than a hundred yards past their hiding place, and when the enemy reached it, their leader called a halt. The communists set about making camp for the night. A fire was lit, and pots were brought out. Soon, despite the almost overpowering stink of the jungle, the four British soldiers were treated to the tantalizing smell of food being cooked.

The sergeant's bold, early-morning front had been gradually deteriorating over the course of the day and now, when he spoke, it was with the voice of desperation rather than command.

'We'll wait until they've gone to sleep, then we'll slip away,' he croaked.

The other two young privates looked to Jacko for leadership.

'Slip away?' Jacko whispered. 'If we can't find our way back to base in the daylight, what chance will we have in the dark? Besides, we've used up most of the water. Even if we did know our way out, we'd die of thirst before we were halfway home.'

The sergeant bowed his head. 'Then we have no choice but to surrender,' he said.

Jacko did not even try to hide his contempt at this. 'If we surrender, we lose face,' he said.

'I don't care,' the sergeant mumbled.

'Well, you should. It would make us less than human in their eyes. There's no telling what they might do to us then.'

'We'll be prisoners of war,' the sergeant whined.

'You're not listening,' Jacko hissed angrily. 'We're the white man, and we'll have lost. They'll use us an example to frighten the coolies.'

'How?'

'They'll think of something. Maybe they'll

65

crucify us on rubber trees. Maybe they'll just carry our heads around on poles. I don't know exactly – and I don't want to find out.'

'So what can we do?' the sergeant whimpered.

'Attack them while they're asleep. At the very worst, we'll get our hands on their water. At best, we might manage to keep one of them alive and force him to lead us out of this hell.'

'We're outnumbered,' the sergeant said. 'There's a good two dozen of them.'

'But we have the element of surprise on our side.'

'How can we surprise them?' the sergeant asked hysterically. 'They'll have sentries posted.'

'Yes, they will,' Jacko agreed. He turned to LH and Socks. 'You're going to have to take the sentries out first.'

Crawling on his belly, LH reached the edge of the clearing. The campfire had died down, but there was just enough light left for him to see that there were only two sentries on guard. One for him, one for Socks. Once they were out of the way, the three privates would spray the sleeping bodies of the enemy with machine-gun fire.

It could work. It had to work!

He edged forward, just as he hoped that Socks was doing on the other side of the clearing. The plan was for him to make the first move, then Socks, who should be watching, would take out his man almost immediately afterwards.

LH's target had his back to him, and from his

stance it was clear that he kept dozing off where he stood. Good. That would make things easier. LH assessed his task, calculating just when he would get up off the ground and exactly where he would grab the guard.

This guard wasn't very tall, even for a Chinese. Not very broad, either. More like a boy than a man. That didn't matter. This was war – and in war being weak was no excuse. LH slowly reached towards his belt, and pulled his knife from its protective sheath.

A knocking on his door!

'LH? LH? Are you all right?'

The stink of the jungle receded. Now all he could smell was furniture wax and his own sweat.

'LH?'

'I'm fine.'

'I heard you crying out.'

'So what? Didn't the nut doctor tell you to expect that kind of thing?'

'You shouldn't call Dr Freedman that. He's a trauma therapist.'

'He's a *shrink*. If you have to go and see him, it's because you're crazy. That's why *I* go – because I've got a screw loose.'

The doorknob rattled. 'Let me in, LH.'

'No!'

'Please! I want to help.'

'*You* can't help. You – and what you've done – are a big part of the problem.'

'If we could just talk...'

'If you don't go away this minute, I'll take my knife out,' LH threatened. 'And once it is out, I'll have to use it – because that's what I've been taught to do.'

'Please don't threaten me!'

'Who says I'm threatening you? Maybe I'm only threatening myself.' LH took a deep breath. 'I'm going to count to five, then I'm getting the knife.'

'You mustn't ... you...'

'One ... two ... three...'

It was on 'four' that he heard the footsteps reluctantly signalling a retreat. He closed his eyes again and let the stinking green hell of the jungle seep back into his nostrils.

The guard still had no idea that he was there ... still didn't know just how close death was...

November the Second

Though rivers of blood
May spill through the crack
The dam has been breached
And there's no turning back.

Eight

Under the cloak of darkness, Mad Jack's Field had seemed a sinister place to Bob Rutter. Now, in the dull light of an overcast November day, any chill he might experience had more to do with the temperature of the air than with any atmosphere which might emanate from the field itself. This was no potential location for a horror film. It was simply a patch of wasteland which no one had yet thought worth developing – just another urban blemish in a declining town which had more than its fair share of such sites.

Rutter shifted his gaze from the charred remains of the bonfire to the edges of the field. A dozen uniformed constables were slowly and meticulously scouring the ground for clues, but it was unlikely they'd have any luck. The earth had been rock-hard the night before, so there was little chance of being able to lift any footprints. Besides – and to use one of the newly fashionable policing phrases which Charlie Woodend affected to

despise – the crime scene had been 'con-
taminated' by two small boys, a passing
couple, a number of police units, several
spectators who had managed to slip through
the cordon (including the one Monika
chased) and two bloody big red fire engines
which, as well as putting out the fire, had
drenched the ground around it.

He turned his thoughts from the crime
scene to the dead woman's clothes. They'd
been bothering him – on and off – since he'd
first examined them the night before.

Her shoes had at once struck a jarring
note. They were bright scarlet, with very
high heels. They seemed totally at odds not
only with the woman's age but also with the
frumpy cloth overcoat and heavy woollen
cardigan she'd been wearing. Then he'd
examined the rest of her clothes, and quickly
understood that it was the overcoat and
cardigan – not the shoes – which failed to
match the rest of the ensemble.

The skirt was black, knee-length and
tightly fitting. The blouse was low-cut, frilly
and electric blue. Underneath these outer
garments, the woman had been wearing a
black lace bra and panty set, stockings and a
suspender belt.

That kind of underwear would have suited
his wife – or Monika Paniatowski – Rutter
thought, but it hardly seemed appropriate
clothing for a woman who was fifteen years

their senior.

Or *was* it inappropriate? he wondered, pulling himself up short.

On more than one occasion, Charlie Woodend had accused him of seeing the world through arrogant young eyes – of assuming that any woman over thirty-five had either lost the urge for sex or, at the very least, the power to attract a partner.

Slightly guiltily, Rutter accepted both the criticism and the extent of his own ignorance which that criticism implied. Perhaps *all* middle-aged women wore the same kind of underwear as the victim. He'd never undressed one of them, so he simply didn't know.

Rutter checked his watch. It was nearly ten twenty-seven and, under normal circumstances, the team should have been able to put a name to the dead woman by now.

Yet that hadn't happened. There'd been no phone calls from anxious husbands who wanted to report that their wives hadn't come home; no children turning up at the police station to say they'd lost their mum; no concerned employers wondering if the reason one of their workers had failed to turn up that morning was because she'd been murdered.

He looked at his watch again.

Ten twenty-nine!

Christ, was it really only a couple of

minutes since the last time he'd checked?

'Calm down!' he told himself.

Calm down? There wasn't much chance of that. His personal life had got his nerves in such a state that he made a spider tap-dancing on a hotplate look tranquil.

When Woodend had briefed the press in the old days, he had done it from wherever he happened to be at the time. Sometimes the briefings were conducted out on the street, sometimes in Woodend's office and some-times – very often, in fact – in a pub. He'd liked doing things that way. He could get to know the journalists, and they could get to know him. When it had been necessary to draw a line over which they should not cross, he'd been able to do it informally, without raising too many hackles. When he'd wanted their help, he could ask for it without having to fill in the mountain of paperwork which was now necessary if he wanted to cover his own back. It had been a good system – one which had actually helped him to get the result he was after.

The Chief Constable did not approve of such effective anarchy. On his return from one of the countless conferences he attended – conferences which, coincidentally, were all within reasonable distance of a good golf course – he'd announced that what the Mid Lancs Police needed, more than anything else in the world, was a good press room. And so one of the larger rooms on the ground floor had been set aside for the purpose, and the criminal records department – which had hitherto been making full use of the room – had been dispatched to a dusty basement.

Thus it was that Woodend found himself standing at the podium in the 'press centre' that morning, addressing three local reporters.

The Chief Inspector made a brief statement, and then asked if there were any questions.

'What was the motive for the murder, Chief Inspector?' asked a pipe-smoking reporter for the Burnley *Telegraph*.

'Come on, Horace, you know it's far too early for me to start speculating about that,' Woodend said.

'Is it true that you think the killer is an escaped lunatic?' asked the man from the Preston *Evening News*, who, like Woodend, smoked Capstan Full Strength.

'If he is a nutter, then it's certainly news to me,' Woodend replied.

'When do you hope to be able to identify the victim?' asked the Accrington *Post* man, who was addicted to short black cigars.

'I can't say when we'll know who she is for sure, but since we're plasterin' Whitebridge with her photograph even as I speak, I'd be surprised if we didn't know by this evenin' at the latest.'

'Are you looking for a serial killer?' the pipe smoker asked.

Woodend frowned. 'We're lookin' for the man who slit that poor bloody woman's throat an' stuffed her into the bonfire. I've no idea whether he's killed before – an' neither have you.' He glared meaningfully at the pipe smoker. 'So if I was in your shoes, Horace, I'd think very carefully before I even *hinted* at anythin' like that in my rag.'

The cigar smoker raised his hand. 'Chief Inspector, would it be possible to comment on—?'

'I've told you all I can for the moment,' Woodend interrupted. 'Keep in touch with the duty desk, and they'll let you know when I'll be available again.'

He stepped off the podium and walked quickly to the door. Behind him, he heard one of the men fire off another question, but he ignored it.

He didn't blame the reporters for trying to squeeze as much information out of him as they possibly could. He would have done the same in their position. They saw this murder as a big chance to make a name for themselves, and were only too well aware of the fact that once the hot shots from Fleet Street arrived, they would be elbowed aside. If, on the other hand, they could come up with a significant angle on the story *before* then, they had a fair chance of seeing their by-lines in the national press. And who knew what that might lead to?

He really *would* have helped them if he could have done, Woodend thought as he approached his office, if only because he got a lot of pleasure from seeing the underdog come out on top occasionally. But the simple truth was that, apart from a black and white photograph of the dead woman, he had very little to give them.

Nine

Rutter sat in his car at the edge of Mad Jack's Field, staring at his car radio. When he'd had it installed only a few days earlier, he'd been like a kid with a new toy, but now even this latest miracle of the 1960s was failing to thrill him.

The problem wasn't that he didn't know what to do to get himself out of the mess he'd fallen into, he thought. He *did* know – he simply didn't want to *act* on that knowledge.

He reached forward lethargically, and switched the radio on. He was just in time for a news bulletin.

'Beatlemania' continued to follow the group on their tour of the country, the announcer said. At their last concert, even a cordon of two hundred policemen had not been enough to stop the screaming fans from mobbing their van.

'Waste of police resources,' Rutter mumbled.

The news continued. Kim Philby, the former British intelligence officer who had gone missing in the Lebanon a few months earlier, had finally emerged in Russia. At his press conference, he had condemned the decadent West and praised the communist system. Ever since the defection of two diplomats, Burgess and Maclean, some twelve years earlier, the newsreader said, the security services had suspected that there had been a third member of their spy ring. Now it was clear that Philby, who had attended university with the other two, *was* that third man.

'That's what I call brilliant detective work!' Rutter said sarcastically. 'MI5 are now sure he's guilty – but only because he's told them he is!'

President Kennedy, seeking a re-nomination no one doubted was his for the asking, was planning to campaign in Texas towards the end of the month, the newsreader concluded. Among the cities he would visit were

San Antonio, Houston and Dallas.

Jack Kennedy was just like all the others, Rutter thought sourly. He might talk about building a new Camelot, but when it came down to it, all he really cared about was getting re-elected. A couple more years, and he would be indistinguishable from every other politician who wanted to be president.

The bulletin ended and the theme music to a popular quiz programme filled the space it had vacated. It was a jaunty tune aimed at lightening the spirit and promising much fun to come. Rutter twisted the off-knob on the radio with such force that it came off in his hand.

For a moment, he just sat there, staring at the knob. Then his mind began to review his reactions to what he had heard on the radio. He had disapproved of the Beatles, for God's sake! He had criticized the security services without any knowledge of the problems and constraints they were working under. And he had slammed Jack Kennedy, whom he had previously regarded as the great shining hope of the free world.

He groaned inwardly. What was happening to him?

'The case!' he told himself. 'Concentrate on the case!'

Why had the killer placed his victim in the bonfire? Because he was playing a game, of course! Because he was trying to draw attention to himself. But weren't there other – perhaps even more dramatic – ways that he could have achieved the same effect?

Why not make an even more public display of his victim?

Why not, for example, hang her from a lamp standard? Or dump her body on the doorstep of the Mid Lancs *Courier*?

And what was so special about bonfires? What hidden significance did they hold for the killer?

Rutter got out of his car, strode rapidly towards the phone box which he had noticed about hundred yards down the road, and dialled home.

'Hello?' said Maria, his wife, her slight Spanish accent now supplemented with a thin overlay of Lancashire.

'It's me,' Rutter said. 'I don't want you leaving the house today.'

'What are you talkin' about?'

'I want you to stay at home.'

'But there is food which needs to be bought. Besides, the baby needs some fresh air.'

'I'll do the shopping,' Rutter promised. 'And I'll take the baby out, too, as soon as I get home. You stay inside. And make sure the doors are locked.'

'Is somethin' the matter?' Maria asked, sounding alarmed.

Damn, he'd frightened her! He'd never

intended to do that. The world was a scary enough place for a woman who could not see it, without him doing anything to add to the sense of menace.

'There's nothing for you to worry about,' he said soothingly. 'You're in no danger. It's just that I'm a bit nervous, and I'd be happier in myself if I knew you were safe.'

'What's happenin' with the case, Bob?' Maria asked.

'Nothing. It's just that I—'

'Robert!'

Rutter sighed. He could rarely fool his wife for long, especially once her suspicions were aroused. Perhaps because she *lived* in the dark, she was adamant that she should not be *kept* in the dark about his affairs.

His *affairs*! He wondered how long he could keep *that* particular secret hidden.

'Tell me, Robert! I need to know!' Maria insisted.

'It's going badly wrong,' he admitted, not sure if he was talking about his life or the case.

'You'll sort it out,' Maria said, deliberately injecting confidence and reassurance into her voice. 'You know that, don't you?'

'Yes,' Rutter replied.

But he didn't mean it, because something deep in his gut told him that this murder was only the beginning – that before the investigation was over, things both professional and

81

personal would have turned a bloody sight worse.

When Woodend reached his office, the phone on his desk was already ringing. He picked it up, and found himself connected to Dexter Bryant.

'Isn't it odd that during all those years you were working for Scotland Yard, and I was working for the *Daily Standard*, our paths never crossed?' Bryant said, after he'd introduced himself.

'Aye, very odd,' Woodend replied noncommittally.

'Is that what you *really* think – or are you just being polite?' Bryant asked, and Woodend could tell by the tone of his voice that he was smiling.

'It's true I was hardly ever in London,' Woodend admitted.

'And I was hardly ever out of it,' Bryant said. 'As far as my editors were concerned, a murder which didn't happen in the London area could scarcely be called a murder at all.'

'Aye, they did tend to think like that,' Woodend agreed.

'And it was scarcely by chance that *you* spent most of your time in the provinces,' Bryant continued. 'If there was one thing that the top brass in Scotland Yard disliked more than your way of conducting an investigation – and they really *did* dislike that, you know – it was the fact that your unorthodox methods usually seemed to produce a result. I don't think they ever slept comfortably in their beds unless they knew that you were at least a hundred miles away from them.'

Woodend found that he was smiling, too. 'If I remember rightly, I wasn't the only one who got up the noses of the brass at the Yard,' he said. 'There were a fair number of them who wouldn't have exactly shed a tear if you'd been transferred from crime reportin' to the *Daily Standard*'s knittin' and sewin' page.'

'You don't hold that against me, I hope,' Bryant said.

'No,' Woodend assured him. 'Not at all. You can tell a lot about a man from the enemies he acquires – an' if you compared your list to mine, I think we'd find a considerable overlap.' He paused for a second. 'As pleasant as it is to chat to you, I take it this isn't a social call you're makin', Mr Bryant.'

'Not *just* a social call,' Bryant agreed. 'I think we need to talk. Are you free for lunch?'

'In case it's escaped your attention, I'm conductin' a murder investigation.'

The Editor chuckled. 'No, you're not,' he said.

'Is that a fact?'

'Did you notice that I didn't send one of my lads down to your press briefing?'

'Aye, I did, as it happens.'

'That's because I knew it would be a waste of time. Your subordinates may be running around like headless chickens, but until you've got a positive identification of the body, you're not actually *conducting* anything. Isn't that right?'

'Close enough,' Woodend admitted.

'So how about we meet up at the Dirty Duck at around twelve?'

Why not? Woodend asked himself.

Bryant was right about there not being much for him to do until the body was identified, so he might as well get a good lunch inside him. Besides, the timing of the Editor's offer intrigued him. It had been several months since Bryant had taken over the running of the *Courier*. So why did he feel the sudden urge to meet now?

Ten

It came as a surprise to Monika Paniatowski to discover that Dr Shastri smoked, because none of the other Asian women she'd met had acquired the habit. On the other hand, she accepted, none of the other Asian women she knew were police pathologists who made jokes about slicing meat.

The last piece of meat that Dr Shastri had sliced still lay on the dissection table. The incision which ran the length of her torso had been neatly sewed back together again with strong black thread.

'Would it be all right if I put her wig back on her head now?' Paniatowski asked.

Dr Shastri giggled. 'What's your problem, Sergeant? Would you rather not be reminded of the fact that where once she had brains she now has balled up pages of the *Daily Express*?'

'No, it's not that,' Paniatowski said. 'I want to get some idea of how she looked to other people.'

'Then by all means replace the wig. It won't bother me. And it certainly won't bother her!'

Paniatowski lifted the corpse's head, slid the wig in place, adjusted it, then took a few steps back. The dead woman must once have had a roundish face, she decided – the sort of face that many men found, in an earthy sort of way, to be highly attractive. But the roundness had all but gone now. Despite the liberal application of make-up, the woman had a haggard appearance which – although having her throat cut couldn't have helped – had already been there while she was still alive.

The same could be said for the body. The ample breasts had begun to wither; skin which had once strained to contain fat now hung as flaps of loose flesh on the thighs.

'Would you like to know how it happened?' Dr Shastri asked.

'How do you mean?'

'Shall I demonstrate how she died?'

'Yes, I suppose that might be a good idea.'

Dr Shastri giggled again. 'Excellent,' she said. 'At last, a moment of excitement in my humdrum day.' She stubbed out her cigarette in one of the stainless steel dishes designed to hold human organs. 'Turn your back to me.'

'What?'

'Turn your back on me.'

Paniatowski turned. She heard the doctor's footsteps, and felt Shastri's left arm go across her chest and grab her right arm.

'Do you happen to know any unarmed combat?' the doctor asked.

'Yes.'

'Excellent again. I'm most delighted for you. But please don't try any of it out on me. Just imagine that you're the woman on the table. Struggle as she might have struggled.'

Paniatowski made a show of resistance, and found that the dainty doctor was stronger than she looked. Much stronger.

'I'm going to draw the scalpel across your throat,' Dr Shastri said. 'It shouldn't hurt at all, because I'm using the blunt side.' She paused. 'At least, I *think* I'm using the blunt side.'

Gallows humour, Paniatowski thought, as she felt the cold steel pass across her throat. You had to laugh!

And she would have done – if her throat hadn't suddenly locked up!

Dr Shastri released her grip and stepped back. 'It would have all been over in absolutely no time at all,' she said cheerfully. 'The windpipe is cut, blood floods into the lungs. Then it is simply a case of "Goodbye, lady".'

Paniatowski massaged her throat. 'Would the killer have to have been a strong man?' she asked in a rasping voice.

'Not particularly. He was taller than his victim – the nature of the wound indicates that – but then that is only to be expected, for the poor woman was no giant.'

'Is there evidence of any other form of assault?'

'Rape, you mean? Or perhaps some other form of sexual interference?'

'Yes.'

'None. Apart from some bruising to her arms and the slash across her throat, he did her no harm at all.'

'What else can you tell me? Had she been drinking?'

'Indeed. She had drunk a great deal of carrot juice.'

'Carrot juice?'

'Yes, but that is only to be expected under the circumstances.'

'She was very sick, wasn't she?' Paniatowski said.

Dr Shastri beamed. 'What a fine detective you are,' she said. 'Most people would have seen the bald head and noticed the huge weight loss, yet still thought that nothing was wrong with the woman. But you, Sergeant, are a trained observer. If you were to see a man with only one leg, for example, it would not take you more than a minute or two to deduce that he had lost the other one.'

Paniatowski grinned. 'And as hard as you may find it to believe, there are people even better at this job than I am,' she said. The grin faded away. 'What was it? Cancer?'

The doctor nodded. 'The enemy within.

Your victim had been on an intensive course of chemotherapy.'

'Was it doing her any good?'

'Virtually not at all. The cancer had reached an advanced stage. Even with the drugs, she must often have been in a great deal of pain. It could almost be said that her killer did her a favour.'

Paniatowski reached into her handbag and produced two miniature vodka bottles.

'Drink?' she suggested.

Dr Shastri walked over to the shelves and returned with two glass retorts. Looking at them, Paniatowski decided it would be wisest not to ask what they contained previously.

'It is against my religion to drink alcohol,' the doctor said. 'So only a small one for me, please.'

Paniatowski unscrewed the caps and poured out the liquid. Dr Shastri knocked hers back with all the panache of a hardened Cossack.

'Can I ask you to do something for me, Doc?' Paniatowski asked.

'Of course. It's what I've been waiting for.'

'You have?'

'Naturally. Or was I wrong to assume that the vodka you have given me was nothing more than a bribe?'

Paniatowski grinned again. If it hadn't been for the other woman's golden-brown skin, she'd have been willing to swear they were twins, separated at birth.

'No, you weren't wrong,' she admitted. 'It was a bribe.'

'So what is it you wish me to do to earn it?'

'I wish you to make one quick phone call,' Paniatowski said.

Eleven

The clock was just striking noon as Woodend entered the upstairs dining room of the pub which the brewery insisted was called the White Swan, but the locals refused to recognize by any other name than the Dirty Duck. He looked around him. There was no sign of Dexter Bryant. But his arrival had not gone unnoticed. An attractive woman in her late forties first smiled at him and then signalled that he should join her.

Woodend walked over to the table. 'I'm afraid you may have mistaken me for somebody else,' he said.

The smile on the woman's face melted away into a look of concern. 'Oh dear,' she said. 'How embarrassing. I'd have staked my life on your being the right man. You *look* so much like a chief inspector! You certainly *ought* to be one, even though you're not.'

'As a matter of fact, I am,' Woodend said.

'Then you *are* Mr Woodend?'

'Yes.'

The smile returned. 'I knew my journalistic instincts hadn't let me down,' the woman said. 'I'm Constance Bryant, Dexter's wife. My husband's terribly sorry but he's going to be late – he has some family matters to deal with – and he said that we should start without him. Do please sit down.'

Woodend sat, and when the waiter came he ordered a mixed grill with all the heart-clogging trimmings. Constance Bryant, in contrast, wanted only a cheese salad.

'You're expecting me to ask you about your current case, aren't you?' Mrs Bryant said brightly.

'It's what people normally do,' Woodend admitted.

'And if I did ask, you'd fob me off with generalities, wouldn't you? You'd say, for example, that it was too early in the investigation to draw any firm conclusions.'

'Probably.'

'And all the time, the thought would be going through your mind that I'd got a real nerve to probe like that. You'd want to say that I'd never dream of asking a doctor about the health of one of his patients, so what gave me the right to question a policeman –

who's just as much a professional as any quack – about his investigation. Or perhaps you'd want to cut straight to the chase and tell me it was none of my bloody business.'

Woodend grinned. 'You sound like a woman who's talked to a lot of bobbies. An' I noticed you talked about *journalistic* instincts. Are you in the same business as your husband?'

'Yes and no. I'm a journalist by trade, and before I married Dexter I was a foreign correspondent for more years than I care to remember.'

'Then you must have married Mr Bryant...?'

'Rather late in life?'

'I wasn't goin' to say that,' Woodend told her, a little uncomfortably.

Constance Bryant laughed. 'Of course you were, and you should be grateful I've pulled you out of a potentially embarrassing situation. Dexter's my second husband. My first died.'

'I'm sorry,' Woodend said.

'It was a long time ago,' Constance Bryant said. Then she shook her head. 'No, I'm lying. I'm very happy with Dexter now – I couldn't imagine being married to anyone else – but whenever I think of Edward's death, it seems to me as if it only happened yesterday.' She paused, and a look of remorse came to her face. 'But now I *am* embarrassing you.'

'Not really,' Woodend said unconvincingly.

'Change the subject. Ask me something else. Quickly!'

'How did you become a foreign correspondent?'

Constance Bryant smiled again. 'A good question,' she said. 'Edward was a businessman, and we lived in India. Have you ever been there?'

'No.'

'Then I'd better explain a little about what life was like for us. We didn't mix with the natives. It wasn't our choice – it simply wasn't the done thing. So we were forced to live in a very closed society. We gave dinner parties, we played bridge at the club – and all we ever saw were the same old faces again and again. At first I had my son, Richard, to distract me, but as he began to grow and need me less, I became incredibly bored. Then I got the idea of writing articles for the English papers, and discovered I was rather good at it. Edward died, and Richard and I came back to England. I needed to do something to earn my own living, and journalism seemed the natural choice. The *Daily Standard* took me on as foreign correspondent, and I travelled the world covering revolutions, famines and natural disasters. I don't suppose it could have been described as an easy life by any means, but I enjoyed it.'

'But all the time, your ultimate goal was to live in Whitebridge an' run the Mid Lancs *Courier*,' Woodend said.

'You're teasing, aren't you?'

No, Woodend thought, with a sudden shock of realization. He wasn't teasing – he was flirting.

'I … er … wasn't suggesting you'd made the wrong decision,' he said, to cover his confusion.

'There's a lot of pressure in working for a national newspaper, and the more important you are, the greater that pressure is,' Constance Bryant said. 'Dexter and I had been at the top of our profession for quite a long time. We decided to slow down a little, and when I inherited the newspaper from my uncle, it seemed as if fate was pointing us in the direction we'd already decided to take.'

'So who *does* run the *Courier*?' Woodend asked. 'You? Or your husband?'

'Our plan was to run it jointly, and that's probably what we'll end up doing.'

'But you're not doin' it yet?'

Constance Bryant shook her head. 'Ever since we've moved to Whitebridge, I've been rather under the weather. My doctor says it's an allergy, but until he has established exactly what *sort* of allergy, he can't prescribe the medication which will clear it up.'

She had been a good hostess, Woodend thought – but not a perfect one. All through the conversation, she had been glancing at the door whenever she thought Woodend wasn't looking, and now, seeing the look of relief come to her face, he realized just how nervous she must have been.

He turned to follow her gaze. Standing in the entrance were two men. One of them was, Woodend guessed, in his early fifties. He was of medium height, had black hair and was wearing a smart blue suit. The other was taller and much younger – possibly no more than twenty-five or twenty-six. His hair was unfashionably long, and his chin was covered with stubble. He was wearing the kind of combat jacket sold in the Army and Navy Stores. Neither man looked exactly comfortable in the other's company.

Constance Bryant rose from her chair.

'Will you excuse me for a moment?' she asked, but she was already moving away before Woodend had had time to answer.

The woman joined the two men in the doorway. The Chief Inspector was too far away to hear what was being said, but he could read enough in the stance of the three people to get a rough impression of what was going on.

The younger man – who was possibly Mrs Bryant's son – had an aggressive air about him. Aggressive *and* aggrieved, the Chief Inspector guessed. The world as it was constituted did not appear to please him, and if he was unhappy with the world in general, then Whitebridge must get right up his nose.

Mrs Bryant, in contrast, couldn't give a hang about the world, but only about her son. She had lost her earlier aura of quiet confidence. Now she hovered uncertainly like a dog which fully expects to be beaten and will accept such a beating – should it come – as entirely justified.

And then there was Mr Bryant. He seemed torn between two opposing forces. On the one hand, he clearly felt sympathy for the younger man, and would gladly have taken on some of his burden, had that been possible. On the other hand, he was well aware of the effect that Richard was having on his mother, and would cheerfully have reduced him to a pulp if that could have alleviated it.

The trio appeared to have run out of things they wanted to say to one another – or perhaps of things they *could* say. Mrs Bryant took hold of her son's arm, and after a token show of resistance, he allowed himself to be led away. Mr Bryant watched them go, then brushed the edge of his hand over the lapels of his jacket, as if his troubles could be swept away like an unwanted piece of lint. That done, he squared his shoulders and turned to face Woodend's table.

Well, it had certainly been an interesting lunch *so far*, the Chief Inspector thought.

Twelve

Rutter stood watching as the uniformed constables continued to search Mad Jack's Field. In theory, he supposed, he was *supervising* the search, but watching the officers' slow and meticulous progress only made him feel useless. He wanted to be away from there. He wanted to be *doing* things.

The screech of car tyres from somewhere close to the edge of the industrial estate made him look up. It was always possible, of course, that the sound heralded the arrival of some other lunatic driver – but he was putting his money on it being Monika Paniatowski.

He caught sight of the bright-red MGA approaching the nearest roundabout at something considerably in excess of the recommended speed. Monika had *always* driven too fast, he thought, but there'd been a time when he'd considered it more the traffic police's business than his. Now things had changed. Now, despite the fact that she was an excellent driver, he worried about her.

The MGA came to a shrieking halt a few

yards from him. Paniatowski gave him a broad smile, and gestured that he should come over to her. It was not until he was halfway there that he realized that in the old days – when they seriously loathed each other – she would never have acted so imperiously towards a man who outranked her.

'I've got a lead on our stiff, and I didn't want to wait until the boss is free before I got the all-clear to follow it up,' Paniatowski said.

'So since I'm the Number Two on this investigation, you're here to ask for my permission?' Rutter asked.

'Exactly,' Paniatowski said casually, as if she regarded the granting of that permission as a mere formality. 'Can you get away from here, do you think?'

'I suppose I could,' Rutter replied. 'You'd feel happier if I accompanied you, would you?'

'Don't know about that, but I should think it'd be more fun for *you* to come with me,' Paniatowski said cheerfully. She patted the passenger seat. 'Get in, then, Inspector!'

Rutter had hardly had time to settle in the bucket seat before Paniatowski slammed the car into gear and was off again.

'If it's not too much trouble, would you mind telling me where we're going, Sergeant?' Rutter asked.

Paniatowski threw the MGA into a dubiously legal U-turn, and once again her tyres screeched out a tortured protest.

'We're going to a street called Rawalpindi Road,' she said. 'It's not far from here. In fact, my guess is that it's no more than five minutes away on foot. A five minute walk from where we found the body! Significant, wouldn't you say?'

'So you think that our victim lived in Rawalpindi Road?'

'Exactly.'

'And just *what* makes you think that?'

'I've just found out that she was dying of cancer. That's why she was bald – because of the chemotherapy.'

'I still don't see...'

'Did you know Whitebridge General Hospital has a wing devoted exclusively to the treatment of cancer?'

'No.'

'Neither did I. Both of us being young and healthy, there's no reason why we should. But apparently it's quite a big unit, and it's where anybody with cancer who lives within a fifteen-mile radius of Whitebridge eventually ends up being treated. Anyway, they've got this one outpatient on their books – a woman called Betty Stubbs – who didn't turn up for her treatment this morning. According to the hospital, that's not like her at all. She's always been so reliable before.'

'That doesn't necessarily mean—'

'And not only that, but she's the right age, the right height and has the right kind of cancer at the right stage of development. In other words, my dear Watson, she fits the description of our stiff to a T.'

'You seem to have learned a great deal,' Rutter said.

'Yes, I have, haven't I?' Paniatowski replied complacently.

'And they really gave out all that information *over the phone*?' Rutter asked, with growing unease.

'Yes, they did.'

'Isn't that against the rules? Isn't it, in all but the most extreme circumstances, actually *illegal*?'

'Possibly.'

'Yet they were perfectly willing to talk to you?'

Paniatowski grinned. 'I didn't say that.'

'Then what *are* you saying?'

The grin widened. 'If either of us had rung up, they'd have given us the cold shoulder. But when it's a doctor who's making the inquiry – a member of their club, the medical equivalent of a fellow Freemason – then it's another matter altogether.'

'And did a doctor make this particular inquiry?'

'Yes.'

'Which doctor?'

'No, not a witch doctor,' Paniatowski said, the grin still in place. 'A proper one, with all the right certificates hanging on the wall.'

'What was the name of this doctor?' Rutter asked, almost – but not quite – adopting a cold official tone.

'And you call yourself a detective!' Paniatowski replied, not noticing. 'You should be able to work it out for yourself.'

Rutter thought for a moment, then the answer became obvious. 'Was it Dr Shastri?'

'The very same. She was most willing to oblige. I think that if she's handled in the right way, she could very well turn out to be a really valuable addition to the team.'

'She broke the law,' Rutter said, his unease having now almost graduated to alarm. 'You *both* broke the law!'

'Possibly,' Paniatowski agreed. 'But only in the interests of speeding up the investigation – of seeing justice done. Besides, things are only wrong if you get caught doing them. And we won't – because we're the only two people who know about it.'

'You're forgetting me,' Rutter reminded her. 'I know about it.'

'Yes, but you don't really count.'

'I am your superior officer. It is *my* job to see that you're doing *your* job within the limits of the law.'

Paniatowski laughed, as if she thought he'd *set out* to be funny. 'Oh, come on, Bob!' she said.

Rutter turned away, so she couldn't see his frown. Monika was cutting far too many corners. Perhaps she always had, but now that he was closer to her – now that she trusted him more – he was starting to see the full extent of the problem. And it *was* a problem, because on occasions like this she was not only cutting corners herself, but also dragging him round them with her.

In the old days he could have pulled her up for such behaviour – perhaps even issued her with a warning. But now, in their changed circumstances, he was not sure he still had that option.

Thirteen

Dexter Bryant took the seat that his wife had recently vacated and gestured to the waiter to take away her unfinished food.

'Sorry to be so late, Chief Inspector,' he said.

'That's all right, I had a nice chat with your missus,' Woodend replied. 'What was the problem? Difficulties with your son?'

'With my stepson,' Bryant corrected him

automatically. Then the Editor's eyes narrowed. 'What makes you ask that?'

'There just seemed to be a bit of tension between you.'

'He was angry, but his anger wasn't directed at me,' Bryant said. 'At least, it wasn't directed *specifically* at me. You must understand that the boy's been through some difficulties, and it's taking him a while to readjust. But I'm not unduly worried. Richard has many fine qualities, and he'll come right in the end.'

The waiter appeared with his notepad. 'Are you ready to order now, Mr Bryant, sir?'

Bryant shook his head. 'No, given that I'm starting a little late, I think I'll skip lunch and just have a gin and tonic.' He turned to Woodend. 'I've been meaning to arrange a lunchtime meeting with you for weeks, but somehow I never quite got round to it. But now's the time, if there ever was one, isn't it?'

'Is it?' Woodend replied. 'Why?'

'Because of the murder last night.'

'Would you like to spell out exactly what you mean – just so there's no misunderstandin'?' Woodend asked cautiously.

Bryant laughed. 'You think I'm here to ask for special access to police sources, don't you?'

'It wouldn't be the first time that kind of thing's happened.'

'Well, it's not happening now. Quite the

reverse, in fact. I'm here to offer you the services of my newspaper – and that offer is unconditional.'

'Again, I'd be happier if you spelled it out,' Woodend said.

'Very well. We're already printing the dead woman's photograph in our next edition, though I've no doubt you'll have identified her by the time it hits the street. We're also more than willing to give prominence to any other appeal you want to make. And, of course, you can rely on a favourable editorial. I'm not in the business of attacking the police.' Bryant paused. 'At least, I'm not in the habit of attacking them unless they're completely incompetent – and even if I didn't know your reputation, I can see just from looking at you that you're far from that.'

'I always get a little bit worried when people start to flatter me, Mr Bryant,' Woodend said.

'I don't blame you,' Bryant responded. 'But it's not flattery to say that you're good at your job, just as it's not conceit for me to say that I'm good at mine. It's a realistic assessment of the situation as it exists.'

'An' the most dangerous kind of flattery is the kind which says it's not flattery at all.'

Bryant laughed. 'I can't really believe you're as cynical as you seem, Chief Inspector.'

'Can't you? Why's that?'

'Because nobody is.' Bryant's gin and tonic arrived, and he took a small sip. 'There is one other way I can help you,' he continued, growing more serious again.

'An' what way might that be?'

'During the course of my career, the police have approached me several times with a request to plant false information in the paper – information aimed solely at misleading the man they're seeking. I'm not unique in this, I know, but I also know that some of my colleagues have refused to cooperate because they say it will damage their reputations. I'm not like that. I've always put duty before reputation, and if it helps, in even a small way, to catch a dangerous criminal, I'll print any lie you want me to print.'

'Thank you,' Woodend said.

'I mean it.'

'I'm sure you do.' Woodend leant back in his chair. 'Most things in this life operate on the tit-for-tat principle. Well, you've just offered me the "tit". Isn't it about time I heard about the "tat"?'

'You're right,' Bryant agreed. 'I do want a favour.'

'I thought so. Let's hear it, then.'

'Last night, when I heard about the fire engines being called out—'

'How *did* you hear about it?' Woodend

interrupted.

Bryant smiled. 'No comment.'

'Was it one of my lads who tipped you the wink?'

'I didn't hear it from the police.'

'So it was somebody in the fire service?'

'Again, no comment. A reporter who reveals his sources doesn't keep those sources very long.'

'So you knew that there'd been a fire and the police were involved. Were you also aware there'd been a murder?'

Bryant frowned. 'No, I wasn't. If I had been, I might not have...' He trailed off.

'Might not have what?' Woodend asked, pouncing on the indecision.

'Might not have sent Jamie Clegg down there,' Bryant admitted reluctantly.

'Is that what this is all about?' Woodend asked. 'One of your reporters?'

'Yes, it is. He's a nice lad, Jamie. Very keen.'

'Go on,' Woodend said.

Bryant's confidence had continued to ebb away, and now he seemed a little unsure how to proceed.

'What ... er ... what happened is at least partly my fault,' he said. 'I've been trying to inject a bit of life into the *Courier*, and it's possible that, as far as my staff are concerned, I've gone a little too far a little too fast.'

'This Jamie Clegg,' Woodend said. 'He

wouldn't happen to be the feller my sergeant ended up chasin', by any chance?'

'He would.'

'You *told* him to sneak on to Mad Jack's Field an' try an' steal one of the petrol cans?'

'Of course not. I would never have done such a thing. Not only is it unethical, but it's stupid – any journalist worth his salt knows you'll get more out of the police by co-operating than you will from trying to pull a fast one over on them. In fact, what Jamie did was *doubly* stupid – because trying to find a vital clue on a large site in the darkness was about as effective as pissing into the wind.'

'Then if you had nothin' to do with it—'

'But the point is, he may have thought that's what I *wanted* him to do – may have imagined that's what I meant when I told my staff they should use their initiative. That's why I say this whole thing might be partly my fault.'

'I'm still not sure what you're after,' Woodend said.

'Now that you know who your intruder was, you're probably thinking of charging him with something.'

'Damn right I am.'

'And indeed, you're perfectly entitled to do so. I couldn't blame you if you did. But the lad didn't mean any harm. And as far as I can ascertain, he didn't *do* any harm.'

'He made my sergeant ladder one of her new nylon stockings.'

'Then I'll make sure he buys her a new pair. Or perhaps even half a dozen pairs, to compensate for the inconvenience he's caused. But as I said, the only thing he's really guilty of is being too eager to do his job well. You and I both know what that's like. So could you let him off this time?'

'If I do—'

'If you do, I promise you I'll give him the biggest bollocking he's ever had in his life.'

'I suppose it would cut down on the paperwork if I looked the other way for once,' Woodend said. 'Besides, we're all entitled to make one mistake. But if he ever oversteps the mark again—'

'He won't. From now on, I'll make sure I keep him on a pretty tight rein.'

Woodend nodded. 'Then we'll say no more about it.'

'Thank you,' the Editor said. 'One more thing.'

'Yes?'

'There's something I need to warn you about. I didn't mention it earlier, in case you thought I was trying to curry favour. But now that I've got what *I* want, perhaps you'll take it at face value.'

'You can be a long-winded bugger when you want to be, can't you?' Woodend said jovially.

Bryant grinned again. 'There's always the danger that when you live off words, like I do, you'll end up strangling yourself with them. Do you want the warning or not?'

'Aye, you may as well tell me, now that you're all keyed up for it,' Woodend said.

'Am I right to think that the name Elizabeth Driver is not entirely unknown to you?'

'It's far from unknown,' Woodend said, an element of a growl creeping into his tone.

There'd been a time when Elizabeth Driver – rising star of the *Daily Globe* – *had* been a stranger to him, but ever since she'd tried to manipulate the facts around the murder at Westbury Hall to her own advantage, she'd been an intermittent thorn in his side.

'I take it from your reaction that you're not one of her greatest admirers,' Bryant said.

'Miss Driver, in my opinion, is to responsible journalism what Ghengis Khan was to market gardenin'.'

Bryant laughed. 'That's pretty much my opinion of the lady, too. So I imagine you'll be far from delighted to learn that, according to one of my old colleagues on Fleet Street who I spoke to less than an hour ago, Miss Driver is already on her way up here.'

'I've heard better news,' Woodend admitted.

Fourteen

A long row of terraced houses on one side of the street gazed across at another long row on the other side. At the top end was the pub, at the bottom end the corner shop. The houses were all two-up, two-down, except where extensions had been built on to their rears. Their front doors opened straight on to the street and their back yards could be entered from an alley. Rawalpindi Road looked exactly like a dozen or so other streets in the same area – and a hundred or so other streets in the rest of Whitebridge.

Paniatowski drove her MGA slowly down the street, one eye on the lookout for children, the other on the numbers on the front doors.

'That's it!' she said, pointing at a house roughly halfway between the grocery store and the boozer. 'Number Forty.'

The adjoining houses had brightly painted front doors – one red, the other blue – with sash windows to match. Number Forty's, in contrast, was an old-fashioned chocolate-brown colour, which was made all the more depressing by the fact that the paint had started to peel and flake.

'It must be hard to get enthusiastic about home improvements when you know you've only got a few months left to enjoy them,' Paniatowski said, examining the door from the driving seat.

'Still, you'd think her husband would make the effort – if only to show that there's always hope,' said Rutter, who always kept the outside of his house smart, even though his wife would *never* be able to see it.

'She doesn't have a husband,' Paniatowski told him. 'According to her hospital records, she's a widow with no children. That's probably why no one's noticed she's missing yet.'

Rutter climbed out of the passenger side of the car and had almost reached the front door before he realized that Paniatowski was not beside him. He turned to see that the sergeant was rifling through the organized chaos which was her glove compartment.

'Are you coming or what?' he asked.

'In a minute,' Paniatowski replied irritably. 'When I've found my spare packet of cigarettes.'

'I'll just hang around till you're ready, then, shall I, Sergeant Paniatowski?' Rutter asked.

'You're an inspector, Mr Rutter, sir,' Paniatowski said, transferring her search for the elusive cigarette packet to the floor of the car. 'You should be able to knock on a door, even without me there to hold your hand.'

How would an outsider interpret that exchange? Rutter wondered. Would he regard it as harmless banter between colleagues? Or might he take a darker view and see it as the sergeant challenging the inspector's authority by pushing back the limits of what was acceptable? Perhaps he would even come to the conclusion which Rutter had pretty much reached himself – that now they were sleeping together, Paniatowski had decided that the equality of the bedroom should set the tone for the rest of their relationship.

He shouldn't need to be asking himself these questions, Rutter thought as he took out his growing frustration on the door knocker – and the fact that he *had to* ask them was nobody's fault but his own.

He heard his knock echo down the hallway of the house, but there was no sound of footsteps in response. He knocked again, even harder this time.

The blue door to his immediate left opened, and a woman appeared on the doorstep. She was in her mid forties. Her hair was in curlers and a cigarette dangled from the corner of her mouth. She placed her hands squarely on her hips – a sign among northern housewives that she was looking for

112

trouble – and turned her angry eyes on Rutter.

'You men!' she said in disgust. 'I know you can't control your instincts – I've got a husband of my own – but why do you always have to be so bloody loud about it?'

'I'm a—' Rutter began.

'I know what you are,' the woman interrupted. 'Hasn't she told you yet that you should use the back door when you come visitin'? That's what all the other randy sods do!'

'Is that what you think he is?' asked Paniatowski, who had now found her cigarettes and joined Rutter on the pavement.

The sergeant's arrival served first to confuse the other woman, then to tell her that she had made a big mistake.

'Oh, I'm sorry,' she said, blushing. 'I thought your friend was...'

'A randy sod?' Paniatowski supplied.

'No, I...' The woman's eyes narrowed with a sudden suspicion. 'You're not Jehovah's Witnesses, are you?' she demanded. 'Because if you are, you're wastin' your time. She'll want no truck with you – an' neither do I!'

She was quick to start closing the door, but not quick enough to stop Rutter preventing the manoeuvre with a strategically placed foot.

'Police!' Paniatowski said, producing her

warrant card.

'Police?' the woman echoed.

'Could we have your name, please?'

'Ryder. Thelma Ryder. *Mrs* Thelma Ryder.'

'What did you mean about Mrs Stubbs' visitors going to the back door, Mrs Ryder?' the sergeant asked.

'Nothin'. I ... nothin'.'

'Just exactly what kind of visitors are we talking about here?' Paniatowski persisted.

The other woman shrugged her thin shoulders, and the ash which had been building up on her cigarette end broke free and fell to the ground.

'Well ... you know...' she said vaguely.

'No, I don't know,' Paniatowski told her. 'I'm convent-educated, you see. The nuns kept us away from the seamier side of life. That's why I need to have everything spelled out for me now.'

'It's ... it's a bit awkward to explain.'

'Try!'

'Well, ever since her husband died, Betty's been a bit strapped for cash, an' so last year she started entertainin' gentlemen callers.'

'Are you trying to say that she was on the game?'

'I wouldn't put it quite like that.'

'Then how would you put it?'

'Like I said, she was entertainin' gentlemen callers.'

Paniatowski reached into her handbag and

produced the photograph she'd picked up from the morgue. 'Is this her?'

The other woman peered at the picture. 'Looks a bit pasty, doesn't she?' Thelma Ryder asked. Then the obvious thought hit her. 'It's not ... She hasn't ... I mean, I heard about the murder on the wireless, but I never imagined...'

'Tell me more about the visitors,' Paniatowski said.

'What do you want to know about them?'

'We could start with how many of them there were.'

'I used to see quite a lot of them goin' in. Then the neighbours complained and she started lettin' them in through the back door, so I wouldn't really know any more, would I?'

'Wouldn't you?' Paniatowski retorted. 'What can you see when you look out of your back bedroom window?'

'The yard.'

'Whose yard? Yours? Or Betty Stubbs'?'

'Well, both of them.'

'And are you seriously trying to tell me that a woman with your natural curiosity didn't notice when her next-door neighbour had visitors?'

Mrs Ryder looked down at her doorstep. 'I might have noticed the occasional visitor when I was upstairs dustin',' she admitted.

Paniatowski sighed. 'How many of them

were there?' she asked with mock weariness.

'It depended,' Mrs Ryder mumbled. 'There could be four or five of them on pay day, but in the middle of the week there might only be one or two. An' she hadn't been seein' as many recently.'

No, she wouldn't have been – not with her cancer – Paniatowski thought. 'What kind of men visited Mrs Stubbs?' she asked.

'Ordinary-enough lookin' fellers, I suppose. Middle-aged men, most of them. Some of them wore overalls, but there were quite a few who were dressed up in suits, or at least jacket and trousers.'

Paniatowski could picture them – down-trodden men who took what they couldn't get at home from a woman in no position to refuse them.

'Did you recognize any of them?' she asked.

'No!' Thelma Ryder said quickly.

A lie – obviously – but one that could be put on the back burner until they'd gleaned the rest of the information that Mrs Ryder would be willing to give up voluntarily.

'If you had to make a guess at how many *different* "gentlemen callers" she had, what figure do you think you'd come up with?'

'Hard to say. Some stopped callin' after a while, but then there were always new ones an'—'

'Just a rough figure. That's all I expect,'

116

Paniatowski said.

'Twenty. Maybe twenty-five.'

So, without looked into any other motives for Betty Stubbs' death, they already had a score of potential killers to investigate, Paniatowski thought.

Cloggin'-it Charlie was going to love that.

Fifteen

As the train began to slow down on its approach to Whitebridge Station, Elizabeth Driver took her pocket compact out of her handbag and examined her face in the mirror.

She was too much of a realist to try and pass as beautiful, she told herself. On the other hand, it would certainly have been the grossest kind of false modesty to regard the image she was seeing in the mirror as anything other than highly attractive.

'And highly available!' she mouthed at her reflection.

That was what they said back in the offices of the *Daily Globe*, anyway:

'She's like the village bike, everybody's had a ride on her!'

'She's had more pricks in her than a second-

hand dartboard!'

While she might have argued with the crude way the thoughts had been phrased, she had no quarrel with the general assertion. She *was* available, though – as some of those same colleagues who'd made an unwanted pass at her had learned to their extreme physical discomfort – not *universally* so.

And why *shouldn't* she be available? She had no real objection to the sex act, and if using it helped to further her career, who could blame her?

The train passed the chipped enamel Whitebridge sign, then slowed to a crawl. Ignoring the fact that she was sitting in a non-smoking carriage – and that the only other passenger in it had already informed her that he suffered from asthma – she lit up a cigarette.

She always had mixed feelings about returning to this grubby little mill town stuck out in the arse end of nowhere. On the one hand, a sensation of keen anticipation raced excitingly through her blood. On the other, a mood of dull dread could sometimes press down so heavily on her shoulders that she had fight the temptation to catch the very next train back to London. She didn't wonder where these feelings came from. She didn't have to – because she knew. They both had their origins in one single source – Chief

Inspector Charlie-Bloody-Woodend.

Once, at the start of their brittle and usually hostile relationship, she'd offered to go to bed with Woodend – and he'd actually had the nerve to turn her down!

Of course, she'd been a blonde then, she thought, excusing her failure. Now that her hair was jet-black – now that she looked more like a 1930s vamp – his jaded middle-aged fancy might find it more difficult to resist her.

'Not that he'll get the bloody chance!' she said aloud – and with some vehemence.

'What?' her fellow passenger asked.

'Nothing.'

The man coughed. 'Look, if you could just go out into the corridor to smoke...'

'Piss off!' Elizabeth Driver said.

And it wasn't just that Woodend had *turned her down*, she thought. It was that he still refused to admit that it had been a mistake. If he'd apologized to her for his stupidity – or perhaps his lack of nerve – she could have put the whole matter behind her. If he'd shown how sorry he was by feeding her information which he denied the other reporters, she might even have considered giving him a second chance to bed her. But he refused to fall under her spell. Worse still, whenever she'd tried to outflank him on an investigation, he'd always seemed to be one step ahead of her, with the inevitable result that while he solved his case, she lost her scoop.

That was where the dread came from – from the knowledge that he'd always beaten her in the past, and might well do so again.

But there was also the anticipation – the thought that history could be reversed and she might one day be able to get one over on him. And this time, there was a distinct possibility that she could – because this time she just might have Dexter Bryant on her side.

She hardly knew Bryant. He had been one of the true aristocrats of Fleet Street when she'd been nothing more than a humble serf. But situations changed. He'd come down a few steps in the world, while she had risen a few. Now they might possibly be able to meet somewhere in the middle.

There was no reason why an alliance between them shouldn't work, she told herself. They were, after all, both crime reporters. They had a mutual interest in wanting to break a sensational – and often fairly accurate – story before anybody else could. They were a natural team.

Besides, she had another ace up her sleeve. She had met Bryant's wife – the world-famous foreign correspondent – and what a sad-looking, middle-aged, washed-out blonde the woman had turned out to be. Constance Bryant couldn't possibly be giving a vigorous man like Dexter what he needed – which meant that he must constantly be on the lookout for someone else who could. And should he choose to take advantage of it, such a person could soon be landing on his lap – both metaphorically and literally! All he needed to do to make his dreams come true was to see the sense of allying his experience and knowledge with the energy and ruthlessness of a young reporter determined to make it to the top by the time she was thirty.

As the train came to a juddering halt in Whitebridge station, Elizabeth Driver took a last drag on her cigarette, then threw it on the floor and ground the butt with the toe of her shoe.

'See?' she said, looking across at her fellow passenger. 'All gone! No more smoke! Are you happy now?'

The man said nothing, but now the train had ceased to clatter, she could hear how badly he was breathing.

Perhaps she'd been a little unfair to him, she thought, feeling the slight mental twinge which was the closest she ever came to guilt. Perhaps, after all, she should have taken her cigarette into the corridor.

Still, it was too late for that now. She'd have to think of some other way to make it up to him.

She stood up. Her small suitcase and her

portable typewriter were in the luggage rack above her head. She reached up for them – stretching more than was strictly necessary – and felt her skirt begin to ride high up her legs. A little more stretch and she knew the skirt had risen high enough to reveal the tops of her stockings.

She held the pose for several seconds before lifting her luggage clear of the rack. The asthma sufferer would have got quite an eyeful of her long, slim legs, she told herself. She was willing to bet he didn't have anything half as nice as that to look at in his own home.

She opened the carriage door, and stepped on to the platform. Whitebridge railway station was just as she remembered it: crenellated woodwork; old gas mantles which were still in place though it must have been decades since the station had gone electric; travel posters for holiday resorts which had long since ceased to be fashionable. What a dump!

This was the town in which she had already lost several battles – but not yet the war. Though the station buildings blocked any view of Whitebridge from her, she still turned to face the direction in which she knew the police headquarters lay.

'Up yours, Charlie Woodend!' she said, not quite under her voice.

Sixteen

The late afternoon was normally one of Rawalpindi Road's quieter times. With the husbands still at work, the children still in school and the wives toiling over a hot stove, the street could normally expect no more foot traffic than the occasional pensioner on a careful measured stroll and the odd door-to-door salesman chasing his quota.

It was a very different story that particular afternoon. Those residents who had yet to be visited by one of the team of police officers working the road waited impatiently indoors for the call to come. Those who had received the visit gathered together in clusters on each other's doorsteps. They looked at No. 40, then at each other, then back at No. 40 again. The street buzzed with speculation and revelation. It was all very exciting.

In the house where the dead woman had lived there was an air of ordered calm. Surfaces were being dusted for fingerprints, and drawers were being opened in the search for clues. The bedding had already been stripped off and sent to the lab, and the drain in the back yard was being dredged on the off chance that it might contain something useful. Now that the team had a centre from which to operate, things were finally starting to happen.

Woodend walked into the front room of No. 40 and looked around him. It was all pretty much as he would have expected it to be from the outside. The floor was covered by a fitted carpet patterned with purple and yellow swirls. There was a cloth-covered three-piece suite which was probably several years old, but looked hardly used. Three pottery ducks of decreasing sizes were in full flight on the wall, and an electric fire with coal-glow effect sat snugly within a polished tiled fireplace.

'All this must look a bit old-fashioned to you, Monika,' the Chief Inspector said to his sergeant.

Paniatowski, who had been to Woodend's home and recognized the similarities, shrugged awkwardly. 'Well...' she said.

'You have to understand what this room represents,' Woodend told her, 'an' to do that, I suppose, you have to have grown up in Whitebridge – or some place like it – in the thirties. We saw pictures in the newspapers of millionaires swiggin' champagne on their private yachts, but we never thought for a second that anythin' like that would ever come our way. What we hoped for – what we *aspired* to – was this. We wanted a nice front parlour full of furniture that we didn't owe a penny on. We didn't have to use it – that wasn't the point – we just had to *have* it. It would be our own little palace in the middle of harsh, grimy Whitebridge. Go into any front room on this terrace, an' you'll find the mirror image of this one.'

'I suppose you're right,' Paniatowski agreed, slightly mystified.

'You're missin' the point, aren't you?' Woodend asked.

'I think I must be.'

'There are places – like that area we went to in Manchester when we were investigatin' the moorland murders – where women grow up almost expectin' to go on the game. They'd never have thought to put together a room like this. What this room says is "respectable". It says that the woman who arranged it was more than willin' to play by all the rules of the society which surrounded her. It's not the room of a woman who ever thought that she'd end up sellin' herself.'

'Yes, I can see that,' Paniatowski agreed.

'But life doesn't always go as we've planned it, does it?' Woodend continued. 'Husbands die when they're not supposed to, an' electricity bills an' rent demands take no account of personal tragedies.' He lit a cigarette. 'She was on the game purely an' simply because she needed the money, wasn't she?'

Paniatowski nodded. 'According to the neighbours, her husband was a heavy gambler who died leaving her nothing but debts. The bailiffs were hammering on the door even before he'd gone cold.'

'When was this?'

'Three years ago.'

'An' how long after her husband's death did she first go on the game?'

'About six months.'

Aye, Woodend thought, that would be just about right. For the first couple of months she'd be feeling too much of a sense of loss to worry about anything as trivial as her debts. For the next few months, she'd be telling herself there had to be a pleasanter way out of her problems. Finally, when no other solution had magically presented itself, she'd have given in to the inevitable.

'How many punters did she normally see in the course of a week?' he asked Paniatowski.

'As far as we can calculate, there were at least a dozen. Of course, it wasn't always the *same* dozen. Some of her original customers stopped coming after a while, and new ones appeared on the scene.'

'Plus – if she's anythin' like the other cases of prostitution I've come across – there'd be the ones workin' on a schedule, who only saw her once a fortnight or once a month,'

126

Woodend said.

'The travelling salesmen who drop in when they're in town?'

'Aye, an' the henpecked husbands who have to wait until their wives are off on a visit somewhere before they'll risk goin' to a prozzie.'

'Of course, she's not been seeing anything like that number of men recently,' Paniatowski said sombrely.

And no wonder, Woodend thought. The poor woman simply wasn't up to it – she was bloody dying!

'We know *why* she went on the game,' he said. 'Now what we need to know is *how* she went about it.'

'That shouldn't be too difficult to discover, should it?' Paniatowski asked.

'You tell me,' Woodend replied. 'Suppose you were a middle-aged woman who'd led a conventional life up to now, but was thinkin' about turnin' her hand to prostitution. Where would you start?'

'The Boulevard?' Paniatowski hazarded.

'There's only two kinds of prozzies who work the Boulevard. The very young ones who don't know any better – an' the very old ones who have no choice. Betty Stubbs didn't fit into either category. Besides, she didn't pick men up off the street – they came to her house.'

'So maybe she had a pimp,' Paniatowski

suggested.

'An' how would she find one? Put an ad in the Mid Lancs *Courier* – "Middle-aged woman, in desperate straits, seeks procurer?" That doesn't seem very likely, does it now?'

'No,' Paniatowski admitted. 'It doesn't.'

'Anyway, pimps like their girls to be young. There are plenty of spring chickens ready to be snapped up. Why would they bother with an old broiler like Betty?'

'And if she did have a pimp, he'd want her to see a lot more than twelve punters a week,' Paniatowski said.

'Exactly,' Woodend agreed. 'Twelve punters a night would be nearer the mark. Did Betty have a phone?'

'No.'

'Then we can rule out her puttin' advertisements in tobacconists' windows as a way of makin' contact. They never include an address on the cards, only a phone number.'

'Maybe she met her customers at some kind of social gathering,' Paniatowski said.

'Like what, for example?'

'I don't know. A church hall whist drive?'

'Aye, you meet some rum buggers at church hall whist drives,' Woodend said, only partly sarcastically.

'Or a social club.'

'It's worth checkin' on. In the meantime, we might get a clearer picture by talkin' to some of her punters. I'll need a list of as many names as you can come up with.'

'That won't be easy,' Paniatowski warned him. 'I might manage to squeeze a few names out of her neighbour, but there aren't many men in Whitebridge who'll be willing to volunteer the information that they pay for sex.'

'We might be able to reach some of them through the *Courier*,' Woodend suggested. 'Get on to the Editor. Tell him I want him to put an appeal in tonight's paper for Betty's clients to come forward. Say he should make it plain that their confidentiality will be respected.'

The idea seemed to trouble Paniatowski. 'Isn't that a bit like putting a box of matches into the hands of a pyromaniac?' she asked.

'You're askin' me if we can trust Bryant not to turn our appeal into a sensationalist front-page story?'

'More or less.'

'We can trust him. He'll do a good job for us.' Woodend lit up a cigarette. 'Not that it really matters *how* good a job he does. I don't expect the appeal will lead anywhere.'

'You don't think the killer was one of her punters?' Paniatowski asked.

'If he was, he'll have taken care to ensure that neither the neighbours nor any of Betty's other customers caught sight of him.'

'Why? Because he always knew that he was

going to kill to ~~kill~~ her?'

'Because he always knew there was a *possibility* that he might.' Woodend took a drag on his Capstan. 'I don't know what game he's playin', Monika, but I don't see him havin' anythin' personal against Betty.'

'You don't? Why?'

'Because the most important thing to him is not that he killed her, but what he did with her body afterwards. He needed a bonfire, an' the kids built one for him. He needed a dead body, an' Betty Stubbs was available. She was nothin' more than a prop to him.'

'Who's he playing this game of his *with*?' Paniatowski asked.

'Partly with the people he expected to gather around the bonfire once the incendiary device had gone off. That particular pleasure was denied to him when those two kids found the body. But mostly I think he's playin' with *us*. He wants to show us how superior he is. He wants to demonstrate that even though he took tremendous risks, we still can't catch him.'

Paniatowski shuddered. 'The problem is, he caught us with a sucker punch – and he'll know that as well as we do.'

'Exactly.'

'If he's really to convince himself that he's superior to us, he's going to give us a second chance – one we'll be ready for.'

'Yes.'

'And the only way he can do that is to give us another body, isn't it?'

'Looks like it,' Woodend agreed gravely.

Seventeen

From her vantage point in the reception area of the Mid Lancs *Courier*, Elizabeth Driver was in an excellent position to observe much of the workings of the newspaper. Not that it was exactly an enthralling sight, she thought. The place could never have been mistaken for Fleet Street – and that was putting it mildly. In fact, it only a shade more impressive than the offices of the Maltham *Chronicle*, the provincial weekly rag on which she'd been working when Charlie Woodend – miffed that she had slightly distorted reality in order to produce a better story – had personally seen to it that she'd lost her job.

Her musing shifted from Woodend to Dexter Bryant. The Editor might well put on a brave face in public about his changed fortunes, but a face was all it could possibly be. The simple truth was that going from the *Daily Standard* to the Mid Lancs *Courier* was the equivalent of moving out of Buckingham Palace and into a small, damp council flat.

131

A young woman in a short blue dress appeared at Elizabeth Driver's side. 'Miss Driver?' she asked.

'That's me.'

'I'm Margaret Pearson, Mr Bryant's secretary. If you'd care to follow me, he'll see you now.'

As she stood up, Elizabeth Driver gave the other woman the automatic once-over. Tall, long legs, nice breasts. She wondered whether Miss Pearson was *just* a secretary or whether her job also involved duties of a much more intimate nature.

The secretary led her into the Editor's office, she and Bryant shook hands, and then they both sat down. His appearance surprised her. She was almost certain he'd only been away from London for a little over a year, yet he looked considerably older than the last time she'd seen him. He was still rather dishy, though – in a mature sort of way!

'What can I do for you, Miss Driver?' Bryant asked.

'Call me Elizabeth,' she said. 'Or Liz, if you prefer.'

'What can I do for you, *Elizabeth*?'

'Even though I've been to Whitebridge a few times before, I'm still what you might call a *comparative* stranger,' Elizabeth Driver said, crossing her legs to reveal a generous expanse of thigh. 'And that's a problem all we reporters have to face at one time or another, isn't it? Reporting crime in the regions is, I'm sure you'll agree, pretty much a case of fighting the enemy on his own ground.'

'Fighting the enemy on his own ground?' Bryant repeated, as if she'd lost him already. 'What enemy? I'm not sure I know who you mean.'

'In this particular case, the enemy I'm talking about is Detective Chief Inspector Charlie Woodend.'

'Is he the enemy?' Bryant asked. 'He struck me as a very honest, straightforward copper.'

'Oh, he's good at giving that impression to people,' Driver admitted. 'Very good. But it's all a façade. Cloggin'-it Charlie is one of the most devious men you'll ever be unfortunate enough to meet. He'd shaft his own grandmother if he thought it would help him to get what he wanted.'

'You're saying he's a master at playing constabulary politics?'

'That's right.'

'Then I'm surprised he's still only a chief inspector.'

'He's made some mistakes in the past,' Elizabeth Driver conceded, 'but, like the cunning old fox he is, he's learned from them. And that makes him even more difficult to handle.'

The phone on the desk rang.

'Excuse me a moment,' Bryant said. He picked up the receiver. 'Yes, Sergeant ... yes, the appeal's gone in ... the paper should be on the street within the hour ... no problem.'

'Was that Monika Paniatowski?' Elizabeth Driver asked, as Bryant placed the phone back on the cradle.

'You're so sharp you're almost in danger of cutting yourself,' Bryant said.

'Woodend's been bedding her ever since she became his bagman. She doesn't like it, but he's made it clear that sleeping with him goes with the job.'

'Indeed?' Bryant said.

'But I didn't come here to talk about Charlie Woodend's sordid little affairs. I've got a proposition to make to you.'

Bryant gave her a smile which might have been interpreted as being encouraging – but then again, might not. 'Go on,' he said.

'The murder last night is sensational copy. It's ages since there's been a real Jack the Ripper-type case for our readers to sink their teeth into. And with a bit of luck it won't stop there.'

'What do you mean? It won't stop there?'

'Our maniac may well decide to strike again. And again! Handled just right, it could be one of the biggest stories of the year.'

'What you say may well be true,' Bryant replied, noncommittally. 'But I'm still not

134

sure why you requested this meeting.'

Elizabeth Driver leant forward a little, partly to give their conversation a conspiratorial air, partly to afford Dexter Bryant a better view of her cleavage.

'We both have our strengths and our weaknesses,' she said, slightly huskily. 'My weakness, as I've already hinted, is that I don't have your local knowledge and contacts.'

'And what's my weakness?' Bryant asked, the smile still hanging tenuously on his face.

'Your weakness is geographical. You'll still have to live in this dump when the case is over, which means that you may think twice about making enemies. I, on the other hand, will soon be off covering another grisly murder in another part of the country, and once I'm gone, I don't give a damn what anybody in Whitebridge thinks about me.'

'It seems to me that Mr Woodend isn't the only one capable of shafting his own grandmother when the need arises,' Bryant said. He stood up and held out his hand for her to shake. 'I really don't think I can help you, Miss Driver.'

'I wouldn't be so hasty if I were you,' Elizabeth Driver warned. 'This story could be your ticket back to Fleet Street.'

She knew she'd made a mistake the moment the words were out of her mouth. Bryant tensed, and all signs of geniality disappeared from his face. He was suddenly a very powerful, frightening man, and Elizabeth Driver began to realize why the reporters who'd known him well still spoke of him with awe.

'Are you suggesting I left Fleet Street under some kind of cloud, Miss Driver?' he asked.

'No, but—'

'But you *are* suggesting that in order to get back there, I need to have some kind of dowry to buy my way in.'

'I never meant—'

'I'm constantly being offered jobs on national newspapers. I turn them down because, for personal reasons which are no concern of yours, I choose to live in White-bridge.'

'I wasn't suggesting—'

'I haven't finished!' Dexter Bryant said, in a voice which made her blood run cold. 'You seem to think we're colleagues – but we're not! We might inhabit the same jungle, but we're about as alike as the elephant and the hyena.'

'If you're trying to—'

'I don't like your kind of crime reporting, Miss Bryant. I never have. The way you present it, it's murder as entertainment. It sticks to the facts only as long as those facts will provide your readers with the morbid fascination they seem to crave. You say I could help you with your story, and you're undoubtedly right. I could make a big difference – but I'm not going to. Would you like to know why?'

She didn't want to ask, yet she heard herself doing so anyway.

'I don't like your style, Miss Driver,' Bryant said, 'and even more than that I don't like your bland assumption that I'd be more than willing to be unfaithful to my wife.'

'I really have no idea what you're talking about, Mr Bryant!' Elizabeth Driver protested.

'Of course you do. You sit there, squirming in your chair and sending out signals that you're available, but it's all a waste of effort. I've had experts try to seduce me, Miss Driver – women well out of your class in all respects. And they've failed!' His anger seemed to be increasing with every word he spoke. 'My wife is older than you are, and she's in ill health. But she's got ten times the sex appeal you have. Or ever could have – even with lessons!'

'I've never been so insulted in my life!' Elizabeth Driver said, outraged.

'It's your own fault,' Bryant told her, his anger gone and his tone now almost mild. 'If you don't want to be treated like a pig, Miss Driver, then stop rolling around in the shit.'

Elizabeth Driver sat in the saloon bar of the

Vines, a pub which had as its main advantage its proximity to the Mid Lancs *Courier* offices. The two gin and tonics she'd rapidly knocked back had calmed her down – but not a lot. She felt humiliated, not only because Dexter Bryant had spoken to her in the way he had, but also because – for reasons she still did not quite fully understand herself – she had allowed herself to just sit there and take it.

She'd come to Whitebridge expecting to have one enemy to deal with. Now it appeared that she had acquired a second. Well, so what? She was Elizabeth Driver – a tough-as-nails reporter, a rising star of Fleet Street – and she could handle them both.

But how exactly should she go about it?

'It doesn't matter who they are or how important they may be, every bleeder's got a hidden weakness of some kind – a skeleton in the cupboard,' her boss at the *Daily Globe* had told her on her first morning at the paper. *'And it's our job to find that skeleton and then rattle it to see which bones fall off.'*

She believed that. More than believed – it had become an article of faith.

She still hadn't found the skeleton in Charlie Woodend's cupboard, though she'd been searching for it ever since he was transferred to Whitebridge. But that wasn't to say that she was going to stop looking for it – not by a long chalk!

Dexter Bryant, on the other hand, seemed a much easier nut to crack. For though his skeleton was equally well hidden for the moment, she thought she had a pretty good idea of where to start looking for it.

She ordered a third gin and tonic and ran her argument through her mind once more. No one in their right mind would give up Fleet Street voluntarily, she reasoned. No one with a shred of self-respect or ambition would willingly accept exile in Whitebridge. Therefore, whatever he might claim, Dexter Bryant's present situation was not of his own choosing. He had done something wrong – and exile to Whitebridge was his punishment!

And where had he committed this blunder which had led to his downfall? In London, of course. London, her home turf – where she had contacts, where she knew how to apply pressure to get what she wanted.

She took a slug of her fresh drink and happily contemplated a future in which both skeletons were uncovered, and she had Woodend and Bryant by the throat. She would use them like fighting cocks, setting one against the other for her own pleasure and the advancement of her career. If they co-operated, she would let them get away with a few scratches. If they didn't, she would force them to fight it out to the death.

Eighteen

The landlord of the Drum and Monkey glanced across at the corner table in the public bar and – as he'd expected – saw that the pint of bitter, the half of bitter and the double vodka were occupying their customary seats.

There was no brass plaque on that table which read, 'Reserved between the hours of nine and eleven in the evening (especially when there's been a murder!)' – but there might as well have been. The regulars knew better than to sit there, non-regulars were quickly shooed away from it. It was not that Charlie Woodend had ever asked for special privileges – such a thought would never have entered his head – but it gave the landlord considerable satisfaction to know that important criminal cases were analysed, debated – and perhaps even solved – under his roof. He was not just serving drinks to these three, he told himself in his more fanciful moments – he was literally lubricating the wheels of justice.

Woodend took a sip of his pint, then

reached into the pocket of his hairy sports coat and produced a copy of that night's *Courier*.

'Seen this, Monika?' he asked, waving the paper in his sergeant's direction.

'I've seen it,' Paniatowski replied.

'Well?'

'You seem to have been right about Dexter Bryant,' Paniatowski admitted reluctantly. 'He's done a good job with the appeal for witnesses.'

Woodend beamed with pleasure. 'By heck, but it is *nice* to be right about people – even if it is only once in a blue moon,' he said. He turned to Rutter. 'How've you got on this afternoon, Bob?'

'We managed to extract the names of five of Betty's clients from Mrs Ryder and the other neighbours,' Rutter said. 'I've spoken to them all.'

'An' I trust that, as an ex-grammar school boy, you were reasonably subtle and discreet about it,' Woodend said.

'I didn't stand on their front steps and ask my questions in such a loud voice that their wives were bound to hear, if that's what you meant,' Rutter told him. 'I caught them either at work or on their way home from work.'

'Good,' Woodend said. 'An' how did these fellers react? Did they greet you with open arms?'

141

Rutter smiled. 'Not exactly. I started out by explaining to them that it was a murder – not their morals or their private lives – that I was investigating, but I might as well have saved my breath.'

'Denied it, did they?'

'In the strongest possible terms. A couple of them threatened that if I did anything to blacken their hitherto spotless reputations, they'd sue the police in general and me in particular. But once they'd realized I could not be intimidated into going away, they soon calmed down and admitted that while they had paid Betty for sex, it had all been a mistake, they hadn't enjoyed it, and they'd never do it again.'

'They'll certainly never do it with *Betty* again,' Woodend said. 'Did you learn anythin' interestin' from these little chats of yours?'

Rutter looked troubled. 'Er ... possibly ... but before I go into that, I'd like to hear what Monika has found out.'

'Any objections to doin' things that way round, Monika?' Woodend asked.

'No, sir.'

But there *would have been*, right up to a few months earlier, Woodend thought. When the pair of them had been fighting each other tooth and claw, Paniatowski would have done anything rather than put her cards on the table before Rutter had shown his.

Woodend lit up a cigarette. 'What have you learned about Betty Stubbs from your background check on her, Monika?'

'I've learned just how frighteningly alone a middle-aged widow can be,' Paniatowski said sombrely.

'She was really *that* alone, was she?'

'Yes. After her husband died, she had no one at all to turn to.'

'No relatives?'

'Her parents died years ago. She had a brother, but he was killed in the war. Her husband, Ted, wasn't from round here, and he'd lost touch with his own family. And the marriage wasn't, as they say, blessed with children.'

'But they must surely have had some friends?'

'Her husband cost them any friends they had. The worse his gambling addiction became, the more he tried to borrow from the people he knew in order to support it. And he turned quite nasty if anybody refused him a loan. For the last couple of years before he died, nobody wanted to know him. And that meant, in effect, that nobody wanted to know Betty, either. I haven't been able to find anybody who'd admit to having any more than a passing conversation with her in the last three years.'

'But did you manage to find anybody who at least caught sight of her in the last hour or so before she died?'

'I'm afraid not.'

'Maybe she was at the Saltney Rise Bowling and Social Club,' Rutter suggested.

'What makes you say that?'

'Four of the five punters I interviewed this afternoon said that the first time they met her, it was at the club. And if she had been at the club last night, she'd have probably passed Mad Jack's Field on her way home.'

'Yes, she would, wouldn't she,' Woodend said thoughtfully. 'Your punters didn't happen to say exactly *how* they met her, did they?'

'They said they'd been told that she was on the game.'

'Did they also say who'd told them this interestin' fact?'

'No. At that point, they started coming over all vague. Said they'd forgotten, or that it was a feller they'd only seen in the club that one time.'

'They're lyin'.'

'Of course they're lying. And if you want me to, I'll sweat the truth out of them tomorrow.'

'That probably won't be necessary.'

'Won't it? Why not?'

'Because I've already got a pretty good idea of who was probably pimpin' for her.'

'I didn't know you knew any of the customers at that bowling club.'

'I don't,' Woodend said. 'But if I'd have been in Betty Stubbs' shoes, I know who *I'd* have talked to.'

Rutter stood in the back yard of the Drum and Monkey. He'd told Woodend and Paniatowski he needed to go the toilet – a lie designed to avoid the necessity of explaining why he suddenly needed fresh air.

He gulped some of that air in now – icy air, blowing off the moorland. It stung his lungs, but made him feel better.

Though he'd never expected it – and at first refused to admit it, even to himself – he'd found talking to Betty Stubbs' customers an unpleasant and disturbing experience.

It hadn't been easy with any of them, he thought, but Barry Eccles had been the worst – Barry Eccles had really managed to get under his skin.

Eccles was a metalwork teacher at one of the local secondary moderns. He was a middle-aged, slightly podgy man, with hard eyes, a shiny suit and a bad haircut. When Rutter met him at the school gates, he'd immediately recognized the man for what he was – a natural playground bully who'd never put his past behind him because he had a teaching certificate which meant he didn't need to.

'Were you already on the lookout for a

145

prostitute when you met Betty at the bowling club?' Rutter had asked.

'No, not really,' Eccles had replied.

'But since you fancied her, you thought you'd give it a go?'

'Fancied her?'

'You presumably liked the way she looked.'

'I've never really thought about her looks before, but I suppose she was quite presentable – for a slag.'

Rutter had pictured Betty Stubbs lying on the mortuary slab – her body riddled with cancer, her throat ripped open – and it had taken all his self-control to stop him planting his fist in the middle of the other man's face.

'Why did you feel the need to use the services of a prostitute?' the inspector asked, not even trying to hide his contempt.

The metalwork teacher had studied Rutter for a moment. 'Are you a married man?' he'd asked.

'I'm asking the questions,' Rutter said.

'Are you married?' Eccles insisted, his tone so similar to a bête noir of a teacher from Rutter's own school days that it brought him out in goose pimples.

'Yes, I am married, as a matter of fact,' the inspector replied, before he could stop himself.

Eccles had grinned knowingly. 'And don't you ever fancy a bit of fresh?'

Standing in back yard of the Drum and Monkey, his arm resting on a tower of empty beer crates, Rutter found that Eccles' words were still bouncing around in his mind.

A bit of fresh!

It wasn't like that with Monika, he told himself. She wasn't just a change – a slight variation in his diet.

'*Well? What's your answer?*' demanded Eccles, *who, like all bullies, was adept at recognizing when he'd hit a sensitive spot.* 'Have *you never fancied a bit of fresh?*'

'*I'd never pay for it.*'

The metalwork teacher had smiled, so wistfully that Rutter almost found himself feeling sympathy for the man.

'*You'd never pay for it,*' *Eccles mused.* '*That's what I'd have said when I was your age. But when you get past forty, you start wondering if you've missed out. You know everything your wife's prepared to do for you by then. If there's any change, it's that she's not willing to do it as often as she used to. And you can't help asking yourself if there's a woman out there who might be more adventurous. When you find one – and she only costs two quid a time – you feel as if all your birthdays have come at once.*'

'*How often did you pay her for sex?*'

'*Once a fortnight.*'

'*And when was the last time you slept with her?*'

'*About two months ago.*'

'*Why did you stop?*'

'*There were things she wouldn't let me do to her any more.*'

147

'Did she give a reason?'

'She said they hurt her.'

'So that was it? That was the end?'

'Yes, that was it. I decided that if all she could give me was what I was already getting at home, then I might as well sleep with my own missus and keep the money in my pocket.'

That was better, Rutter had thought. He was happier with this Eccles more than the wistful one – because he found it much easier to despise him.

'One more question,' he'd said. 'You found Betty Stubbs was much more adventurous in sexual matters than your wife. Why was that, do you think? Because she was born sexually liberated? Because her sexual adventurousness had always lain beneath the surface, and it took a real man like you to finally awaken it?'

'What do you mean?'

'Or could it be that she badly needed the two quid you gave her every time you climbed off her – so badly, in fact, that she'd even submit to the disgusting caresses of a bucket of shit like you?'

'You can't talk to me like that!' Eccles had exploded.

'Can't I?' the inspector countered. 'Funny, I thought I just had.'

Rutter took in another lungful of crisp moorland air.

Eccles was a toe-rag, he told himself. He was scum! A bully!

And though he accepted that all comparisons were odious, he reasoned he would be being unfair to himself if he didn't distinguish between his own actions and those of the metalwork teacher just once.

Eccles had probably treated his own wife as shamefully as he had treated Betty Stubbs. He himself, on the other hand, loved his wife with all his heart yet could still find space in one corner of it for Monika Paniatowski.

They were two totally different cases! He didn't sleep with Monika, as Eccles had slept with Betty, merely to practice perversions denied to him at home. He didn't search out fresh diversions, as Eccles had, because what was waiting for him in his own bedroom had started to bore him.

It wasn't the same at all! Not by any stretch of the imagination!

Was it?

Nineteen

Lucy Tonge hated mirrors. She had done for as long as she could remember. They were malicious. They lay in ambush for her in all sorts of places – in shops, in buses, in toilets, and even in offices. And they were so cruel – so unremittingly cruel.

She had, over the years, developed strategies to circumvent most clashes with these relentless reflectors. She would, for example, work out in advance where a mirror was likely to be located, and deliberately look the other way as she approached the spot. Or if there were so many mirrors in a place that she could not avoid them whatever she did, then she would avoid the place instead. And she had perfected the art of brushing her hair – her best feature, her only *good* feature – without once catching a glance of the face which lay below the hairline.

But that was all about to change, she resolved. Why should a woman who was facing the thought of her approaching death so calmly be worried about facing mirrors? Why should a woman who had finally found

150

love be repelled by the very features which were the object of that love?

Stiffened with her new resolve, she rose from the armchair and walked down the narrow passage between it and the bed. She came to a halt in front of the door which led on to the communal corridor. The mirror was there – hanging from a hook – but old habits died hard and she was still not looking at it.

She took a deep breath, and forced her eyes towards the mirror. And what did she see? She saw just what she had expected to see! A nose the size and shape of a tulip bulb. A jaw which was square without being resolute. A complexion which resembled a moonscape.

'Is this what *you* see when you look at me, Roger?' she asked in a tiny, plaintive voice.

It couldn't be. It simply couldn't be. The mirror must, in some strange way, distort her features, because if she really *did* look like that, it was impossible that any man could ever love her.

There was a sudden ringing sound. Someone was calling on her new phone – the phone Roger had had installed for her.

It could be a wrong number, she thought, cautioning herself in advance against hope.

But if it wasn't a mistake? If it wasn't, then it had to be the one person in the world who she really wanted to talk to.

She grabbed at the receiver and breathlessly delivered her phone number.

On the other end of the line, a voice said, 'Good evening, madam, can I interest you in house insurance?'

'It's not my house,' she said, disappointedly. 'It's a bed-sit, and I only rent it.'

Then the man laughed, and she realized it had been Roger all along.

'You're so *easy* to fool, my darling,' he said.

'I know I am,' she replied. 'I'm sorry.'

He laughed again. 'Don't apologize. Your naïveté is part of your charm.'

She hadn't even known she *had* charm until she met him. 'I'm so glad you rang,' she said.

'I nearly didn't. It's not always easy for me, you know, and I wasn't sure if you'd be in.'

Where else did he think she'd be? Didn't he know that she had no life which didn't involve him?

'I would have gone out,' she said in an attempt to make herself seem less pathetic, 'but it says in the paper that there may be a killer on the loose, and women shouldn't leave the house without a gentleman friend to escort them.'

'You can be very hurtful sometimes, you know,' he said.

She raised her hand to her mouth in dismay. 'I didn't mean that, Roger. I only...'

'Don't you think I'd *like* to be seen outside

with you? Don't you think I'd be *proud* to have other men notice you on my arm?'

'I really didn't mean...'

'Let's not fight,' he said. 'Let's both imagine we're in a place where there's no need to hide – where we can be ourselves without fear of the consequences.'

But would they ever get to this paradise he had promised her? she wondered. She was trying not to be impatient, because she knew how difficult it was for him to arrange things. But the longer it took, the less likely it was that it would ever happen. However much he might love her and want to be with her, the clock was still ticking – slowly but inexorably – towards the final countdown.

'Are you still there?' he asked.

'Of course I am.'

'Only you sounded a little distressed – sounded as if you thought I was letting you down.'

He was hurt. How could she hurt him – the only man she'd ever met who *hadn't* let her down? She searched her mind for some diversion.

'Do you think this killer will strike again?' she asked.

'No!' he replied, suddenly sounding alarmed. 'What makes you ask that? What have you heard?'

'Nothing,' she confessed. 'I just wondered.'

He laughed, the tension in his voice gone.

'My silly little Lucy,' he said. 'It was a prostitute who was murdered, not a sweet little shop assistant. Why ever should he want to kill you?'

'I never said he wanted to kill me.'

'Of course you didn't.' He paused. 'I expect the murder will be the main topic of conversation at the supermarket tomorrow.'

'Yes, I expect it will.'

'Don't get involved. Don't listen to gossip.' Another pause. 'I don't think I want you working there any more.'

'But I thought we'd agreed that—'

'Why should you, when we'll soon be going away?'

'It's better being at the supermarket than staying here alone.'

Better – but not much!

'I won't tease you any more,' he said. 'It's not fair.'

'What do you mean?'

'If I were you, I'd go into work late tomorrow. Very late indeed. And when that nasty Mr McCann starts shouting at you for it, I'd hand in my notice.'

'You've got the tickets!' she said excitedly.

'I've got the tickets,' he confirmed. 'We sail the day after tomorrow.'

'So we really will be going?'

'Yes, we really will be going.'

'For how long?'

'Two weeks.'

She'd been hoping for a month. But perhaps that had been asking for *too* much, she told herself, doing her best to dampen down her disappointment. And anyway – looking at it from the purely practical viewpoint – while she was sure she could manage two weeks, there was no guarantee that in a month she'd still feel up to enjoying herself.

'We're going to have a lovely time,' she promised. 'The best time in the world. I'm going to make you so happy.'

'I know you are,' he said.

November the Third

There is danger in quiet
For who is to say
What evils are planned
'fore the ending of day?

Twenty

The previous morning, the murder of an unknown woman on Mad Jack's Field had been *the* topic of conversation at the bus stops and in the cafes. That the corpse had a name in time for the evening papers had rekindled some interest in the subject, even among those who had no idea who Betty Stubbs was. But now it was old news, and the first thoughts of the majority of people waking up that dark November morning were about personal matters – work, money, sex, Bonfire Night – rather than the fact that there was a killer on the loose.

Even for those most closely involved in the whole sorry business, Betty's death did not necessarily occupy their consciousness as they emerged slowly from sleep. Charlie Woodend awakened wondering how his daughter Annie was getting on in nursing college, and pledging that as soon as this case was over, he and Joan would make the time to visit her. Elizabeth Driver rolled out of bed feeling resentment against both Woodend and Bryant, and promising herself that she would have her revenge on them, whatever it took. Monika Paniatowski was thinking of her unhappy childhood and wishing she could put it all behind her. And Bob Rutter, lying in bed next to his pretty, blind wife, asked himself what kind of man he could be to even think of betraying her.

At nine o'clock, with the thoughts of his own problems pushed temporarily to the back of his brain, Bob Rutter arrived at the morgue. He was not alone. The man who accompanied him was approaching fifty, had iron-grey hair, and marched rather than walked. In the past, Rutter had taken members of the general public to view a body and had seen them either vomit or faint – and sometimes do both. He had no such concern this time. Sergeant Frank Atkins, late of the Royal Marine Commandos, had seen enough violent death during the course of his career to be able to take Betty Stubbs' body in his stride.

'It's a very neat cut,' Atkins said, looking down at the body. 'Very neat indeed. No jagged edge, which means you can rule out most hunting knives. My guess – and it's only a guess – is that the weapon which inflicted this wound was a Fairbairn Sykes.'

'A what?' Rutter asked.

Atkins laughed good-naturedly. 'I keep forgetting how young you are, son,' he said.

'The Second World War must seem like ancient history to a lad like you.'

'Not quite,' Rutter said, feeling stung and slightly defensive – as he always did when anyone commented on his comparative youth. 'I remember the war. I was too young to fight, but I had to live through the Blitz. Still, I've no idea what a Fairbanks—'

'Fairbairn. Fairbairn Sykes.'

'I've no idea what that is.'

'When the Commandos were formed in 1940, Captains Fairbairn and Sykes were appointed as the first instructors in close-combat fighting. Nice harmless term, isn't it? "Close-combat fighting!" But what it actually meant was *dirty* fighting – fighting that definitely didn't stick to the Marquis of Queensbury Rules. Anyroad, Fairbairn and Sykes decided straight away that one thing their men really needed was a good knife. The problem was, they couldn't find a suitable one.'

'That's amazing,' Rutter said.

'But true,' Atkins told him. 'The last big advance in knife development had been the Bowie knife in the 1830s. So, the pair of them went to the Wilkinson's Sword factory – you may have used their razor blades – and told the managing director exactly what they wanted. And he had it made for them.' A faraway look came into Atkins' eyes. 'It's a lovely weapon. Heavy grip that sits nicely in the palm of your hand. Double-edged blade and a point that's as sharp as buggery. Even an amateur can do a good job with a knife like that.'

'How difficult would it be to get hold of one?'

'I wouldn't exactly call them rare.'

'So what would you call them?'

'Let's just say there's just enough of them about to make them a collector's item – which means that if you're prepared to pay the asking price, you could get your hands on one easy enough.'

'That really wasn't what I wanted to hear,' Rutter told him.

By nine thirty Elizabeth Driver had breakfasted, smoked her first three cigarettes of the day, and was placing a long-distance call to London. She was well aware, even as she dialled, that the reporter she was ringing would not welcome hearing from her at that time of the morning. Well, screw him! He owed her, and if collecting her debts caused him to lose some of his beauty sleep, she really didn't give a damn.

The man was as gruff and annoyed as she'd expected him to be. 'Didn't get to bed till two,' he complained.

'But *before* you went to bed, you found out what I need to know?'

'Some of it.'

'Let's have it, then.'

'Wait while I go and find my notes,' the reporter grumbled.

He kept her on hold for a full five minutes. 'Did you say you were going to *fetch* your notes, or were you carving them into stone?' she asked, when he eventually came back on the line.

'Had to go for a piss,' he said grumpily. 'Scotch goes straight through me these days.'

'Then you should drink less,' she said tartly. 'What have you got for me?'

'Dexter Percival Bryant,' the man read. 'Born 1915. Father was a major in the artillery and was killed in action in 1917. Dexter was educated at Westminster School, then at St John's College, Oxford.'

'What!' Elizabeth Driver exclaimed. 'St John's College? He went to *university*?'

'Yes.'

'Journalists don't go to university.'

'He did.'

'What did he study?'

'Languages. Came away with a First Class degree, so he must be bright. No wonder he was the best crime reporter on the Street.'

Some people started out with all the advantages, Elizabeth Driver thought bitterly. But that didn't matter. Bryant *had been* the king of Fleet Street crime reporters – but he wasn't there now, and the crown was up for grabs!

'What did he do in the war?' she asked, half-expecting to be told that the bastard had been awarded the VC.

'He applied for active service, but was turned down. Flat feet, apparently. Spent his war in the pay corps at Kettering.'

Well, that was something, at least, Driver thought. 'Any scandal ever stick to him?' she asked. 'Any suggestion he might have been involved in black marketeering?'

'Not a whisper. Got an honourable discharge in '45, and went straight to Fleet Street as a junior reporter.'

Damn! Elizabeth Driver thought. 'What else have you got?' she asked.

'Not a great deal. He turned out to be very good at his job. Was chief crime reporter of the *Standard* by the time he was thirty-five. The other papers tried to poach him, but he wouldn't go. They say he even turned down a couple of editorships.'

This wasn't going at all well.

'He must have got his hands dirty at some time,' Elizabeth Driver said hopefully. 'You never get anywhere by being pure as the driven snow.'

'Seems he did.'

'What about his first marriage? How did that break up?'

'First marriage? What are you talking about?'

'I just assumed that—'

'There wasn't a first marriage.'

Incredible! Everybody was divorced on the Street, and the more important you were, the more divorces you were likely to have had.

'All right, tell me about his one and only wife,' she said.

'They got married about two and a half years ago. She'd been a widow for nearly fifteen years. She's got one son, in his twenties now. I think he lives with them, but I'm not sure.'

'Why did he and his wife give up the Street and move to a dump like Whitebridge?'

'They said they'd had enough of the pressure of working for the nationals. Said they wanted a quieter life.'

'I know that! But what's the *real* story?'

'As far as I can tell, that *is* the real story.'

Nobody could be quite as clean as Dexter Bryant appeared to be, Elizabeth Driver thought. It would quite destroy her faith in human nature if they were.

'Keep digging,' she said.

'Oh, come on, Elizabeth! I've got a living of my own to make, you know.'

'Keep digging!' she repeated fiercely. 'If you can't find anything on Bryant himself, then expand the search. Find out if there's anything dodgy about his brothers and sisters—'

'He doesn't have any. Like I said, his father

was killed in 1917.'

'His mother, then! Or his wife's mother. Give me some dirt on the family hamster, if that's all there is.'

'Be reasonable, Elizabeth.'

'I need a lever – something I can use against the smug bastard. And if you can't find it, then I might just be tempted to drop some papers I've been collecting on to your Editor's desk.'

'You wouldn't!'

'Papers, you shouldn't need reminding, which will prove conclusively that at the same time as you were claiming extortionate expenses for that story you were supposed to be covering in Dublin, you were, in fact, shacked up with a little typist in Chippen-ham.'

'You're a bitch!' the man said. 'A real twenty-one carat bitch.'

'Oh, please! It's far too early in the morning for compliments,' Elizabeth Driver said, hanging up.

Twenty-One

The clock on the wall in the Saltney Rise Crown Green Bowling and Social Club said it was ten minutes past eleven in the morning, and the only customers were the four regulars who had already been pacing nervously up and down outside when Rodney Whitbread had opened the doors on the stroke of the hour.

Whitbread himself leant against the bar, smoking a cigarette and musing about life in general. He liked his job as bar steward. The work wasn't unduly heavy, and while others had to drag themselves from their beds at seven, he got to lie in for a couple more hours. Besides, there were the perks. He never had to pay for his own ale, for example. And if he kept his wits about him, there was always the chance of making a little extra money on the side.

But it was that bit of extra money that could be the problem, wasn't it? he reminded himself. You thought you weren't doing no harm – that you were helping other people as well as yourself. And suddenly you found yourself in a hole so deep that you could see no way of ever climbing out.

He looked up when he heard the door swing open, and saw the big man in the hairy sports coat.

Trouble! There was no doubt about it.

This man was the law. And not the friendly uniformed bobby who came round for a drink after closing time. He was the real thing.

'Sorry, sir, this is a members only club,' Whitbread said, without much conviction in his voice.

Woodend ambled over to the bar. 'I don't want a drink, lad,' he said. 'An' even if I did, I wouldn't waste my time suppin' the neck oil you sell here.' He looked down at the pumps. 'Baldwin's Premium Bitter?' he continued, pulling a face. 'Premium! Bitter! I wouldn't use it to drown slugs.'

'Our customers seem to like it,' the bar steward said, unease giving way to professional offence.

'Aye, they would. They're a funny lot, are crown green bowlers,' Woodend replied. 'Me, I think ordinary bowlin's complicated enough, without stickin' a bloody great hump in the middle of the pitch.'

'We'll have to agree to differ on that,' the bar steward said huffily.

'True enough,' Woodend agreed. 'Would you like to see my warrant card now?'

The steward's stomach did a somersault. 'You're police?' he asked.

'I am. But I'm not tellin' you anythin' you didn't know already. You had me spotted the moment I walked in.'

'We stick to the law in this club,' the steward said. 'Never open before eleven, always close on the stroke of three.'

'Bollocks!' Woodend said, good-naturedly. 'There's no point in belongin' to a private club if you can't squeeze in a few extra drinks after closin' time, now is there? Anyway, that's not why I'm here. You'll have heard about what happened to Betty Stubbs, will you?'

The steward shrugged. 'Somebody might have mentioned it to me.'

'So you knew her, did you?'

'She used to come in a lot when her husband was alive. Ted was a fair bowler.'

'But you haven't seen her since?'

'She ... she may have dropped in a couple of times since the funeral.'

'That's it? Just a couple of times?'

'Possibly a bit more than that,' the steward admitted.

'Meanin' what, exactly?'

'I suppose you might have called her a regular.'

Woodend ran his hand thoughtfully along his chin. 'Do you know, I think I might risk a pint of Baldwin's Best Horse Piss after all.'

'We're not allowed to serve non-members.'

'In that case, I shall be forced to arrest myself. But I can't do that before I've actually committed the crime, now can I?'

When the pint had been pulled, Woodend slid a two-shilling piece across the bar.

'Have that on me,' the steward suggested.

'Not a chance, lad,' Woodend replied. He took a sip of the beer. 'God, it's even worse than I remembered. Where's it from? London?'

'Yorkshire!' the steward said, outraged.

'Funny, I could have sworn it had a southern taste about it,' Woodend told him. He took another swallow. 'Still, maybe I'll get used to it.'

'You don't mind if I go an' check on the stock, do you?' Rodney Whitbread asked hopefully.

'That can wait for a few minutes,' Woodend replied, in a voice which was not *quite* commanding. 'How did Betty Stubbs get by after her husband died, do you know?'

'I expect she had a widow's pension.'

'She did – but she had a lot of debts, as well. Or hadn't you heard about them?'

'I may have heard somethin'.'

Woodend took another sip of his pint. 'You see, this isn't a big city, like Manchester,' he said. 'We're simply not geared up to runnin' vice operations in the same way that they are.'

'I'm not followin' you.'

'Oh, I think you are. When I learned that Betty Stubbs was on the game ... I'm sorry, I'm gettin' ahead of myself. You did *know* she was on the game, didn't you?'

'I ... uh...'

'Anyway, I began to wonder how she got started. Where would you go if you wanted to get your end away?'

'I'm a married man!'

'Then you'll have a lot in common with most of the fellers who visit prostitutes.' Woodend lit up a cigarette. 'Anyway, I'd already come to the conclusion that she'd most likely want to start out in some surroundin's where she was known an' felt comfortable. Then my inspector came up with the interestin' fact that most of her punters met her here.'

'I wouldn't know anything about that. I just serve the drinks.'

'The thing is,' Woodend continued, as if the barman had never spoken, 'she'd have needed someone to help her out – to recommend her to those fellers who were feelin' randy but didn't know where to go to get satisfaction. See what I'm sayin'?'

The bar steward looked down at the counter, and said nothing.

'Now in a lot of trades, you can rely on word of mouth,' Woodend continued. 'You get a good plumber – if such a thing really

171

exists outside the realms of fiction – an' you have no hesitation about recommendin' him to your friends. But while nobody's ashamed to say they've used a plumber, there's a lot of men who'd think twice before admittin' to havin' gone to a prostitute. So what she will have needed is somebody who not only knew what she did, but had the opportunity to talk to all the customers. He'd probably be the sort of feller that customers would tell their troubles an' frustrations to anyway. A bar steward, for example.'

'If you think that I—'

'Oh, I do, lad,' Woodend interrupted. 'I thought it even before I came in here. Now that I can see the look on your face, I'm sure of it.'

'I don't want to say any more.'

'An' I don't want Whitebridge Rovers relegated to the Second Division at the end of the season. But I've got to be realistic – and so have you.' Woodend took another drag on his Capstan. 'Look, son, I'm investigatin' a murder here. That's all that matters to me at the moment. If you're fiddlin' the books or sellin' off some of the stock when the committee's not lookin', I don't care. An' I don't care if you were pimpin' for Betty Stubbs. But if you hold out on me, I'll have your guts for garters. So let's hear what you've got to say.'

'I wasn't pimpin' for her,' Rodney Whitbread muttered. 'Not exactly, anyway.'

'So what, exactly anyway, *were* you doin' for her?'

'Sometimes I'd point a bit of business her way.'

'An' what was your cut of the deal? Half of what she made?'

'It wasn't like that. She'd slip me a couple of quid now an' again, but I never asked her to. I only helped because I felt sorry for her. She needed the money, and she told me that goin' on the game was the only way she knew to get it. Am I in trouble now?'

'Not as long as you keep tellin' me the truth,' Woodend assured him. 'I'll need a list of her punters' names. An' you'd better not try to hold out on me, because we already know who some of them are, an' if those names don't appear on your list—'

'I couldn't do that! You can't ask me to!'

'It's more in the nature of tellin', rather than askin',' Woodend said. 'But don't worry, nobody need know that they came from you. In fact, I'll go out of my way to suggest I got the list from somewhere else entirely. But I have to have it. Understand?'

'I suppose so,' Rodney Whitbread said, defeatedly.

'An' I'll especially need to know if she had any favourite punters.'

'I couldn't say about that.'

'You're feedin' me a line again,' Woodend

growled.

'No, honestly, I'm not,' Whitbread protested. 'She saw her customers at home. I've no idea whether any of the fellers I recommended her to saw her just the once, or whether they saw her a dozen times. That's the truth. I swear it is!'

'What about her most recent punters?' Woodend asked. 'The newest ones? Can you tell me anythin' about them?'

'She's ... she's not really been on the lookout for new business recently. She hasn't been feelin' too well.'

'But?'

'No buts.'

Woodend sighed. 'Do you think you're the first one who's ever found himself in this position, lad? Because if you do, you couldn't be wronger.'

'I don't know what you're talkin' about. What position?'

'When you heard Betty Stubbs had been murdered, your first thought was to go down to the station. Then you started worryin' about how it would make you look. An' you're still worryin' – because though you've told me some of it, you're still holdin' part of it back.'

'She told me about this new feller she was seein',' Rodney Whitbread admitted. 'She said he was different to the others.'

'In what way?'

'Even though she couldn't do ... couldn't do what she used to do to him ... he still wanted to see her. An' he paid her the same amount of money, even if all she could manage was to toss him off.'

'What else did she say about him?'

'Nothin'.'

'Age? Description? Background? Where she met him? Where they went together? Did she go to his house or did she go to his?'

'I swear that's all she said. That he wasn't like the others. That he promised he'd never abandon her.'

'There must be somethin' you've forgotten – or are holdin' back!'

'I got the impression that he was younger than she was. But that was only an impression.'

'When was the last time you saw her?'

'The night before last. About seven o'clock.'

'Not long before she was killed?'

'I suppose it must have been.'

'Tell me about it.'

'She dropped in shortly after we'd opened. There weren't any other customers. She didn't want a drink, or anythin'. She just wanted to talk. To tell you the truth, I don't think there were many people, apart from me, who she felt she *could* talk to.'

'An' what did she have to say for herself.'

'She said her friend, Mr X—'

'Mr X?'

'That's what she called him. It was a bit of a joke between us, like. Man of mystery an' all that.'

'Go on.'

'She said ... I did tell you she hadn't been feelin' too grand recently, didn't I?'

'Aye, you did. What was wrong with her, by the way?'

'I don't know for sure. Maybe it was women's troubles. Somethin' to do with her plumbin'. Anyway, as I was sayin', she told me Mr X was goin' to help her with her health problems – that he knew a doctor who'd performed miracles in the past.'

He'd traded on her hope and used her vulnerability against her, Woodend thought angrily.

The bastard! The schemin', lying, cold-hearted bastard!

'An' after she'd told you about this doctor and his miracle cure, she left, did she?' Woodend asked the bar steward.

'Yes.'

'To meet Mr X?'

'I think so,' Rodney Whitbread said. Then a single tear slid down his cheek. 'Oh God!' he moaned. 'Why didn't I try to stop her?'

Twenty-Two

Lucy Tonge should have reported for work at the supermarket at half-past eight, but it was nearly twelve when she waltzed through the main door wearing the skirt and jacket that she'd spent most of the morning shopping for.

She smiled at the girls on the cash registers as she walked past them. To think that she had once envied them their jobs – had once desperately wanted to be one of them.

She had almost begged Mr McCann to let her take over one of the tills.

'Can't do it, Lucy,' he'd told her.

'Why not?'

'Anybody can work a cash register, but not one in a hundred girls could run the stock room like you do. You're far too valuable where you are to be moved anywhere else.'

She'd believed him. She'd even been flattered. And then she'd overheard him talking to the assistant manager later in the day.

'Got to draw the line somewhere,' McCann had said. 'None of the girls are what you might call beauty queens, but we certainly don't want

somebody with a face that could turn milk sour sitting at the cash desk.'

How she'd wept that night – and on the nights which followed. But that didn't matter now. It hadn't been her *real* life she'd been living – only a badly lit, badly plotted rehearsal. And though she could have been bitter about finally being given a starring role so late in her career, she wasn't. To go out in a blaze of glory – that was all she asked for! And that was what her knight in shining armour was about to give her.

'Mrs Tonge!' said a booming voice.

'Mr McCann,' she replied, turning to the man in a khaki coat.

'What time do you call this, Mrs Tonge?'

'Five minutes to twelve, Mr McCann.'

'And do you have an explanation for your extreme tardiness?'

'I'm afraid I don't, unless it's that I just didn't feel like coming in any earlier.'

'You're sacked,' McCann said. 'Go to the office immediately. Ask for your cards and two weeks' pay in lieu of notice.'

She hoped he'd say that. 'Mr McCann, you take your two weeks' pay and stick it up your ar—... up your bottom,' she told the manager. 'You're not sacking me, because I quit.'

She turned and walked out of the supermarket with as much flair as she could summon up.

McCann probably thought that she would

run straight home, weeping tears of regret at her rash decision. But she didn't do that at all. Instead, she walked quite calmly into Mario's Coffee Bar and ordered herself a pot of tea and a round of toast. She had planned this in advance, just as she had deliberately staged her row with McCann shortly before some of the cashiers were due to take their break.

The girls would arrive soon. Though they had never invited her to join them, the cashiers always came to Mario's, and this time she would be waiting for them. She would be perfectly civil to them. She wouldn't brag or gloat. She would simply tell them – in the most matter of fact tone – where she was going the next day. And then, though they would hate themselves for doing it, they would envy her as much as she had once envied them.

It was pure coincidence that Rutter and Paniatowski ran into each other at the main entrance to police headquarters, and yet, given his current mood, it seemed to the inspector like the hand of fate was pushing them together.

'We need to talk, Monika,' Rutter said.

Paniatowski looked at him bemusedly, as though she knew something was going on – but hadn't yet quite figured out what it was.

'So talk,' she suggested.

Almost as an involuntary action, Rutter glanced quickly up and down the street.

'Not here,' he said. 'And not now. We need to be somewhere quiet.'

'This wouldn't be about us seeing each other, would it?'

'I've already told you, now's not the time,' Rutter said.

'What's the matter with you?' Paniatowski asked. 'Since yesterday afternoon, you've been acting as if I was a complete stranger.'

Rutter knew he should shut up then and there, yet somehow he couldn't bring himself to do it. 'It's because of talking to those men,' he blurted out.

'What men?'

'Betty Stubbs' punters.'

'I still don't understand what you're saying.'

'At first, I was disgusted at the thought of even being in the same room with them. I felt so bloody superior, you see. But then I started to question myself – to wonder if I was any better than they were.'

'Are you trying to say there's no difference between me and Betty Stubbs?' Paniatowski demanded furiously.

'No! Of course not!'

'Then just what *are* you saying?'

'This has nothing to do with you. It's all to do with me. I made wedding vows, just as Betty's punters did. Does the *way* I choose to break them really matter all that much?'

'You mean that as far as you're concerned, you're equally guilty whether or not you pay for it.'

'Yes,' Rutter said. 'I mean, no!'

'What am I to you? Nothing more than a piece of meat?'

'That's a really crappy thing to say.'

'And what you've been saying *isn't* crappy?'

Rutter put his hand on Paniatowski's arm. 'Look, Monika, I really care for you. But what we've been doing is not right. And it's not fair on Maria.' He hit his forehead with his free hand. 'Does the fact that she's blind make it even worse? I don't know. I just can't say any more.'

'I've never wanted to break up your marriage,' Paniatowski said, her eyes misting slightly.

'I know that.'

'I've never made any demands on you. I've never asked you for any assurances.'

'I know that too.'

'So if you want to stop seeing me, just stop seeing me.'

'But I don't want to stop seeing you,' Rutter said. 'I love you.'

'Don't try to make a fool out of me – and don't lie to yourself. It's Maria you love! Can you deny that?'

'Of course I don't deny it. I don't *want* to

deny it. I do love her. And maybe what I feel for you isn't the same kind of love at all. But it still *is* love.'

It was no longer just moisture in Monika's eyes – it was real tears. 'My God!' she said. 'What a bloody mess!'

Standing on the opposite side of the road to police headquarters, Elizabeth Driver had been watching the little scene develop between Paniatowski and Rutter with some interest. Of course, she was too far away to hear what they were actually saying, but from their stance and their gestures she could draw the reasonable conclusion that whatever it was about, it was certainly serious.

Suddenly Paniatowski bowed her head.

Was she crying? Elizabeth Driver asked herself. Surely not! Monika Paniatowski didn't cry – ever!

But if she wasn't crying, why had Rutter taken her head between his two hands? And why was he now lifting it up again and kissing her on the forehead?

This was wonderful, Driver told herself. This was just too good to be true.

Twenty-Three

Woodend looked, with some concern, at the other two members of his team who were facing him across the desk. There'd been a time when Rutter and Paniatowski had found it a strain even to be in the same room, he thought. Then things had changed. For the previous few weeks, they'd been so close he couldn't have slid a piece of paper between them. Now their relationship seemed to have reached a third level. Now they were united – but only by pain.

'Is there somethin' the pair of you would like to tell me?' he asked.

Paniatowski shook her head.

Rutter mumbled something which may have been, 'No.'

'Are you sure about that?' Woodend asked, 'because, to be honest, I've seen star attractions at autopsies who put on a better show than you two are managin' at the moment.'

Paniatowski favoured him with a weak smile.

Rutter couldn't even manage that.

Neither of them seemed the least inclined

to say what was on their minds.

'Well, since nobody seems to have anythin' more interestin' to talk about, we may as well discuss the investigation,' Woodend said. 'Would either of you happy-go-lucky folk care to give an opinion on how my little chat with the bar steward has altered our view of the case?'

'We always knew our killer was probably playing games with us,' Paniatowski said, making the effort, 'but until this morning we didn't have enough information to even begin to speculate on his relationship with his victim.'

'An' now it's all crystal clear, is it?'

'No, but there are certain things we can rule out. Assuming that this Mr X is our murderer—'

'An' seein' that Betty Stubbs was settin' out to meet him just before she was killed, it seems more than likely that he is.'

'Assuming that, we can rule out the idea that he was looking for a woman – *any* woman – and she happened to be in the wrong place at the wrong time. We can also discard the theory that she was killed simply because of *what* she was. He didn't just know she was a prostitute – he knew her as a *person*. So whatever sickness is driving him, it's specific rather than general.'

'I'm not at all happy with this automatic assumption that he *is* sick,' Rutter said.

'Oh, you've finally woken up, have you?' Woodend asked. 'So you don't like the idea that he's a nutter. What's your alternative?'

'That he had a much more conventional, down-to-earth motive for killing Betty Stubbs.'

'Like what, for instance?'

'We know he was one of her punters. Perhaps they had an argument over how much money he owed her. Or perhaps she tried to blackmail him – threatened to tell his wife what had been going on if he didn't cough up a lot of cash.'

Woodend shook his head sceptically. 'Leavin' aside the 'northodox way he chose to dispose of the body for the moment, I still don't buy that. You're basin' your argument on the fact that he was one of her punters, an' I don't think there's any doubt that he was. But he wasn't a *normal* punter, like your Mr Eccles.'

'How can you be sure of that?'

'Because she wouldn't have let a normal punter know that she was sufferin' from cancer.'

'Why not? She might have told a *lot* of people she had cancer.'

'She won't have,' Paniatowski said. 'People *don't*! They have no problem telling you about any other diseases. Far from it. There are professional invalids who'll trap you in a corner in the library and entertain you for hours with tales of their various ailments. But if it's cancer they've got, they keep quiet about it.'

'I'm not convinced that's true,' Rutter said.

'That's because your head is so full of your own ideas of the way things *should* be that you never bother to listen to what other people say or do,' Paniatowski countered angrily.

'Monika!' Woodend warned.

Paniatowski took a deep breath. 'I'm sorry,' she said.

'That's all right. Just tread a bit more carefully,' Woodend advised her.

'I was being unfair to you, Bob,' Paniatowski continued, in a more reasonable tone of voice. 'If you've never known a family which has had to deal with cancer, you probably have no idea what it's like. The victim says nothing, and even when the victim's relatives tell you about it, they do it in a whisper.' She pursed her lips. ' "Have you heard about our Wilfred? He's got cancer." '

'Monika's right, you know, Bob,' Woodend agreed. 'Looked at logically, cancer's no worse than any other serious illnesses – but that's not how most families see it. They act as if was somethin' shameful. It's almost like they think the victim is unclean – an' should have a bell round his neck, like a leper.'

'Surely that's an exaggeration,' Rutter protested.

'But not much of one,' Woodend said firmly. 'We all *do* think of cancer as somethin' different – maybe because, of all the things that might happen to us, it's the one we fear the most. What was it that new mate of yours, Dr Shastri, called it, Monika?'

'The enemy within.'

'Aye,' Woodend agreed. 'That just about sums it up as far as most folk are concerned.'

'What you say *may* be true,' Rutter conceded, 'but can we say with any certainty that Betty *didn't* tell any other people?'

'We know she didn't tell Rodney Whitbread, the bar steward,' Monika pointed out. 'And he was about the closest thing to a friend that she had towards the end.'

'All right, so she kept it quiet,' Rutter agreed, shifting his ground. 'In that case, how can we be so sure that she told Mr X?'

'Because Mr X had promised to introduce her to a doctor who could work miracles,' Woodend said. 'An' to be able to make that claim, he'd have to have known what *kind* of miracle needed performin'. You see—'

'Enough! I'm convinced!' Rutter said, holding up his hands in surrender. 'Maybe he did know about her disease. Maybe that's why he killed her.'

'Do you want to expand on that?' Woodend asked.

'Mr X becomes one of Betty's punters with no other thought in mind than getting his end away. But then the unexpected happens – he grows to like her, perhaps even to love her.' Rutter turned his head so that he was looking at neither Woodend nor Paniatowski. 'Then he learns she's about to face a slow and painful death, and he decides to put her out of her misery before any of the real suffering starts.'

'A mercy killin'?'

'Yes.'

'Havin' your throat cut is quick enough – but it's also terrifyin',' Woodend said. 'If he'd really cared about her, he'd have poisoned her. Or smothered her while she was sleepin'. If he'd cared, he'd have left her lyin' on her own bed, perhaps with a bunch of flowers in her hands. But he didn't do that. He stuffed her in the bloody bonfire.'

'I've had a thought about why he told her she could be cured,' Paniatowski said.

'Go on,' Woodend encouraged.

'I used to have a friend whose father was a gamekeeper on the Earl of Sutton's estate. He took us around it once, and let us feed the pheasants. Do you know *why* they feed the pheasants?'

'To fatten them up?'

'Partly. When you go shooting, it *is* nice to come home with a nice fat bird. But the real reason they do it is so that the pheasants have no reason to wander off somewhere else. It's a way of making sure that the birds

188

will still be there when the shooting season opens.'

'An' you think that's what the killer was doin'?' Woodend asked.

'Yes, I do. He was feeding her hope, for no other reason than to ensure that she'd be around when the time came to kill her. And it's possible she wasn't the only one he was feeding up, isn't it?'

'More than possible,' Woodend agreed gloomily.

Twenty-Four

The baby – poor little thing – had been unsettled all afternoon, and had only just quietened down when the doorbell rang.

'*Hijo de puta!*' Maria Rutter said exasperatedly – though she spoke the words softly in order not to awaken the sleeping child.

The bell rang again, more persistently this time. Maria closed the nursery door gently behind her, then walked rapidly down the hall. Though she could not see it, her hand found the latch immediately, and after checking that the safety chain was in place, she opened the door a few inches.

'Mrs Rutter?' said a woman who, Maria

guessed from her voice, was probably in her late twenties.

'Yes, I am Maria Rutter.'

'What a lovely accent you have. So soft and yet – dare I say it to another woman – so sexy.'

'Who are you?' Maria asked.

The visitor laughed. 'Sorry, didn't I mention that?'

'No, you didn't.'

'I'm Liz Driver. I assumed you'd know it was me, since you were expecting me.'

'But I *wasn't* expecting you.'

'You weren't?' Elizabeth Driver asked, apparently mystified. 'Are you sure that Bob didn't tell you?'

'Certain.'

'Well, I suppose he's got so much on his mind at the moment that it's hardly surprising he forgot. But even if you didn't know I was coming, you at least know who I am, don't you?'

'I don't think so.'

Elizabeth Driver sighed. 'Such is the fleeting nature of fame. I'm a reporter from the *Daily Globe*. I've worked with Bob before. I'm almost hurt that he hasn't mentioned me to you.'

'I would have remembered.'

'Anyway, he arranged to give me an interview, and he said that since he'd be in this area, it would be easiest to do it at his home. And that's why I'm here.'

'That doesn't sound like Bob at all,' Maria said.

'I can assure you that—'

'He never brings his work home. And if anyone was going to make a statement to the press, it would be Charlie Woodend.'

'I hope you don't think that I'm here under false pretences,' Elizabeth Driver said.

'That's *exactly* what I do think,' Maria told her. 'There are people who suppose that once you lose your sight, you lose your brain as well. But that isn't the case at all. I didn't know what to think of you at first, but now I do. I don't like you, and I don't trust you. And if you don't leave immediately, I'll call the police.'

'Listen, Mrs Rutter—'

'I have some influence with the police in this town, you know,' Maria said.

And then she laughed, more to show she was not to be intimidated than through genuine amusement.

There was silence from the other side of the door.

'I'm serious,' Maria said.

'I'm sure you are,' Elizabeth Driver replied, sounding thoroughly ashamed of herself. 'You're quite right not to trust me. In fact, you're right about everything. I *didn't* arrange to meet your husband here. And I *did* think that because you're blind, it would be easy to fool you. I promise I won't make that mistake again. I promise I'll treat you – and all blind people – with the respect you deserve.'

'It's too late to win me round,' Maria said. 'But I still want to know why you pretended you had an interview with Bob.'

'I'm doing a background piece on your husband. "Rising star of police force." That kind of thing. I thought it might help if I could see his home. Whatever you think of me, I can assure you that I meant no harm.'

'I still don't believe a word you say,' Maria told her. 'And I really would like you to leave now.'

'Of course. I'll go at once. I'm so very sorry to have bothered you, Mrs Rutter. Truly I am.'

'You can apologize as much as you like. I shall still tell my husband about your visit.'

'Yes,' Elizabeth Driver said, smiling slightly to herself. 'Yes, I'm quite sure that you will.'

One of his doctors had told him that his flashbacks, like an old photograph, would fade with time. LH had believed it – and believed in *him* – for quite a while. Not any more. The doctor had been just another in a long line of charlatans who had all peddled their false hopes and soft reassurances. The flashbacks had not faded. They were as vivid now – as heart-stoppingly real – as they had been that day he had staggered out of the jungle.

Him on one side of the clearing, Socks on the other. Two guards. The one closest to Socks is big for a Chinese, but the one LH must deal with is so slight he looks as if one of the rare jungle breezes would blow him away.

LH reaches into his sheath and pulls out his knife. A Fairbairn Sykes, specially made for killing by Wilkinson Sword. It is a terrible and terrifying instrument, with a point which could prick out the heart of a mosquito and an edge which could slice through a brick.

He is two feet from the guard now, and the guard is two seconds from death. He makes his move — left arm wrapped around the guard's chest, right hand drawing the knife across the guard's throat. The guard gurgles and twitches, and then goes limp. LH drops him and reaches for his sub-machine gun.

All hell breaks loose in the clearing as the three British soldiers spray hot metal death into the sleeping Chinese. The enemy have no chance. Some never wake. Others have only moments to realize that something is wrong before they forfeit their lives. Prone bodies are twitching, dying men are groaning all around the clearing. If all war is hell, then this is the inner circle.

'Cease fire!' Jacko screams. 'Cease fire, you mad bastards!'

It takes some time for the order to work its way

into LH's brain, and even longer for the brain to persuade the finger to release its grip on the trigger.

The clearing itself relapses into silence, though beyond it countless jungle creatures shriek, scream or howl. LH can hear none of this. His ears are still reverberating with the sound of gunfire. But though he cannot hear, he can still smell, and he knows that the clearing stinks of cordite and blood.

Jacko is already checking through the bodies, hoping that one of the Chinese is still alive and able to walk – because if they cannot find a guide to lead them out of this green, sweating prison, then all the killing has been for nothing.

He finds what he is looking for. A boy. If he had been English, LH would have said he was seven or eight, but being Chinese he could be as much as twelve. Jacko holds on to the boy's thin arm and speaks soothingly to him in Chinese.

The boy looks around him wildly, then breaks free of Jacko's too-gentle grip. For a moment they think he is about to make a run for it, but that is not his intention. Instead, he falls on his knees before the sentry LH has killed, and starts to moan, 'Jia mu! Jia mu!'

'What's he saying?' LH asks Jacko.

Jacko looks sick. 'He's saying "Mother, mother",' he replies.

Twenty-Five

Woodend could remember evenings around this table in the Drum and Monkey when heated discussions of the current case had produced enough energy to light up the whole pub.

Where was that energy now?

Paniatowski looked as if she were about to break into tears at any moment. Rutter had the appearance of a man who had just completed an assault course in full kit and carrying his platoon leader on his back. Worst of all, Woodend thought, not only did the other two seem to have no fight left in them, but they seemed, just by their presence, to be sapping his.

'Run through Betty Stubbs' background again, will you, Monika?' he asked half-heartedly.

'She went to one of the local elementary schools, where she wasn't much of a scholar,' Paniatowski droned. 'She left school at fourteen, and got a job at Woolworth's. Her father kept a pretty tight rein on her socially, by all accounts, and her first real boyfriend was her husband, Ted. They were married as soon as she turned twenty-one. They lived with her parents for the first couple of years, then they bought the house in Rawalpindi Road. About ten years ago, Betty had a burst appendix and had to give up work. And that's it.'

'There's nothin' at all in that to make her particularly attractive to our killer, is there?' Woodend asked.

'Nothing at all.'

'Yet we know he didn't select her at random. We know he's been planning this for quite some time.' Woodend turned to Rutter. 'What about you, Bob? Did you get any leads on the knife?'

'After Sergeant Atkins told me the wound looked as if it had been inflicted by a commando knife, I sent some of the lads round all the shops in the area which might have sold it – including the ones dealing in second-hand goods. The shopkeepers came up with names of three customers who'd bought sharp knives. I interviewed all three personally. They seemed non-starters, but I gave their knives to the lab for examination anyway.'

'What about old soldiers?' Woodend asked.

'What about them?'

The Chief Inspector sighed. 'Old soldiers often bring souvenirs of their wars home with them. Anybody who might have been in a position to get his hands on a knife while he was in the services needs to be checked on.'

'I hadn't thought of that,' Rutter admitted.

No, Woodend thought. But there was a time when you *would have.*

'Mr Woodend!' the barman called.

'Yes?'

The barman was holding up the phone. He had his hand over the speaker. 'Phone call for you. Are you here?'

Woodend sighed again. 'Aye, I'm here, I suppose.'

He levered himself out of his chair and walked over to the bar. The moment he had gone, Rutter said, 'He knows.'

'Knows what?' Paniatowski asked.

'About us.'

'Is there still any "us" to know about?'

'Look, we still need to find the time to talk. I've got an idea. You leave your car here tonight, and I'll drive you home.'

'It's only a short journey to my flat. You must think we don't have much to talk *about.*'

'Monika ... please...' Rutter said.

'And are you really sure that once we're alone together in your car, you'll want to talk? Isn't it more probable that you'll give in to your base animal instincts, and try to screw me rigid? Or has your new-found morality left you impotent?'

'It's not like that!' Rutter protested. 'You know it isn't.'

'I'm sorry to break up this meetin' of Agony Aunts Incorporated,' said a grim voice above them, 'but if you can possibly spare the time, I'd like you to come along with me.'

Rutter and Paniatowski looked up. They had not noticed Woodend's return, but then they'd been so intent on each other that the chances were they wouldn't have noticed a herd of elephants rampaging through the pub.

'What's happened?' Paniatowski asked. 'Something important?'

'That depends what you classify as important,' Woodend said tartly. 'As important as the conversation the pair of you were just havin'? Probably not! But it could possibly prove to be of minor interest to a team of detectives who are supposed to be investigatin' a murder case. Can you guess what it might be?'

Rutter and Paniatowski exchanged glances, and both saw in the other's eyes that they were thinking the same thing – and hoping that it couldn't be true.

'Another bonfire's been set alight, hasn't it?' Rutter said.

'Spot on!' Woodend agreed.

Even from a distance, Woodend could see

the headlights of the cars pointing towards the extinguished bonfire. This time it was a real field, rather than merely a strip of waste ground. And this time, it was located on the edge of Whitebridge rather close to the inner-city industrial centre. Other than that, the scene which was being enacted in the east meadow of Sourbrooke Farm was almost a mirror image of the one at Mad Jack's Meadow two nights previously.

Woodend parked his Wolseley next to a squad car, and saw that Rutter and Paniatowski were also pulling in close by. Perhaps he had been too rough on them back in the pub, he thought. But he liked them both, and did not want to see either of them getting hurt. And then there was Maria to consider – dear, sweet, blind Maria.

He climbed out of his car and walked towards the centre of the field. The arrival of the fire brigade had prevented the bonfire from completely burning to the ground, though the firemen had still not been able to save much of it.

But maybe there'd been no need to save it, Woodend thought hopefully. Maybe this time it really *was* nothing more than an act of vandalism carried out by one gang of small boys against another gang of small boys.

And then he saw the stretcher-bearers and, standing beside them, a woman wearing a sheepskin jacket over her bright sari.

Woodend looked down at the corpse on the stretcher. 'If she was in the bonfire, why isn't the rest of her burnt as badly as the left arm and leg?' he asked the sergeant in charge.

'She *wasn't* in the bonfire, sir,' the sergeant replied. 'She was *beside* it. I assume that was where the murderer laid her out.'

'Do you really mean "laid her out"? Or is that just a fancy way of sayin' "dumped her"?'

'Laid her out,' the sergeant reiterated. 'You'll see that for yourself when you examine the photographs, sir. She was a few feet from the bonfire, parallel to it, if you see what I mean. Her right arm was by her side, and her right leg was stretched out straight in front of her. But her left arm an' left leg had been moved, so they were pointing at the bonfire. It was all neat an' careful, sir. There's no chance it could have happened accidentally.'

'So why do *you* think he did it in that way, Sergeant?'

'Seems to me that the only possible explanation is that he wanted exactly what did happen *to* happen.'

'In other words, he wanted part of the body burned, but not all of it?'

'Yes, sir.'

'But *why* should he have wanted that?'

'Beats me, sir,' the sergeant admitted. 'I'm pretty much a traffic an' petty larceny man. All this is a bit out of my league.'

'There are times when I wish that it was out of mine,' Woodend told him.

A constable appeared with a torch in his hand. 'Inspector Rutter thinks you'll want to see what we've found, sir.'

Woodend followed him to a spot about halfway between the bonfire and the edge of the field. Rutter and Paniatowski, both with flashlights in their hands, were bending over something on the ground. As he got closer, Woodend could see that it was a small suitcase. It was bright red, and looked newly bought.

'I take it the suitcase belonged to our victim?' Woodend said.

'It's more than likely,' Rutter agreed. 'Especially since all the clothes are about the right size and the right style for a woman her age.'

Paniatowski had been carefully searching through the suitcase. Now she held up a blue booklet in her gloved hand. 'British passport.'

'Open it,' Woodend told her, bending down to take a closer look.

The document had recently been issued to a Lucy Tonge.

Lucy Tonge's body had been taken away for

post-mortem at roughly the same time as door-to-door inquiries were establishing that Lucy lived alone and her neighbours knew little or nothing about her. A further search of the meadow had been postponed until daylight. Until the town woke up again, there was little to do but wait – and Woodend decided that he and his disjointed team might as well do the first part of their waiting back in the public bar of the Drum and Monkey.

Paniatowski and Rutter looked a little more alert and a little more motivated than they had earlier, Woodend thought – but there had to be a better way to keep his team up to speed than by relying on a fresh murder every few days.

'I want to examine the murders from two different angles,' he announced. 'First the similarities between them, then the differences. Do you want to run through the similarities, Monika?'

Paniatowski nodded. 'Both women lived alone. Both had their throats cut, and both were dumped in fields with bonfires, which were then set alight. And both knew Mr X.'

'Are you certain?' Woodend cautioned.

'The suitcase and passport make it a more than reasonable supposition. Just as Mr X had promised to get Betty Stubbs cured, so he promised to take Lucy Tonge away from all this. It's a case of the gamekeeper fattening the partridges again.'

'Good point,' Woodend agreed. 'Now in what way were the cases different? Bob?'

'We never found Betty Stubbs' handbag, which probably means the killer took it away,' Rutter said. 'On the other hand, he left Lucy Tonge's passport where we were sure to discover it. Then there's the way he chose to position the bodies. He put Betty's in the middle of the bonfire, where – if all had gone according to plan – it would have been badly burned. But he went to great pains to see that didn't happen to Lucy's.'

'So what conclusions can we draw from that?'

'He arranged things so it would take some time for us to identify Betty, but he either actually *wanted* us to identify Lucy Tonge immediately, or didn't *care* if we did or not.'

'An' what was the thinkin' behind that?'

'Caution,' Paniatowski suggested. 'Betty was his first murder. He hadn't quite got the measure of us. Now he thinks he has, and he's confident that we won't catch him whatever he does.'

'Does that mean that you think he's plannin' another death?' Woodend asked.

'I don't know,' Paniatowski said. 'What do you think, sir?'

'I don't know either,' Woodend admitted. 'But if he *is* goin' to kill again, he's only got tomorrow night to do it.'

November the Fourth

While treachery rules
No wise man will say
Who'll still be alive
At the end of the day.

Twenty-Six

There was a thick fog that morning. It was the kind of fog which seems to take malicious pleasure in the chaos it is causing – a fog which insinuates its way into noses and throats; a fog which caresses the skin with the icy touch of death. It was such a fog as most people imagined when they thought of Jack the Ripper haunting the streets of old London. It was the last thing that Whitebridge – a town slowly being engulfed by the fear a second murder had brought to it – needed at that moment.

'The last time we saw her was yesterday mornin',' the blonde cashier said. 'She was already in Mario's Coffee Bar when we got there on our break.'

Bob Rutter looked around the supermarket stock room which the manager had reluctantly agreed he could use to conduct his interviews. It was a cramped airless room, a room in which it was impossible to move without squeezing between towers of cardboard boxes. He wondered what it must have been like for Lucy Tonge to spend most of her working day in this place.

'Did you notice anything unusual about Lucy yesterday morning?' he asked.

'She was drinkin' *tea*!' said the second cashier, who was a brunette and had her hair in a beehive. 'Fancy drinkin' tea in a *coffee* bar! Course, she never did have any style about her, however hard she tried.'

The blonde nudged her friend in the ribs. 'Shut up!' she said. 'You shouldn't talk about her like that now. She's dead!'

He was not exactly dealing with rocket scientists here, Rutter decided. 'Apart from her drinking tea in a coffee bar, was there anything else odd about her behaviour?' he asked.

'How do you mean?' the blonde girl replied.

'Did you *often* see Lucy in the coffee bar, for example?'

The two girls shook their heads.

'Matter of fact, it was the first time,' the blonde said. 'And I think the only reason she was there then was to talk to us.'

'To swank to us, you mean!' the brunette said.

'To swank about what?' Rutter asked.

'Her Prince Charmin'! The man who was goin' to take her on a glamorous cruise.'

'Had she ever mentioned him before?'

'No. She told us he'd asked her not to talk

about him, on account of him bein' married. We didn't fall for that, of course.'

'You didn't believe he was married?'

'We didn't believe he *existed*. She was always makin' up stories. Called herself *Mrs Tonge*, didn't she? Said she was a widow.'

'And wasn't she?'

'Course she wasn't! She's from Preston, like my Auntie Gladys, an' my auntie told me she'd never been married.'

'So why do you think she pretended she had?'

'For the same reason she invented her Prince Charmin'. To try an' convince us that she could pull men if she wanted to. We weren't fooled. A man'd have to be blind *an'* stupid to want anythin' to do with Lucy Tonge. If you ask me, whoever killed her probably mistook her for somebody else.'

Poor Lucy, Rutter thought. Poor miserable Lucy. Even in death, she was being denied her due.

The note on his desk said the Chief Constable wanted to see him as soon as he came in. Well, he should have expected that, Wood-end supposed. Sharks could smell blood, vultures could smell death. And Henry Marlowe – who had the worst characteristics of both of them – could smell a threat to his career even with the wind blowing in the wrong direction.

209

Woodend walked along the corridor and knocked on the Chief Constable's door.

The previous chief constable had always got off his chair to greet his visitors at the door. Marlowe, believing that his desk enhanced his position, had never been tempted to indulge in such a dangerously democratic experiment, and merely called out that Woodend should enter.

The Chief Constable was not alone. Sitting next to him – on the authority side of the desk – was Detective Chief Superintendent Newton.

Newton was a comparatively new boy to the Mid Lancs Force. Woodend had not expected to like him, and the Chief Superintendent had lived up to that expectation. He reminded Woodend of some of the sergeants he had known in the Army – men who would lick their superiors' boots as long as that gave them the right to inflict the same humiliation on those below them.

The Chief Constable looked woefully at Woodend. 'Two murders, by the same man, in only three days,' he said. 'This is a very bad business, Charlie.'

'I'm aware of that, sir,' Woodend replied.

'The papers aren't at all happy about it. And who can blame them? Scotland Yard already thinks we're country bumpkins, and you're not doing anything to persuade them otherwise.'

'Do you have any specific complaints, sir?' Woodend asked.

'Specific complaints?' repeated Marlowe, who had an almost pathological fear of being pinned down to a definite opinion. 'No, I have no *specific* complaints. They are, by their very nature, operational matters, and it would be quite improper of me to interfere.' He turned to Newton. 'Isn't that right, Duncan?'

'Quite so,' Newton replied. 'Operational matters, by their very nature, are *my* concern.'

Two people, one voice, Woodend thought. And that voice was undoubtedly Henry Marlowe's. Woodend wondered if Newton quite appreciated how willing the ventriloquist would be to throw his dummy to the wolves, should the need arise. There was a pause, while Newton waited for Marlowe to speak again. Then, when it became plain that the ventriloquist intended the dummy to have the next line, he cleared his throat, then said, 'Would you like to outline to us the way in which you're conducting this investigation, Chief Inspector?'

'I'm followin' procedures, sir.'

'And what does that mean, exactly?'

You shouldn't need to ask, Woodend thought. You should already bloody-well *know*!

'We're tryin' to trace the movements of

both victims,' he said. 'We're lookin' for witnesses. We're investigatin' the victims' backgrounds to see if there are any common factors which link them.'

'And it's all getting you precisely nowhere,' Marlowe said.

'Solving a case of this nature isn't always easy, sir,' Woodend said, adding silently: If it *was* easy, you'd be doing it yourself, you bastard!

'As you know, DCS Newton is not a man to second-guess those under his command,' Marlowe said. 'Apart from that sort of thing being inappropriate, he's far too busy with his own responsibilities to keep looking over anybody else's shoulder. But there may come a time when, for the sake of the Force's reputation, he will feel compelled to step in and take charge himself. Isn't that right, Duncan?'

'Yes, that's right,' Newton agreed.

'So there you have it, Chief Inspector,' Marlowe said. 'Get a result soon, or the case will be taken over by someone who can.'

'I wouldn't want you to think I don't appreciate your custom, but two bodies in three days is rather too much of a good thing,' Dr Shastri said.

Paniatowski, weighed down by the case, weighed down by her *life*, nevertheless managed to force a weak grin to her face.

'Sorry about that, Doc,' she said.

'And where will it end?' the doctor asked. 'I had planned to spend next July with my family in India. Will that still be possible, do you think? Or will trade be so brisk by then that you will be sending the bodies to me on a conveyor belt?'

'This should be the last one for some time,' Paniatowski said, praying that it was.

The doctor nodded her head. 'Good. And now, would you like to know what I and my little scalpel have discovered?'

'If you wouldn't mind.'

'The woman was in her mid-twenties—'

'We know that. We've got her passport. She was twenty six.'

Dr Shastri feigned a frown. 'Please, no more!' she said. 'Every job has its perquisites. In the case of a real butcher, he has the opportunity of selecting the finest cuts of meat for his own use. In the case of we medical butchers, we have the satisfaction of telling people things they do not already know, and thus demonstrating how clever we are. Do not deny me that simple pleasure.'

'Sorry!' Paniatowski said, and this time her grin was genuine.

'The woman was in her mid-twenties,' Dr Shastri repeated, now that the ground rules had been made clear. 'She had had her tonsils cut and her appendix removed. Rather unusual for a non-Asian woman of her age, she was still a virgin, though she was wearing a diaphragm – so perhaps she had hopes of getting lucky. It is difficult to say with absolute accuracy, but I would guess that she had between six and nine months left.'

'Left?' Paniatowski repeated. 'Left to do what?'

'To live, of course.'

'She was *dying*?'

'Did I not mention that before?'

'No. Believe me, I'd have remembered if you had.'

'Then let me tell you that this woman was suffering from the same kind of inoperable cancer as the last one you brought me.'

Twenty-Seven

'So now we've got our common factor,' Woodend said heavily, sliding his over-spilling ashtray from one side of his desk to the other and then back again. 'One single point at which the life of a middle-aged prostitute an' that of a timid young shop worker intersect. Both women, in now appears, were out-patients of the Whitebridge General Cancer Wing.'

'Which, you must admit, narrows it down *a little*,' Bob Rutter said, attempting a note of optimism.

'Well, aren't we the Happy Little Bunny this mornin',' Woodend said sourly. 'You're quite right, of course, Inspector. Now, instead of our murderer bein' any man in Whitebridge an' district, we've narrowed it down to the doctors, the male orderlies, the cleaners, the maintenance staff, the caterers, men who happened to be there visitin' other sick people, people with access to the hospital's medical records, and any feller who bothered to hang about outside the hospital so that he could follow Lucy and Betty an' find out where they lived. So it should be a doddle from here on in, shouldn't it?'

This wasn't the DCI Woodend she knew, Monika Paniatowski thought, shocked. It was Cloggin'-it Charlie's way to encourage his team, not to make them feel like something the cat had dragged in. And then she realized that the anger he was showing was not directed at his inspector and his sergeant at all, but at the people behind the ranks – and the way he thought they'd screwed everything up.

'At least we've built up a clearer picture of the murderer,' she said, attempting to steer Woodend's attention back on to the investigation.

'Have we?' Woodend asked incredulously.

'In what way?'

'We now know why he chose Betty and Lucy as his victims.'

'Is that right? Well, I'm probably bein' thicker than usual, but I can't say that *I* know.'

'He chose them because they were particul arly vulnerable,' Paniatowski said. 'Because, in addition to their other troubles, they had cancer to worry about. He selected them because he knew they were so desperate that they'd probably believe *whatever* he told them.'

'So we know he's a meticulous planner. I'd call for a drum roll if we hadn't *already* known it.'

'We knew, but perhaps we weren't *fully* aware of either the depth of his planning or the extent of his ruthlessness,' Paniatowski persisted.

'Good God, if that's all we can learn from one extra death, then we really are in trouble,' Woodend said. 'How many more women have to be killed before we get our next clue, Monika? Two? Three? An' how many murders will it take before we're finally in a position to make an arrest? A dozen? A hundred? We're lettin' down the people we're supposed to protect. An' the *reason* we're lettin' them down is that we're distracted – me included – with what's goin' on between the pair of you.'

216

'With respect, sir, I think you're wrong about that,' Rutter interjected. 'I don't claim that the relationship is making our jobs any easier, but I don't think it's clouding our judgement either. We're too professional for that.'

'Then why aren't we gettin' anywhere with the investigation?' Woodend bellowed.

'Because this is the cleverest killer, and the most complicated case, that we've ever had to deal with,' Rutter said.

Woodend grabbed at his ashtray, and for a moment it seemed as if he was intending to hurl it at his inspector. Then he released his grip on it, and lit up a cigarette.

'Aye, perhaps you're right,' he said, when a few seconds had passed. 'Perhaps we'd still have been in this hole even if you had both managed to keep your pants on.'

'And perhaps I'm wrong,' Rutter admitted. 'But Monika and I will both try harder from now on.'

Woodend nodded. 'There are other potential victims out there who need to be warned,' he said crisply. 'Women who attend the Whitebridge cancer wing an' have suddenly found they've got a new friend who seems too good to be true – because he bloody well is! I'll get on to the BBC local news an' the *Courier*. We can rely on both of 'em to get the message across without creatin' a panic. As for you two...' he paused, undecidedly, '...do

217

you think you can work together without your private affairs gettin' in the way?'

'Yes,' Paniatowski said.

'No question,' Rutter agreed.

'Then get down to the hospital with all the manpower you can muster. I want everybody who works there interviewed, and all the interviews cross-checkin'. I want a list of all the patients who've been admitted in the last six months, so we can question their male visitors. An' if anybody has noticed a man on his own loiterin' outside – even just the once – then I want to know about that, too. Understood?'

'Understood,' Rutter and Paniatowski said in unison.

'Then bloody get on with it before we have another stiff to explain away,' Woodend told them.

LH had had his first nervous breakdown only days after coming out of the jungle. He'd been pronounced completely cured a year later. Three months after that, he'd tried to hang himself.

It had been during his second stretch in the mental institution that he'd begun to fumble in the darkness of his own insanity for a strategy which might help him to survive. And he'd found it. *He* had found it! Not the doctors who claimed to be curing him – but he himself!

Everyone had said that what he had done in the jungle had not been his fault, he'd argued. So whose fault was it?

Not the fault of war! Such abstract concepts were of no value to a man who had spilled hot blood.

Then on whom *could* he lay the blame? On the woman he had killed, of course! If she hadn't have been there that night, he couldn't have slit her throat. And it was her choice that she had been there – not his!

War was men's business. That had been accepted throughout the ages. The woman should have known this. It was her job to stay at home – to be ready to minister to her husband when *he* returned from the fighting.

From there it had been just a small step to seeing all women as traitors – traitors to the role they had been given in life, traitors to the men they had married. The enemy was not the foreigners with guns lurking outside the camp, but the women within it.

Women had a sacred duty to their men. And even if the men died, the obligation was not at an end, for now the duty was transferred to preserving the dead men's memory. Yet how many women took these duties to heart? Virtually none!

It was a crime. It was a sin. And these women – these betrayers – should not go unpunished.

Twenty-Eight

Rutter and Paniatowski sat opposite each other in the main office of the cancer wing of Whitebridge General. It had taken a court order to get their hands of the mountains of files which they both had piled up beside them – and it would take a miracle to work their way through them in less than a week.

In other parts of the hospital wing, detective constables were questioning the staff.

– *Do you remember either of these two women? Did you contact them outside the hospital?*

– *Did you notice any male visitors who paid particular attention to any patient other than the one he was visiting?*

– *Did you see anyone suspicious hanging about the grounds?*

It was a procedure which had to be followed, and it was always possible that it would get results, but neither Paniatowski nor Rutter had any faith in it.

Mr X had been seeing both Betty Stubbs and Lucy Tonge, yet the investigation so far had not been able to turn up a single witness who had noticed him with either of the women. How likely was it then that, having walked the subtle tightrope with his victims, he would allow a casual encounter with a hospital worker to bring him crashing down?

The phone on the desk rang, and Rutter picked it up. Paniatowski heard him say, 'Hello? Oh, it's you, my darling,' and developed a sudden interest in the file in front of her.

'Yes?' Rutter said. 'What! ... You're sure about that? ... Why didn't you tell me last night? ... You thought I looked too tired to bother me with it ... Yes, you were probably right ... You're sure that's the name she gave you? ... First she said she'd arranged an interview with me and then she admitted she hadn't ... No, don't worry, I'll take care of it ... . Me, too.'

Me, too, Paniatowski thought.

I love you, darling.

Me, too!

Rutter slammed the phone down on the cradle. 'I have to go out for a while,' he said, his voice thick with anger. 'You can hold the fort, can't you?'

'I suppose so,' Paniatowski said, wondering if Bob would ever run so fast to protect her. 'Where are you going? Is it personal business?'

'Why should you even need to ask that?'

Rutter said. 'Didn't you hear who I was talking to?'

'No,' Paniatowski lied.

'So let me be sure I've got this completely clear,' Dexter Bryant said. 'You think that their having cancer was not the main factor which contributed to their deaths. Is that right?'

'The murderer could have chosen some other group to draw his victims from,' Woodend said. 'Women who'd recently been deserted by their husbands, for example. Or women who'd lost their jobs, and were facin' financial hardship. The determinin' factor, we believe, was that they should be feelin' especially vulnerable, an' have nobody they could turn to.'

'So why didn't he consider one of these other groups you mentioned?'

Woodend sighed. For an intelligent man, Bryant was taking a long time to understand this simple point.

'He probably *did* consider them,' the Chief Inspector said. 'But in the end, he must have decided that nothin' is as likely to make a woman as vulnerable as the thought of her imminent death.'

'Let me ask you another question,' Bryant said. 'Is it your opinion that if there is another death, the victim will be one of the women who attended the outpatient department of the casualty ward?'

'We're hopin' there *won't* be another murder. That's why we're havin' this conversation now.'

'But if there *were* another murder?' Bryant insisted.

'If there was another murder, then yes, I would expect the victims to be one of the outpatients.'

Bryant finally seemed satisfied. 'Right, then. I'll run a competition with a big prize. A holiday would probably be the best idea.'

'You'll do *what*?' Woodend asked. 'Have you lost your mind?'

For a moment it seemed as if Bryant couldn't understand why Woodend looked so outraged. Then comprehension dawned.

'I'm sorry, that must have sounded awful, the way I put it,' he said. 'Here you are, talking about life and death, and here's me coming up with the idea of a competition. But the two *are* connected – it's just that my mind was running ahead of my words, and so you couldn't see what the connection was. Shall I explain?'

'I think you'd better,' Woodend said.

'If we want to see newspaper sales jump by ten or fifteen per cent, we announce a competition with a wonderful prize. We can't do it too often, of course, because it's so damn expensive, but it's never been known to fail.'

'I'm still not with you.'

'You've seen the placards that newspaper sellers have in front of them, haven't you?'

'Yes.'

'If the one this evening reads, "Police issue warning to single women", we'll probably sell a few more papers than usual, but we can't guarantee we'll reach all the people we'll need to. If, on the other hand, the placard reads, "Win a fabulous two-week holiday in sunny Spain", we'll sell as many papers as we can print. And before the readers ever get to the bit of the paper about the holiday, they'll see your warning on the front page. *Now* do you see?'

'Yes,' Woodend said. 'The problem is, the Force is clogged with red tape, an' to get permission to finance a holiday like that would take me two or three days at least. Even then, I can't say for sure that I'd be successful.'

Bryant laughed. 'There's red tape in the newspaper world, too, but not when the Editor's wife owns the newspaper in question. The *Courier* will cover the cost of the holiday. We're the local newspaper. It's the least we can do for the community we serve.'

'I owe you for this,' Woodend said.

'No, you don't.' Bryant checked his watch. 'It's going to be a push to get it organized in time,' he said, 'but I think I should just about be able to manage it if I get started now.'

Elizabeth Driver was sitting in the bar of her hotel. She didn't particularly want to be there, but if anyone were looking for her it would be one of the first places they'd try. And after all the groundwork she'd done, somebody – a very special somebody – certainly *should* be looking by now.

The door of the bar suddenly burst open, and an obviously furious Bob Rutter swept into the room.

'What the hell did you think you were playing at?' he demanded.

'Why don't you take a seat?' Elizabeth Driver suggested sweetly.

Rutter treated the invitation with the contempt he felt it deserved. 'How dare you call at my home like that?' he asked. 'I could probably have you prosecuted for telling my wife we'd arranged to meet there. And apart from the legal consequences, it's a gross breach of professional ethics. It could well cost you your job on the *Daily Globe*.'

Driver laughed. 'Do you really think the *Globe* is as namby-pamby as that?' she asked. 'If you told my Editor what I'd done, he probably give me a rise for showing initiative.'

'Why *did* you do it?' Rutter asked.

'Ah, I was wondering when you'd cool down enough to start worrying about that,' Elizabeth Driver said.

'Worrying? I'm not worried.'

'Well, you should be. I didn't go to your house as a reporter, I went as a *woman*. It was only when I decided not to say what I'd been intending to that I put my reporter's hat on again.'

'I have no idea what you're talking about,' Rutter told her.

'It seemed to me, as a *woman*, that your wife had the right to know what was going on between you and Monika Paniatowski.'

Rutter looked pole-axed. 'I ... I haven't...' he spluttered, and, though he was probably not aware of doing so, he sank heavily into the seat that Elizabeth Driver had offered him earlier.

'Don't try to deny you're having an affair,' Elizabeth Driver said. 'I've made a couple of phone calls, visited one or two discreet country hotels within easy driving distance of Whitebridge, and I've already dug enough to more than prove my case.'

Rutter willed his heart to slow down. 'So why *didn't* you tell Maria?' he forced himself to ask.

'Like I said, I had second thoughts. I felt a certain duty to your wife, but I also felt a duty to you.'

'To *me*?'

'Yes. After all, Bob, we both make our living out of crime, don't we?'

'You're attempting to blackmail a police

officer!' Rutter said, with growing incredulity.

'Of course I'm not. That wouldn't only be wrong, it would be stupid. But if you wanted to slip me the odd tit-bit of information, as a way of showing your gratitude, then I certainly wouldn't complain about it. And who knows, it might just tip the balance in your favour the next time I have another crisis of conscience about telling Maria the truth.'

'I won't do it,' Rutter said.

'I don't think you quite appreciate what I'm willing to give up here,' Elizabeth Driver told him. 'You're not exactly important enough to be front page news, but the fact that the person you're committing adultery with is another police officer should be enough to persuade my Editor to run it as an inside story – especially considering your wife is blind! Human interest, you see. My readers are bound to wonder what kind of man it is who'll betray his blind wife, don't you think?'

'Yes,' Rutter agreed. 'It's something I've been wondering about myself.'

Twenty-Nine

During the course of the day, the autumn sun had managed to gather enough strength to temporarily vanquish the fog. Now, as darkness fell, that fog was back, more virulent – more malevolent – than ever.

Looking out of his office window at the swirling menace below, Woodend found himself wondering if there had been a fog like this on the night of 4th November 1605.

He pictured Guy Fawkes, hiding in the cellar beneath the Houses of Parliament.

Had he been afraid, as he crouched there behind his barrels of gunpowder? Probably!

But had he been beset by doubts? Definitely not!

Fawkes had not needed to search for any justification for his actions. The king was suppressing the True Faith; therefore the king must be removed. Small wonder, then, that with right, justice and the Lord on his side, he had been willing to commit murder – even though, in the process, many innocent people would die. Small wonder that he had elected to become the enemy within, a human bomb at the heart of England's centre of government.

Woodend turned his mind from thoughts of the past to the enigma of the man who had so recently become the centre of his own existence. What motivated this particular killer? Did he, like Fawkes, see some justification for what he was doing? Did he, too, see the loss of innocent lives as a necessary price to be paid? And if so, as a price for *what*?

He did not recall asking himself this sort of question about any of the other cases he had investigated. But then no other case had *been* like this one. The killings were not random or spontaneous – they were carefully planned in advance. And though he could not produce a shred of evidence to back up his theory, Woodend was becoming convinced that the murderer was on a mission – that he saw himself as killing for something greater than himself.

Elizabeth Driver was feeling very pleased with herself. And why shouldn't she? It wasn't every day that she got to put the squeeze on a police inspector, especially a police inspector who was so much in his boss's confidence.

Yes, Rutter was a rare prize, she thought, but life would be even better if she could also get a handle on Dexter Bryant.

She picked up the phone and dialled her reluctant helper in London. For once, he did not seem to resent her calling. In fact, he seemed almost eager to speak to her.

'I've found out something juicy,' he said.

'On Bryant?'

'No, not on Bryant. He's clean as a whistle. There are even some people on the Street who call him *Saint* Dexter.'

'Then if you've nothing on him, I don't see how you can say—'

'It's not him – it's about a member of his family. And once I've told you, you'll be able to make him dance to whatever tune you want to play.'

Elizabeth Driver felt a churning in the pit of her stomach. This was going to be *great*!

'Now I've taken the trouble of ringing you up, I suppose I might as well hear what you've got to tell me,' she said casually.

'You don't fool me,' her informant told her. 'You're excited. I can sense it, even at this distance.'

Damn! She should have been able to hide it better than that.

'So I'm *interested*,' she conceded.

'If I tell you, does that wipe out my debt? Does it mean I don't owe you anything any more?'

'That all depends how good it is.'

'Oh, it's good.'

'Then let's hear it.'

He gave her all the details.

'Well?' he said when he'd finished.

'You've cleared your debt,' she told him, and hung up.

What a bloody fool the man was, she thought. No wonder he'd never amounted to anything. How could he uncover such invaluable information – and still not see how to use it properly?

She could make Dexter Bryant dance to her tune, he'd said.

What a waste that would be! Like using a precious silver spoon to eat cabbage soup! Like squandering precious jewels in order to buy worthless trinkets!

With what she knew now, she could gain huge influence within the police force. And not just at the level of detective inspector. Not even at the level of detective *chief* inspector. No, armed with the bombshell her unwilling helper had given her, she was going right to the top.

It was as she was closing one of the White-bridge General files and reaching across for another that Monika Paniatowski noticed the expression on Bob Rutter's face. The anger it had been displaying when he return-ed to the hospital had all but gone, to be replaced by a look of anguish and hope-lessness which quite shocked her.

She wanted to comfort him, but didn't

dare. She wondered what could possibly have happened to him, but didn't feel she had the right to ask.

Rutter closed the file he had been attempting to study, and pushed it to one side.

'What time are we meeting the boss?' he asked.

'Eight thirty.'

'Do you think there's any chance he'll be in the Drum before that?'

'He could be.'

'Then I think I'll go and see if he's there now.'

'Any particular reason?' Paniatowski wondered aloud.

'There's something I want to talk to him about.'

'And does it have anything to do with us?'

'No, not directly.'

'But *indirectly*?'

'I suppose so.'

Paniatowski stood up. 'In that case, I'm coming with you.'

'I'd rather you didn't.'

'I don't care what you'd "rather"!'

A freshly agonized look crossed Rutter's face. 'I just need half an hour in private with Charlie. It *does* concern you in some ways, but I promise you I won't say anything to harm you. In fact, it's partly for you I'm doing it.'

'Then tell me what it's about.'

Rutter shook his head. 'I can't. Trust me, Monika. Just this one more time.'

A frown of indecision appeared on Paniatowski's brow.

'Please!' Rutter said.

'Half an hour,' Paniatowski told him. 'You've got half an hour, then I'll be joining you whether you've finished what you want to say or not.'

Thirty

Woodend looked across the table in the Drum and Monkey at the man who had once been his protégé.

'So Elizabeth Driver knows all about it,' the Chief Inspector groaned. 'Whatever were you thinkin' of when you started this affair?'

'I'm not sure I was even *thinking* at all,' Rutter confessed. 'It was almost as if there was an evil angel deep inside me, whispering that it would be all right.'

Woodend raised his hands to his forehead, but said nothing.

'I knew I shouldn't listen,' Rutter continued. 'I understood that the angel's main aim was to destroy me – but I did what it wanted me to do anyway.' He paused, and

233

looked appealingly at his boss. 'Do you know what I mean, sir?'

Woodend maintained his silence.

'*Do you know*?' Rutter persisted.

'Aye, I know,' Woodend said heavily. 'How could I not? We've *all* got our evil angel.'

'That's what I'm saying.'

'It can spread like a cancer, until it's taken over us completely.'

'Exactly.'

'But unlike a real cancer, there's always somethin' we can do about it. We can fight back – an' if we're strong enough, we can defeat it.'

'It's not as simple as that,' Rutter said defensively.

'Yes, it is,' Woodend argued.

'That's easy for you to say.'

'Easy!' Woodend repeated. 'Don't you think I've ever been tempted? Have you forgotten Liz Poole?'

She'd been involved in the first case they'd ever worked on together, Rutter reminded himself – and she'd made it plain to Woodend that if he wanted her, he only had to ask.

'No, I've not forgotten her,' the inspector said.

'An' neither have I,' Woodend said. 'I don't think I ever will. But if I've got regrets, then they're regrets I can live with.'

'What's your point?' Rutter asked snappishly.

'You think it's Elizabeth Driver whose holdin' a gun against your head, but you're wrong.'

'I never said—'

'She may actually have it in her hand, but you're the one who put it there in the first place.'

The few creaking props by which Rutter had been holding up his sense of self-justification finally buckled and collapsed, almost burying him in the process.

'You're right, of course,' he confessed. 'I'm the one who put it there.'

'An' how are you goin' to deal with the situation?'

'Not in the way Elizabeth Driver wants me to!'

'Aye, I gathered that, or we wouldn't be sittin' here talkin' about it now,' Woodend said. 'So what *are* you goin' to do?'

'As soon as this case is over, I'm going to tell Maria about the affair. What she does then is up to her. I wouldn't blame her if she kicked me out.'

'Neither would I,' Woodend agreed. 'But that's only one part of your problem, isn't it?'

Rutter nodded. 'When Driver realizes I'm not going to co-operate with her, her first thought will be to run the story of Monika and me as a sort of consolation prize for herself. I'm going to try and pre-empt that.'

'How?'

'By resigning. The story will lose most of its appeal if one of us is no longer on the Force – so maybe it won't be worth printing after all.'

'I hope you're not expectin' me to try an' talk you out of handin' in your resignation,' Woodend said.

'No, I'm not. But even if you did try, it wouldn't do any good. Now that Driver's got the story, I'm finished whatever happens. Even if they don't dismiss me, they'll shunt me into some kind of job in which I'll never see real policing again. But if I go now – and go voluntarily – there's just a chance I'll be able to save Monika's career.'

A half-wistful smile came to Woodend's face. 'I used to take pride in you, Bob,' he said. 'Then all I felt was disappointment.' He held his hand out across the table. 'After what you've just told me, I think I may be able to start admirin' you again.'

Rutter shook the hand. 'Thank you, sir. That means a lot to me.'

'I'm goin' to miss you when you've gone, lad,' Woodend said.

'I'm going to miss you, too, sir,' Rutter told him.

No one had bothered to give a name to the piece of wasteland, though in shape, isolation and origin, it could have been a close relative of Mad Jack's Field. It was located about a mile and a half from the town centre. Minor roads bounded its north and south borders. Its east and west edges were marked by a row of houses and an old tannery respectively. In the centre stood one of the biggest bonfires in Whitebridge.

Constable Ernie Rowse looked longingly up at the stack of branches and timber, then blew into his hands for warmth.

'How long are we goin' to be stood here?' he asked his partner, PC Ken Blake.

'We get relieved at two in the mornin'.'

'We could freeze our balls off by then. I'll tell you what! Why don't I light this bloody bonfire?'

'Have you lost your mind?'

'No, listen, it's a brilliant idea. As long as it's burnin' we'll keep warm. An' when it's finished burnin', there'll be nothin' left to guard any more.'

'An' we'll not lack for company, either.'

'What do you mean?'

'I mean that before it had even got properly goin', we'd have a couple of fire engines, half a dozen squad cars, an' an ambulance down here. Still, you wouldn't have to worry about your balls freezin' off any more – you wouldn't *have* any balls by the time Cloggin'-it Charlie had finished with you.'

'So maybe it was a daft idea, now I think

about it,' Rowse admitted grumpily, 'but I still think it's a waste of time us bein' here.'

Blake switched on his flashlight. 'I should not be away for more than about ten minutes,' he said.

'What are you talkin' about? Are you goin' off somewhere?'

Blake sighed. 'Don't you *ever* listen to orders? One of us is supposed to patrol the perimeter of the site once every half hour.'

'That's another daft idea,' Rowse said dismissively.

'Maybe it is,' Blake agreed. 'But if I'm questioned by the sergeant later on, I want to be able to say, hand on heart, that I did what I was supposed to do.'

Rowse watched the bobbing light in Blake's hand travel across the field to the boundary, and turn and continue along it parallel to the road. Eventually, as was bound to happen, Blake's light disappeared, hidden by the bonfire.

If he'd wanted to, Rowse could have walked around to the other side of the bonfire, and continued to follow Blake's progress with his eyes. But he didn't want to! That was the difference between him and his partner, he thought – he took a sensible approach to the job and Blakey was too keen by half!

The clock which hung over the bar – a

perpetual warning to customers that even in paradise there were time limits – said that it was a quarter to nine.

'I told you that I'd posted constables at all the bonfires in the Whitebridge area, didn't I, Monika?' Woodend asked.

'No, sir, you didn't.'

'Thought I had. Must just have mentioned it to Bob, shortly before you got here.'

Monika looked from Woodend to Rutter, and then back to Woodend. What else had the boss mentioned to Bob shortly before she got there? she wondered. Had they been talking about her? And if so, what had they been saying? Had the two men, *being* men, decided they would cast her in the convenient role of vamp and home-breaker?

She became aware that Woodend was looking quizzically at her – as if he expected her to ask some detective-like question.

'What's the idea behind posting guards?' she said, when she'd worked out what he was waiting for. 'Are you working on the assumption that the killer needs the bonfires as part of his ritual – and if he can't get at them, he won't bother to kill?'

'More or less,' Woodend agreed. 'An' if that it *is* the case, then we're safe after tonight's over – at least until next Bonfire Night rolls around.'

'But you're not sure they *are* necessary to him, are you?'

'No, I'm not. If all he's interested in is burnin' his victims in *some* way or other, then there's a hundred other methods he could use. Which means that the only thing that's goin' to stop his killin' spree is that we catch him – an' we're no closer to that than we were at the start of this bloody investigation.'

'We must know *something*,' Rutter said. 'It's just that we don't *know* we know it yet.'

'I admire your optimism,' Woodend said. He glanced up at the clock. 'Another ten minutes an' I'll be off to make my round of the bonfires.' He coughed, awkwardly. 'An' as for you two, if I was in your shoes, I think I'd call it a night an' go your separate ways.'

And what did he mean by that? Paniatowski wondered. It was almost as if he were suggesting that it would be wiser for them not to be seen alone together. But why *should* it be wiser? They were colleagues. They'd *often* been seen together. It would only seem significant to someone who knew of their affair, and so far, the only person who knew was Woodend himself. Or *was* he the only person? From the way Bob Rutter was behaving, she was beginning to have her doubts.

'If you don't mind, I'll come with you on your tour of inspection, sir,' Rutter said.

'I don't mind at all,' Woodend said. 'Glad of the company.'

That's right, Paniatowski thought bitterly.

You lads go off together and leave the home-breaker on her own!

It occurred to Ernie Rowse that it must have been at least five minutes since the beam from his partner's flashlight had disappeared behind the bonfire, and that by now he should be seeing it re-emerge on the other side of the waste land.

He walked around to the far side of the bonfire, and scanned the distance. There was no sign of Ken's light.

Maybe his partner had stopped for a jimmy-riddle, he thought. That would require both hands, if Ken's bragging were to be believed. But even Ken – as proud as he claimed to be of his equipment – wouldn't leave his torch on while he was relieving himself, because shining a light on the goods would be a very difficult thing to explain when you came up before the magistrate on a charge of indecent exposure!

Rowse laughed at his own whimsy. That was a good one! He'd have to remember to tell Ken when he got back. But when *would* he get back? Even allowing for the fact that he might have had a full bladder, his torch should still have come on again by now.

'Are you all right, Ken?' he called across the waste ground.

There was no answer.

'Come on, Ken! Stop playin' silly buggers!'

Again, nothing but silence greeted him.

He wondered if he should radio in to the station, but if he did that, he would have to explain that his partner had gone missing – which would make him look foolish and might actually get Ken into trouble.

'Stop pissing about, Ken!' he shouted.

It was then that he heard a noise from somewhere behind his left shoulder. He whirled round, shining his beam on the spot. There was no one and nothing there.

'This might be your idea of joke, Ken, but it's certainly not mine,' he said, drawing his truncheon.

Another noise – this time to his right. He turned to face it. It sounded like a stone landing, he thought. Then he heard the quick footsteps behind him, and realized that was exactly what it had been.

The man and his dog turned the corner and headed towards the tannery. They had taken this same walk, at this same time, every night for nearly seven years, the man reflected. No, not every night, he corrected himself. There was one night every year – November the Fifth – when they gave it a miss.

Once the man had tried explaining to the dog that the fireworks – the bangers and rip-raps, the rockets and Catherine wheels – presented no danger to them, but the thick bugger had refused to understand. So now they stayed in on Bonfire Night, with the telly turned up to full volume to block out the sound of the explosions.

As they drew level with the tannery, the man sniffed, and thought he detected the scent of wood smoke in the air. But it was not until he was clear of the building and had an unimpeded view of the waste ground that he could actually see that the bloody bonfire was ablaze.

Thirty-One

The uniformed sergeant whose job it had been to secure the crime scene was waiting for Woodend and Rutter when they pulled up at the edge of the field.

'The body's still here, sir,' he said. 'We thought it would be wiser not to remove it until you'd got a look at it yourself.'

Woodend looked across at the burned-out bonfire. Two ambulance men were standing close to it, holding a stretcher between them. The sheepskin-coated Dr Shastri was kneeling on the ground, examining what could easily have been a pile of rags – but wasn't!

'You go an' look at the corpse, will you, Bob?' he said to Rutter. He turned to the sergeant. 'I think the first thing *I'd* better do is see the lads.'

'The lads?' the sergeant repeated.

'The two young bobbies who got hurt.'

'Oh, the lads!' the sergeant said. 'If you'd care to follow me, sir.'

He led Woodend around the edge of the waste ground to a police Black Maria. Constables Rowse and Blake, both with their heads heavily bandaged, were sitting in the back of it, drinking large mugs of heavily sugared tea. To Woodend's immense relief, they didn't seem to have come out of the experience too badly.

'How are you doin', boys?' he asked.

Blake smiled, and then winced. 'It's all right as long as I don't move at all, sir.'

'Are you up to tellin' me about it?'

Blake started to nod, then thought better of it. 'I was patrollin' the perimeter in accordance with instructions—' he began.

'You're not in court, so you can forget all the crap!' Woodend said. 'Just tell me what happened in your own words.'

'I was walkin' along the edge of the road. I heard a noise, like somebody was followin' me, but bein' very quiet about it. I turned round an' saw the man. Then he hit me.'

'Did you get a good look at him?'

'Not a *good* look.'

'But somethin'?'

'Yes.'

'Tell me about it.'

'He was around six foot tall, with a strong build. He was wearin' one of them thick pullovers you can buy at the Army an' Navy Stores, an' a woollen Balaclava helmet.'

'What about his face?'

'It was all blacked up, sir, like the commandos in the war films.'

'So you couldn't say whether he was young or old?'

'He didn't move like an old feller, but I couldn't give you any idea of his age.'

Rowse had even less to say than his partner. He hadn't so much as caught a glance of the man who'd hit him.

'You'll be taken to the hospital for a thorough check-up,' Woodend told the constables. 'After that, I suggest you go home an' get a good night's kip. An' don't have a drink, however much you feel like it, because that'll play merry hell with your heads in the mornin'.'

'Sorry we messed up, sir,' Blake said.

'You didn't mess up,' Woodend told him. 'We're dealin' with a professional here. There's not a man on the Force who would have spotted him until it was far too late.'

'Would you like to see the body now, sir?' asked the sergeant who had accompanied him to the Black Maria.

'Aye,' Woodend agreed heavily. 'I suppose I'd better.'

The two men stepped out of the van and began to walk towards the bonfire. Monika Paniatowski's bright-red MGA had just pulled up at the edge of the field, Woodend noted.

It was a pleasure to work with her, he thought. She represented the future of decent, humane policing, and he would do all he could to protect her. But he was not sure how effective that protection would be. Elizabeth Driver would be furious that Rutter had chosen resignation over black-mail and, in a fit of pique, might choose to run the story of the affair anyway. And if she did, there was very little doubt about how the Chief Constable would react to it.

Monika would be joining Bob on the unemployment line. Two fine careers would be sacrificed in the interests of developing one sordid one.

'Shit!' Woodend said.

'What was that, sir?' the sergeant asked.

'Nothin'. Thinkin' about somethin' else entirely. Tell me about the latest body.'

'The woman was in her late forties or early fifties, I'd say. She had her throat cut just like the other two.'

'What position was she in?'

'Close to the bonfire, but at right angles to it. Her feet were badly burned, her lower legs somewhat burned. Her skirt had started to smoulder, but we were there quick enough to stop it combusting.'

'Any identification?'

'Yes, sir. A handbag. We've sent a man round to her house to pick up her husband an' take him to the morgue.'

'So this one had a husband, did she?'

'Yes, sir.'

'The other two didn't.'

They were close enough to the bonfire now to see the drama which was being played out in front of it. A civilian stood between two uniformed constables. The man was struggling, and the officers were attempting to restrain him without having to resort to too much force.

'Who's that?' Woodend asked.

'Probably the husband. The constable won't have told him where the body was found, but if he listens to the news—'

The man broke away from his escort – and Woodend saw that he was Dexter Bryant.

'The victim?' the Chief Inspector said.

'Yes, sir. What about her?'

'She wasn't called Constance Bryant, was she?'

'That's right. But how did you—?'

'Sweet Jesus!' Woodend groaned.

The constables grabbed hold of Bryant again, but not before he had managed to move far enough forward to get a look at the body. By now, Woodend was close enough to observe the look of agony on the other man's face.

Bryant noticed him. 'You told me my wife was safe!' he screamed 'You told me she was *safe!*'

'You're wrong, Mr Bryant,' Woodend replied, puzzled. 'We never even mentioned your wife.'

'I asked you if *all* cancer victims were at risk, and you said they weren't. You said only the ones who'd attended Whitebridge General were in any danger. But my wife didn't go there. She went to Manchester! To Christie's Hospital!'

'Your wife had *cancer*?' Woodend said.

But of course she did. She'd never have been lying where she was now if she hadn't.

'She could have beaten it!' Bryant shrieked. 'We could have beaten it together. But you can't beat a slashed throat, can you? There's nothing you can do about that.'

'I'm so sorry,' Woodend said. 'I didn't know ... I never thought...'

'I'll see you crucified for this,' Bryant promised, still struggling against the officers who were holding him. 'It won't be just the *Courier* that goes after you. I've still got friends on Fleet Street. Lots of friends. Lots ... lots of ... of...'

And then he stopped struggling – and started to cry.

There was an air of unease in the pub about

the presence of the three police officers who were sitting at their usual table. All sense of pride – all sense of proprietorship – was gone. This wasn't the crack team which quickly resolved difficult cases. This was the bunch of incompetents who had simply stood by while two innocent women were brutally murdered.

'Bryant was right about one thing,' Woodend told the others, after gulping down a full half pint of best bitter with no obvious sign of enjoyment. 'I *should* be bloody crucified.'

'You couldn't have foreseen the way things would turn out,' Paniatowski said. 'All the evidence pointed towards Whitebridge General being a common factor. Even if you'd known it wasn't, there isn't any way you could have predicted Mrs Bryant would be next on the murderer's list.'

It wouldn't be long before she reached across and stroked his arm as if he were an injured child, Woodend thought.

He took a deep breath. 'Right, that's enough of me wallowin' in self-pity for one night,' he said firmly. 'What has this latest killin' taught us?'

'That the killer's not just after lonely women any more,' Rutter said.

'But he must have had *some sort* of relationship with Mrs Bryant,' Paniatowski added. 'Otherwise she'd never have been persuaded to leave the house.'

'Wouldn't she?' Woodend asked. 'Not even after her husband had assured her that she was perfectly safe?'

'We don't know for sure that he did do that,' Paniatowski said. 'Besides, that's not really the point. There must have been a *reason* why she went out – and the chances are that the reason was provided by the killer. What could it have been? What was her relationship with her murderer?'

'The killer didn't really harm the constables!' Rutter said suddenly, as if his mind had been working on some other track entirely.

'What was that?' Woodend asked.

'He's never shown any compunction about killing his female victims, but he didn't kill the officers. And why not? It would have been as easy to slit their throats as to club them. Safer, too. Blake would never have been able to give a description if he'd been dead. So it's not just that he's *only* killed women so far, it's that he's only *interested* in killing women.'

'Are you sayin' that he's got some twisted code of behaviour? That he thinks it's *wrong* to kill men, whereas it's almost his *duty* to kill women?'

'That's what the facts would seem to indicate.'

'The facts have pointed us in the wrong

direction before,' Woodend said gloomily. 'An' even if they're right this time, where does it bloody get us?'

'I've thought of another connecting factor,' Paniatowski said. 'Widows!'

'The only widow was Betty Stubbs,' Rutter said.

'No, she wasn't,' Paniatowski countered. 'Before she married again, Constance Bryant was a widow.'

'An' Lucy Tonge?' Woodend asked.

'She called herself *Mrs* Tonge. *We* know she only did it because she wanted to make herself seem less pathetic, but perhaps the killer didn't. Perhaps he believed she really had been married.'

Maybe Monika was on to something, Woodend thought. But the brief flare of hope she had fired quickly died away, and he was once again surrounded by the darkness of confusion and incomprehension.

Thirty-Two

It was not until he had almost reached his Wolseley that Woodend noticed the two men standing beside it. They were both wearing camel-hair coats and bowler hats – articles of dress as alien to Whitebridge as an aborigine's loincloth. One of the men was very tall, and built like a brick outhouse. The other was a dapper little man with a neat silver moustache. They were the kind of fellers who would hand an anvil to a man already sinking in a swamp – and Woodend was in no doubt who they had brought the anvil for this time.

'Chief Inspector Woodend?' asked the man with the silver moustache.

'Depends,' Woodend replied. 'Who's askin'?'

'My name's Perkins, *Superintendent* Perkins.'

'You look a bit of a short-arse to be a bobby,' Woodend said.

The other man should have taken offence, but didn't – which was very worrying indeed.

252

'Have you got some identification on you?' the Chief Inspector continued.

Perkins – if that really was his name – reached into the pocket of his overcoat, produced a warrant card, and held it in front of Woodend for a couple of seconds at the most.

'Satisfied?' he asked.

'Not really,' Woodend said. 'But you're not goin' to let me take a closer look at it, are you?'

'No, I don't think that would serve either of our interests,' Perkins said, returning the card to his pocket. 'Shall we get into your car, Chief Inspector?'

'Just the two of us?'

'Yes.'

Woodend looked across at Perkins' companion. 'What about King Kong here?'

'Rodney is perfectly content to stay where he is.'

'Good for Rodney,' Woodend said, opening the door of the Wolseley and climbing into the driver's seat.

Perkins slid in from the passenger side. 'Sorry for the melodrama,' he said, 'but we really *do* need to have a little chat.'

'Is that right?' Woodend replied, non-committally.

'It is indeed. You are currently involved in investigating a series of murder cases. Would I be right in assuming that you consider the man you're looking for to be a maniac?'

Woodend scratched his nose. 'Aye, that's how I'd describe a feller who's slit three women's throats.'

'How *exactly* do you plan to go about the investigation of Constance Bryant's death?'

'She died sometime in the last three hours,' Woodend countered. 'How the bloody hell have you managed to get from London to here so fast?'

'We flew.'

'On a commercial flight?'

'Not exactly. You still haven't answered my question, Chief Inspector. How do you propose to investigate Constance Bryant's death?'

'If you're a bobby, as you claim to be, you shouldn't need to ask me that,' Woodend pointed out.

'I *am* a policeman. But I'm not *your* kind of policemen.'

'Then what are you? Special Branch?'

Perkins sighed. 'I could have had you summoned to London easily enough, if I'd wanted to. Instead, I was courteous enough to come and see you – thus causing minimum disruption to your investigation. I think that entitles me to a little consideration.'

'In other words, you're the one who asks the questions, an' I'm the one who answers them?'

'Precisely. And now we've got that clear,

we can start anew. Why do you think Constance Bryant was killed?'

'Because the murderer, for his own peculiar reasons, has decided to target women with inoperable cancer.'

'So you'll be focusing the thrust of your investigation on the killer himself, which means that there'll be no need to examine the backgrounds of the victims too closely, will there?'

'What a load of bollocks you do talk,' Woodend said disgustedly.

'Would you care to explain that?'

'We don't know that inoperable cancer is the *only* common factor. Bloody hell, I haven't seen the statistics, but it wouldn't surprise me to find out there are hundreds of women in Mid Lancs dyin' of the same thing. So what makes the killer choose the women he does? We know his victims probably hadn't met each other socially. We know they didn't go to the same schools, or belong to the same organizations. But that's not to say there isn't *somethin'* linkin' them *other than* the cancer. So in answer to your question, we'll be lookin' into their backgrounds very closely indeed.'

'I'm afraid it's not convenient to have you look too closely at Constance's,' Perkins said.

'An' why's that?'

'Because she was one of us.'

'A spy?'

'An intelligence operative. As a journalist with a roving foreign brief, she proved very useful to us.'

'Was she workin' for you when she died?'

'No, she'd retired.'

'Because of her health? Or because her uncle had left her the Mid Lancs *Courier* in his will?'

'Her health. There was no uncle.'

'Then who did she inherit the paper from?'

'From a man who would have gone bankrupt years ago if we hadn't been subsidizing it. A man who agreed to be called her uncle as the price of keeping his newspaper afloat.'

'So the *Courier* was no more than Constance Bryant's pension plan – an' when she found out she was ill, she decided to cash it in?'

'Exactly.'

'Do you buy a newspaper for all your retirin' agents?'

'Of course not. Most of them wouldn't want it.'

'But Constance Bryant did?'

'All our agents have different dreams – a different crock of gold they hope to eventually find at the end of the rainbow. One might want a small commercial fishing boat. Another might wish to run a quiet country pub. In Constance's case, it was a small provincial newspaper.'

'An' you always give them what they want?'

'Whenever possible. It's the thought of their eventual reward which keeps them going under pressures which would break most people.'

'I can't help thinkin' it was very convenient for you that Constance's "uncle" chose to die at just the right time,' Woodend said.

Perkins laughed, with what sounded like genuine amusement. 'That's the trouble with dealing with members of the general public like you,' he said. 'You've watched too many films. You all see conspiracy and dirty operations where none exist.'

'So you didn't kill the paper's previous owner?'

'Of course not. It was convenient that he died when he did, but it wouldn't have mattered if he hadn't. He'd long understood that when Constance wished to take over, it would be time for him to retire.'

'Who knows about her background?' Woodend asked.

'One more person than knew about it half an hour ago.'

'Your mates in Whitehall may consider that a clever answer,' Woodend said, 'but you're in the North now – an' we'd just call it smart-arsed.'

Perkins sighed again. 'Her head of section knew, naturally, as did her controller. Two or three other operatives had to be made aware, plus a couple of people in finance and accountancy. The Prime Minister and Foreign Secretary probably know – but not *necessarily*. It amounts to little more than a handful of people.'

'Did her husband know?'

Perkins laughed again, unmistakably contemptuously this time. 'I knew Dexter Bryant when we were both up at Oxford. He had quite a good mind. Might have done quite well in the Foreign Office. Instead he became a *crime* reporter.'

'Meanin' what?'

'If Constance had married someone following a gentlemanly profession, it might have been operationally convenient to make her husband aware of her position. But no one was going to risk informing a grubby little hack.'

'So you're sayin' that he *didn't* know?'

'I should have thought that was obvious.'

'You don't think there's any chance *she* might have told him?'

'All our operatives are rigorously trained to keep their professional and private lives completely separate.'

'He's an intelligent man. He might have guessed.'

'He may well be intelligent – if all those years on Fleet Street haven't rotted his brain. But we are very, very good at providing cover stories for our operatives. I can assure you, Chief Inspector, that Mr Bryant won't have had a clue what was really going on.'

'Shouldn't he be told now?'

'What on earth for?'

'Did Constance run any risk when she was workin' for you?'

'Yes, of course.'

'I mean *real* risk?'

'If she'd been arrested – and there was always a fair chance she would be – the Russians could have put her on trial and sentenced her to twenty or thirty years in prison. But that's by no means the worst thing that could have happened to her. Over the years, several of our operatives have simply disappeared. They'll be dead now, of course, but God alone knows what happened to them *before* they were executed.'

'So she was a heroine?'

'We tend not to use emotive terms of that nature ourselves, but I suppose I have no objection to you employing it.'

'An' you don't think it might be some consolation to the man who's just lost her to know that?'

'I think it might be of some consolation to *you* to know that it is of some consolation to *him.*'

'I'm not followin' you.'

'Oh, I think you are. You feel guilty about not being able to prevent Constance's death.

You think if you can bring a little comfort to her husband, it might help to assuage some of that guilt.'

The bastard was spot on, Woodend thought. But the fact that he'd hit the nail on the head didn't alter the fact that telling Dexter Bryant about his wife's heroism was still the right thing to do!

'Espionage is a complex business,' Perkins continued. 'If we expose Constance as one of our agents, we will be putting at risk other agents who had contact with her. We simply couldn't allow that to happen.'

'You can't *stop* it happenin'!' Woodend retorted. 'You may have signed the Official Secrets Act, but I certainly bloody haven't.'

'True,' Perkins agreed. 'But could you actually reveal the secret, knowing it might lead to further loss of life? Could you really stand to have *more* deaths on your conscience?'

'You're enjoyin' this, aren't you?' Woodend demanded.

'I'm merely doing what needs to be done. And so must you. You will not tell Mr Bryant that his wife was ever an agent of ours. And as for the officers under your command – that's Detective Inspector Rutter and Detective Sergeant Paniatowski, is it not—?'

'You know bloody well it is!'

'—you will instruct them not to investigate Constance Bryant's background any further.

You may give them any reason you wish for this, except, of course, the correct one. Do you understand?'

'Yes.'

'And you'll do as I've instructed?'

'I don't have much bloody choice, do I?'

'You have no choice at all,' Perkins said. He reached into his pocket and handed Woodend a card. 'You can contact me at this number, should the need arise. Just give your name and you'll be put straight through.'

Woodend examined the card. 'This is a London number,' he said.

'Yes, it is,' Perkins agreed.

'But you won't be *in* London, will you? You'll be right here until this whole mess is cleared up.'

'My exact whereabouts should be no concern of yours,' Perkins said smoothly. He opened the car door and stepped out on to the pavement. 'Well, since that seems to be all, I'll wish you a pleasant good night, Chief Inspector.'

'An' I'll wish *you* a bloody long walk on a bloody short pier!' Woodend said morosely.

November the Fifth

Each soul has a cellar
Of deepest dark sin
And there may be found
The enemy within.

Thirty-Three

'It's not often we get children listening to the morning weather forecast, but I'm willing to bet there's a goodish number of you tuning in today,' said the cheery voice over the car radio. 'So here it is, kids. There's a fair amount of cloud about, and it may rain a little round about lunchtime, but if you keep your fingers crossed and wish very hard, we just might have a dry Bonfire Night after all.'

Woodend switched the radio off. Wet or dry, how many parents in the Whitebridge area would let their kids out when there was still a triple-killer on the loose? he wondered.

He had just entered Hill Rise. It was one of those prosperous estates which had sprung up as soon as the post-war period of austerity was over. Well-heeled solicitors lived on Hill Rise, as did successful businessmen. And until the previous evening it had been the home of Constance Bryant, newspaper proprietor and retired spy.

The Bryant house was located at the end of a cul-de-sac. It was a handsome building – though, like the man whose home it was, not ostentatious. As Woodend walked up the path, he found himself wondering what kind of reception he would receive.

It was Bryant himself who answered the door. He looked as drawn and haggard as might have been expected in the circumstances, but at least he was in control of himself enough to have shaved and put on fresh clothes.

'If it's inconvenient—' Woodend began.

'It's never going to be easy, but it has to be done, so we might as well get it over now,' the Editor interrupted. 'If you'd care to follow me, Chief Inspector.'

Bryant led Woodend down a wide hallway into a large, open-plan living room. There was a picture window at one end of the room, overlooking an immaculately laid-out garden. A staircase connected the living room to the house's upper floor.

'Please sit down,' Bryant said dully, indicating a cream-coloured leather sofa.

Woodend hesitated. 'Really, Mr Bryant, if you'd rather that I came back later—'

'Sit!' Bryant ordered, taking a seat himself. 'I want to apologize for my outburst by the bonfire last night, Chief Inspector.'

'It was quite understandable.'

'No, it wasn't. However much distress I may have been suffering, it was totally inexcusable of me to try to lay the blame for the tragedy at your door. You could not possibly have guessed that Constance would be the killer's third victim. If anyone should take the blame, that person should be me. I should not have been at the office last night. Whatever reassurances you might have given me about her safety, I should have been at home protecting my wife.'

You might *say* you don't hold me accountable, Woodend thought, but there's a large part of you that still does. A large part of me, too.

He wondered if there was something he could do to ease Bryant's obvious suffering, and thought back to his conversation with Perkins the previous evening. The man with the silver moustache hadn't quite said that he'd be in deep trouble if he revealed any of the contents of that conversation, but the threat had been clear enough. Well, screw him!

'Did you know your wife worked for the security services?' he asked.

'What?!'

'She was a spy.'

Bryant laughed uneasily. 'That's impossible,' he said. 'We had no secrets from each other. If she'd been involved in that kind of work, I would certainly have known.'

'There are some things you can't tell even those you trust and love,' Woodend said. 'There are very strict rules about it.'

'It's totally impossible!' Bryant protested.

'You have every reason to be proud of her,' Woodend told him. 'She fought for her country as bravely as any soldier. If she'd lived,' he continued, calculating that he could get away with at least one lie, 'she'd have been awarded a medal for her work – though, of course, the Queen would have given it to her in closed session.'

For a moment, Bryant looked as if he had no idea of how to answer. Then he said, 'You're very kind.'

'Kind?'

'To pretend that Constance had been involved in some work of national importance. But you really don't have to pretend at all, you know. My wife didn't have to *do* anything special – she *was* special!'

And she'd done a brilliant job of fooling her husband, Woodend thought. Still, he was glad he'd spoken out. Bryant didn't believe what he'd said now, but later, when he came to appreciate what a gaping void his wife's death had left in his life, he might come to accept the truth and draw some comfort from it.

He cleared his throat. 'I have to ask you about the circumstances surrounding your wife's death,' he said regretfully.

'Of course,' Bryant agreed.

'You said you weren't here when she left the house?'

'That's right. I was down at the paper.'

'We think she may have gone out to meet someone. Do you have any idea who that might have been?'

Bryant shook his head. 'None. Constance tired very easily and spent a good deal of the day resting. As a result, she didn't have much of a social life, and even what little there was came through me. I can think of no one she might have wanted to see on her own.'

'Where was your stepson last night?'

A look which was a mixture of wariness and anger appeared in Bryant's eyes. 'Why do you ask that?' he demanded.

'He's the son of a murder victim,' Woodend said gently. 'I have to know.'

A little of the tension drained out of Bryant's body. 'Of course,' he said. 'Pardon me for being brusque. LH was probably here. He rarely leaves the house.'

'So he might know if—'

'I doubt if he'd have noticed Constance going out, if that's what you were going to ask. Sometimes he's in such a trance-like state that he wouldn't even notice if the house fell down around him.'

'Why do you call him LH?' Woodend asked. 'I thought his name was Richard.'

Bryant laughed weakly. 'It's a nickname my wife gave him. He was quite small when his father died in India, but he was very brave about it. Hence the name Lionheart, you see.'

'Richard the Lionheart. Like the king.'

'Exactly. He's always been brave.' Bryant paused for a second. 'Did you see any action in the last war, Chief Inspector?'

'Yes.'

'A lot?'

'More than enough.'

'I never got to do my share of the fighting. I volunteered, but I was turned down on medical grounds. I don't think I've ever quite learned to accept that rejection. Richard, on the other hand, *did* fight for his country. He was a hero, and any personal problems he's having now are as a direct result of that heroism.'

'Personal problems?'

'He has a nervous disposition as a result of his experiences. He doesn't relate well to people, even the ones who want to be close to him. He made his mother suffer sometimes, but I – as the man who dared to replace his real father – bore the brunt of the attacks. I've never minded that. However unfair and unreasonable he is, I'll keep on trying to get through to him, because though we all owe him a debt for what he had to endure in Malaya, those of us who have never endured war ourselves owe it most of all. I feel responsible for him. Does that sound foolish?'

'No,' Woodend said sympathetically. 'It doesn't sound foolish at all.'

There was a sudden loud thud from up-stairs.

'Is Richard at home now?' Woodend asked urgently.

'Yes, he—'

'Which is his room?'

'Second to the left at the top of the stairs,' Bryant said.

But he was talking to empty space, because Woodend had jumped up from his seat and was already dashing towards the staircase.

The bedside cabinet lay on the floor, where Richard Quinn had kicked it. Quinn himself hung from the high-ceilinged light fitment by a pillowcase which he had twisted to form a rough cord. He could not have been hanging there for long – only since Woodend had heard the thumping sound from downstairs – but he had already started to change colour.

The Chief Inspector grabbed hold of the young man's trunk, and lifted it to take pressure off the neck. Behind him, he heard the sound of Dexter Bryant entering the room.

'Find somethin' to cut him down!' Wood-end shouted. 'An' be quick about it!'

Bryant looked wildly around the room for a moment, then rushed over to his stepson's dresser and opened the drawer. The knife he pulled out of it had a long blade and a wickedly shaped edge. When he drew it across the stretched pillowcase, the fabric gave instantly.

Bryant dropped the knife on to the floor. Woodend hoisted Richard Quinn into a carrying position, took him over to the bed, and laid him gently down on the cover. Perhaps while Quinn had been hanging there, his whole life had flashed before him – but in real time no more than a few seconds had passed.

Quinn's eyes had begun to bulge slightly, and he was making choking noises, but Woodend guessed that no permanent damage had been done.

'Why did you do it, LH?' Dexter Bryant asked anguishedly. 'Why did you try to kill yourself?'

'Mother...' Quinn gasped.

'What about her?'

'Wanted her dead ... often enough. Now ... she is.'

There was a loud imperious banging at the front door. Bryant clapped his hand to his forehead, as if this, on top of everything else, was enough to make his head explode.

'What in God's name...?' he said.

The banging continued.

'You'd better answer it,' Woodend said.

'But LH...?'

'He'll be fine for a minute. Go and see who's there. Maybe they'll be able to help.'

Bryant nodded, and left the bedroom.

Woodend knelt over Richard Quinn. 'What did you mean when you said you wanted her dead – and now she is?' he asked.

'Shouldn't wish for bad things to happen,' Richard Quinn croaked.

'Is that all you did? Wished for bad things to happen?'

'That was ... enough ... wasn't it?'

Woodend became aware of several sets of footfalls on the stairs, and then the room was full of people. The Chief Inspector looked first at Dexter Bryant and then at DCS Newton and the two uniformed constables.

'What's goin' on?' he demanded.

'Thank you, Charlie, I'll take over from here,' Newton said.

'Take over what?'

Ignoring Woodend, Newton walked over to the bed. 'What's happened to him?' he asked, looking first down at Richard Quinn and then turning towards Dexter Bryant.

'He ... he tried to hang himself.'

'I'm not in the least surprised about that,' Newton said, returning his gaze to the man on the bed. 'Can you hear, Mr Quinn?'

'Yes,' Quinn said faintly.

Newton cleared his throat. 'Richard Thomas Quinn, I am arresting you for the murders of Elizabeth Stubbs, Lucille Tonge and Constance Bryant.'

'This is insane!' Dexter Bryant screamed.

273

'Please don't interrupt, sir,' Newton warned him. 'You are not obliged to say anything, Mr Quinn, but anything that you do say—'

'Richard was at home all evening,' Bryant protested. 'With me! He couldn't have killed his mother.'

'I understood that when you were informed of your wife's death, you were at your office,' Newton said coldly.

'I ... I...' Dexter Bryant stuttered.

'Were you at your office or not?'

'Yes, but...'

'It's a serious matter to lie to the police,' Newton said sternly. 'I may have to charge you.'

'For Christ's sake, his wife's been murdered and his stepson's just about to be arrested!' Woodend thundered. 'Cut the man a little slack, you unfeeling bastard!'

'Escort Mr Bryant downstairs,' Newton told the two constables. 'And as for you, Chief Inspector, we'll discuss that last remark of yours later.'

The constables each took one of Bryant's arms, and the Editor started to struggle.

'Don't!' Woodend advised him.

'But I can't just let them—'

'You'll be of no help to Richard if you're locked up in a cell.'

Bryant nodded, accepting the logic of the argument, and allowed himself to be led out of the room.

'Now perhaps we can get on with the business in hand,' Newton said. Then he noticed the knife that Bryant had used to cut through the pillowcase and was now lying on the floor. 'Nasty looking instrument, that,' he told Woodend. 'I'd say it'd be just about right for cutting throats. Wouldn't you?'

Thirty-Four

Woodend flung open the Chief Constable's door, and stormed into the room. Marlowe was, as always, sitting behind the protective cover of his large desk. Seeing Woodend standing there, he first feigned surprise, then – obviously deciding that was not something he could carry off convincingly under the circumstances – he rapidly switched to an expression of mild annoyance and bureaucratic censure.

'This can scarcely be considered appropriate behaviour, Chief Inspector,' he said sternly. 'If you wish to schedule a meeting with me, then there are certain channels which must be gone though.'

'What the bloody hell do you think you're playin' at?' Woodend demanded.

'I'm not sure that I quite understand your

question. What am I *playing* at? Is that what you said?'

'All right,' Woodend said, exasperatedly. 'If it makes you feel any happier, what the bloody hell is Newton playin' at?'

'I should have thought that was obvious. Since you seemed unable to come up with a good line of inquiry in your current investigation – or, indeed, any line of inquiry at all – DCS Newton has stepped in. I did warn you that might happen, you know.'

'Oh, you did,' Woodend agreed. 'Indeed you did. An' the first thing Newton does – *havin'* stepped in – is to arrest Richard Quinn!'

'I can't say with absolute certainty that it *was* the first thing that Mr Newton did. But it is certain that he's arrested Richard Quinn.'

'On what grounds?'

'That's an operational matter. I'm afraid you'll have to ask DCS Newton about it.'

'Operational matter – bollocks!' Woodend said. 'You know everythin' he knows – an' more. He wouldn't dare to do so much as fart without getting' your permission first.'

Marlowe sighed the sigh of a man who is trying to be reasonable, but, in fairness to himself, knows he cannot permit the interview to carry on for much longer. As a performance, it was better than his earlier attempts at surprise and annoyance – but not much.

'If you can bring yourself to calm down for a moment, Chief Inspector, I might be willing to outline as much of the evidence against Richard Quinn as I currently have access to,' he said.

Woodend took a deep breath. 'I'm calm,' he promised.

'Very well. Let's first consider means. Did you know that Richard Quinn had combat training in Malaya?'

'His stepfather mentioned that he'd served in Malaya an' won medals,' Woodend conceded.

'He was a Royal Marine Commando, and the attacks on the three women bear all the hallmarks of commando training. In addition, the wounds are entirely consistent with a dagger called the ... the...'

'The Fairbairn Sykes,' Woodend supplied.

'Exactly. It was standard issue for the commandos, and we found such a dagger in Richard Quinn's bedroom during our search.'

'But do you know it was the knife which was used in the killin's?'

'You certainly believe it is, and no doubt the lab will soon confirm that we are right. Now we'll go on to motive. In this case it is very simple. Richard Quinn hated his mother for marrying his stepfather – we will produce witnesses who will confirm that fact

– and he wanted to see her punished.'

'Then why didn't he do just that? Why did he bother to kill the other two women first?'

Marlowe brushed the question away with a wave of his hand. 'Quinn had a nervous breakdown at the end of his period of service in Malaya. Who knows what goes on in his poor sick mind now? Perhaps the fact that the other women were also suffering from cancer made it easier for him to identify them with his mother. Perhaps he was only using them for practice, and it was pure coincidence that they had the same disease as Constance Bryant.'

'There's absolutely nothin' coincidental about this bloody case!' Woodend protested. 'The killer planned the whole operation long in advance. An' why would a trained commando need practice? That kind of trainin's so thorough that it's like learnin' to ride a bike – once you have learned, you never forget.'

'You obviously consider that you know the way he thinks much better than I do,' Marlowe said. 'In which case, could you please explain to me why the murderer – if he wasn't Quinn – put his victims in the bonfire.'

'I don't know,' Woodend admitted.

'Neither would I – if the murderer *was* anybody else,' Marlowe said. 'But if it was *Quinn*, then I can explain it very easily. He was brought up in India, you see, which means that he will have been aware of the Indian tradition of suttee.'

'The British banned that practice over a hundred years ago.'

'Nevertheless, it is deeply ingrained in the Indian consciousness, and no doubt young Richard would have learned of it. Would you like to explain to me exactly what suttee involves, Chief Inspector?'

'When a man died, he was cremated on a funeral pyre,' Woodend said dully. 'An' once the pyre was burnin' properly, his wife was expected to throw herself on to it after him.'

'Bonfire, funeral pyre – there's very little difference between the two,' Marlowe said. 'Now do you see where I'm going?'

'No,' Woodend said.

'You don't see because you don't *want* to, Chief Inspector! Very well, I'll spell it out for you. Richard Quinn adored his father, and when the father died he expected his mother to die too – or, at very least, to go into perpetual mourning. But that didn't happen. She met Dexter Bryant, and made a new life for herself. And Richard couldn't tolerate that. In placing his mother on the bonfire, he was only correcting the balance – doing to her what she, symbolically or otherwise, should have already done to herself years before.'

'Doesn't all that strike you as just a little

too neat an' tidy? Just a little *too much* like a cleverly constructed crime novel?' Woodend asked.

'No,' Marlowe said. 'It strikes me as an explanation which has the ring of truth about it.'

'All right, I can see we're never goin' to agree on that,' Woodend said, 'so would you mind if we looked at it from another angle?'

'No, as long as that will ensure you leave my office sooner than you would otherwise have done.'

'You've covered means an' motive. What about opportunity? Can you place Richard Quinn anywhere near the scene of any of the murders?'

'We will,' Marlowe said complacently.

'Meanin' you haven't even tried yet. Meanin' that you've charged straight in, like bulls in a bloody china shop, without even botherin' to put a proper case together first.'

For once, Marlowe looked a little uncomfortable. 'We could have waited, but we had the press to consider.'

The press! Of course! The bloody press! Always the bloody press!

He'd been asking the wrong questions, Woodend suddenly realized. He'd got himself so bogged down in the details of the case that he'd completely ignored the much bigger picture.

'How did you get your sights fixed on

Richard Quinn as a suspect in the first place?' he asked.

'That scarcely matters now that we've put together our case and the arrest's been made,' Marlowe said airily.

'You didn't have access to my case notes. You could have asked for them – you'd have been perfectly entitled to – but you never did. You were startin' from scratch. So what made you single out Quinn from the tens of thousands of other men in Whitebridge? How could you have become so convinced he was your man that you'd go to the lengths of doin' a full background check on him?'

'I'm sure Mr Newton will give you any of the details he considers it appropriate you should know.'

'He was fingered, wasn't he?' Woodend said.

Marlowe made no reply. He didn't need to – because his face said it all.

'How was it done?' Woodend asked. 'An anonymous letter? No, your informant wouldn't have taken the risk of bein' dismissed as a crank. Besides,' he continued, beginning to understand more and more of what must have gone on behind the scenes, 'there'd be a price attached to the information, now wouldn't there?'

'I don't see how you could make that assumption.'

'I can make it because if the Force didn't

investigate Quinn's background – an' it's quite obvious that it didn't – then somebody else did. An' that somebody had to have the resources to do the job properly. So who could that *somebody* possibly have been?'

'You're making a fool of yourself with all these wild speculations,' Marlowe said.

'A journalist!' Woodend exclaimed, as if the idea had come as sudden inspiration, instead of having been developing in his head for the previous couple of minutes. 'An' if I had to make a bet on *which* journalist it was, I'd put my money on Elizabeth Driver.'

'You don't know what you're talking about.'

'So if tomorrow's *Daily Globe* runs a bigger story on this case than any other newspaper does – an' if it seems to have inside knowledge of what went on – that'll just be coincidence, will it?'

'Coincidences happen.'

'You can't let the newspapers run your investigations for you!' Woodend said, outraged. 'You can't make a case based on headlines. Police work's about dozens of small details which finally mesh together to give you the answer you've been searchin' for.'

Marlowe smiled, now sure of his ground again. 'And what dozens of small details do you have to offer me, Chief Inspector? Which of your dozens of small details point a finger at the murderer?'

'I admit we're not there yet,' Woodend replied, knowing it was a weak response, yet not having the ammunition which would enable him to produce any other.

'Whereas DCS Newton has his murderer,' Marlowe said. 'Consider yourself off the case, and go back to your office to await a fresh assignment.'

'I want to continue my investigation.'

'I'm afraid that won't be possible.'

'Look,' Woodend said, trying to sound reasonable, 'it's always conceivable that you've made a mistake. An' if you did, that could prove very embarrassin' later on. Whereas, if you were to just let me keep diggin'—'

'I've already told you what I want you to do.'

'If you take me off the case, I'll go public,' Woodend said. 'I'm sure there's any number of other newspapers which will be most interested to discover how the *Globe* got its exclusive.'

'If you do that, you'll be finished,' Marlowe growled.

'Aye, probably – an' there's a good chance that you will be too,' Woodend countered.

'That sounds like a threat.'

'Good! That's what I intended it to sound like.'

Marlowe had been running a pencil

through his hands. Now he snapped it in two. 'You do realize what you're asking, don't you?'

'Yes.'

'And you do realize that the fact we may have got most of our information from the *Globe* – and I'm still not admitting that we did – will be of no interest to anyone if you can't prove that Richard Quinn wasn't the killer?'

'Yes.'

'And that that will leave you totally defenceless? A deer caught in the crosshairs? A fox cornered by the hounds?'

'You've made your point.'

Marlowe's smile returned, and this time it was broad and triumphant. 'Very well,' he said. 'Find me a different killer – or put your own neck in the noose.'

Thirty-Five

The landlord of the Drum and Monkey stood behind the bar counter, polishing glasses and casting the occasional furtive glance at the table in the corner.

Something was wrong, he thought. Very wrong!

He'd been watching these three at work for over two years, long enough to have become an expert on them. And while he'd seen the detectives in all kinds of moods – elation and depression, mystification and triumph – he'd never seen them looking as they did at that moment. They seemed to have lost their team spirit – their sense of common purpose. They seemed, not to put too fine a point on it, to be a team no longer.

'Let me be sure I've got this straight,' Bob Rutter said. 'What you've done is to blackmail the Chief Constable into letting you continue investigating the case, even though an arrest has already been made. Is that right?'

'Close enough.'

285

'But why?'

'I don't like journalists settin' the pace an' direction of an investigation, especially when the journalist in question happens to be somebody like Elizabeth Driver.'

'But what if Richard Quinn really *is* guilty?' Monika Paniatowski asked. 'Have you thought of that?'

'He's not,' Woodend said.

'You've only seen him twice,' Paniatowski pointed out. 'The first time was at the Dirty Duck – and only from a distance – and the second was just after he'd tried to hang himself. I simply don't see how – based on that – you can be so positive that you're right.'

'You had to have been there to properly understand what I'm sayin',' Woodend argued. 'The lad's a mess. He'd never have been able to convince Betty Stubbs that he knew a doctor who could cure her cancer. He couldn't have persuaded Lucy that he was goin' to run away with her. It's just not in him.'

'He tried to top himself,' Rutter said. 'Couldn't that have been because of remorse?'

'Yes, if he'd really killed his mother – and *only* his mother. But we're all agreed our killer's not like that. He's a long-term planner with nerves of steel. The man who organized those three murders so carefully wouldn't have botched a suicide attempt in the way he did. Besides, he *told* me he didn't kill Constance, an' I believed him.'

'He said something, in a state of shock, which might possibly be interpreted as a denial,' Rutter said. 'But it's not the *only* possible interpretation of his words.'

'Are you sure you've not just been swayed by personal factors?' Paniatowski asked.

'Like what?'

'Like the fact that you've got so much against Elizabeth Driver that you can't bear the thought that she might be right – even by accident?'

'The lad didn't do it,' Woodend said stubbornly. 'I'd stake my reputation on it.'

'You *are* staking your reputation on it,' Paniatowski reminded him. 'You're staking your *career* on it.'

The twists and turns of life never ceased to amaze him, Woodend thought. Only the day before, Rutter and Paniatowski had been on the defensive in his company because of their affair. Now *he* was on the defensive because, once again, he'd put his neck on the line.

'I'll ask DCS Newton to assign the pair of you to another investigation,' he said.

'No you bloody won't,' Paniatowski said angrily. 'We've stuck together so far, and we'll stay stuck together – even if you are steering the ship on to the rocks.'

'Talk to her,' Woodend said, appealing to Rutter.

'I agree,' Rutter replied. 'If we go down, we'll all go down together.'

Woodend shook his head. 'It's not that I'm unaffected by your kamikaze instincts,' he said, 'but you wouldn't be much use to me anyway. Somewhere out there, there's a bloody big clue that will lead me straight to the right answer. If I find it, solvin' the case will be a doddle on my own. If I don't find it, it wouldn't matter if I had the whole of the Mid Lancs CID behind me – I'd still get nowhere.'

'And where are you hoping to find this bloody big clue of yours?' Rutter asked sceptically.

'I'm not sure,' Woodend admitted. 'But the offices of the *Courier* are as good a place to start as any.'

'Why there?' Paniatowski asked.

'Because Constance Bryant didn't just *leave* her house last night – she was *lured out*. Which means that she had to have a special relationship with the killer, just like the other two victims did. Her husband has no idea what it might be, but somebody at his office might. That's why I want to talk to everybody who works there.'

'And thus, as ever, does the drowning man clutch at a straw,' Paniatowski said sadly.

★ ★ ★

Woodend had gathered all the *Courier*'s staff in the newspaper's reception area, where they stood in a semicircle. It was a bit of a squeeze, but at least it enabled him to see how they interacted with each other.

'I wanted to get Mr Bryant's permission before I talked to you all,' he said, 'but I haven't been able to contact him. Which I suppose is hardly surprisin' under the circumstances. Nevertheless, if I had managed to speak to him, I'm sure he'd have been more than willin' for me to go ahead with this.'

A balding, young-middle-aged man raised his hand tentatively in the air.

'Yes?' Woodend said.

'Jack Donovan, Deputy Editor,' the man announced. 'I believe I speak for all of us when I say we're more than willing to do anything we can to help.'

Woodend nodded. 'Good. Now, as you all know, Mrs Bryant wasn't a well woman an' didn't get out much. But nobody lives in a complete vacuum, an' what I'm tryin' to get a lead on is anybody who might have had more than casual contact with her. So if you know anythin', I'd be grateful if you'd speak now.'

He scanned the row of faces in front of him. Some of them looked genuinely distressed at the news of Constance Bryant's death, some merely mildly uncomfortable, and a few almost completely blank. None seemed to offer the hope of any useful leads.

'It doesn't matter how trivial the information you have might seem to you,' he encouraged. 'It could provide the vital link we need. Even if it's only office gossip, there still might be an important grain of truth in it.'

The paper's staff were becoming restive. Several shuffled their feet, and a couple of them coughed unnecessarily. And then – from the very edge of the semicircle – came the distinct sound of a snicker.

Woodend focused his attention on the person who had made the sound. He was a boy, scarcely out of school, with sly eyes and an unpleasant mouth. The Chief Inspector recognized the type easily enough – snide, cocky and malicious – and for a moment he almost ignored him. Then he decided that even if this *was* one of the straws Paniatowski had talked about, it was still better than nothing.

'Have you got somethin' to say?' he asked.

The boy grinned, obviously pleased to be the centre of attention. 'If you want to know about Mrs Bryant, why don't you ask Jamie Clegg?' he said.

'An' why should I do that?'

'Because he had the hots for her.'

There was a low rumble of disapproval from the rest of the staff.

'That's not the kind of thing the Chief Inspector needed to hear, Bains,' the Deputy Editor said angrily. 'When this is over, I'll see you in my office.'

'Who's Jamie Clegg?' Woodend asked.

At the other end of the semicircle, Clegg raised his hand. He wasn't much older than the boy who'd just spoken, Woodend noted, and the fact that he was blushing furiously showed he had none of Bains' self-assured cockiness.

'You're the reporter who tried to take the petrol can away from the scene of the first murder, aren't you?' Woodend asked.

Clegg's colour deepened. 'I didn't know ... I never meant to...' he mumbled.

'None of that matters now,' Woodend told him. 'What did your friend Mr Bains mean when he said you had the hots for Mrs Bryant?'

Jamie Clegg looked down at the floor. 'She took me out for coffee a couple of times,' he admitted.

'*She* took *you*? You didn't ask her to go?'

Clegg muttered that no, he hadn't, and around him several people started to giggle.

'*Why* did she ask you out for coffee?' Woodend asked.

'She said she could see I wanted to get on in newspapers. She said she'd been a young reporter herself once, and she'd help me in any way she could.'

That made sense, Woodend thought. Constance Bryant's maternal instincts had been rebuffed by her own son, so what could be more natural than that she should choose to lavish them on this earnest – and obviously decent – young man?

'Did you talk about anythin' else?' he asked.

'No.'

'She didn't tell you about any of her friends? Didn't talk about some project she'd become involved in?'

'She just wanted to give me tips on how to be a good journalist.'

Well, that seemed to lead nowhere. 'Does anybody else have something they want to say?' Woodend asked.

Nobody had.

Thirty-Six

The map of the park classified the stretch of water as a lake, but it was really nothing more than a pond with pretensions. Still, Woodend thought, it did well enough for the ducks. They seemed perfectly happy on it, bobbing up and down on the surface with the occasional dive to the bottom to break the monotony. They didn't have to worry about seeing justice done. They didn't give a quack about whether the right man had been arrested or not. And God, how he envied them!

He had been in the park for around about half an hour, he guessed. He'd been hoping that getting away from the bustle of the centre of the town might, in some way, open his mind – suggest a new line of inquiry for him to follow. No chance! The park had failed to work its magic, and amidst all this nature there wasn't even a brick wall for him to bang his head against.

'Hey, sweetheart, come over 'ere an' show us your tits!' called a loud rough voice behind him.

He turned. Two large – obviously drunken men – were lounging on one of the benches. A schoolgirl, who couldn't have been more than thirteen or fourteen, was rapidly walking away from them.

The Chief Inspector walked over to the bench. 'You're causin' a disturbance,' he said.

'An' what if we are?' one of the men asked belligerently, bunching his fists. 'What are you goin' to do about it?'

The other man recognized Woodend, and poked his companion in the ribs.

'Police!' he warned. 'We're sorry, Chief Inspector,' he said to Woodend. 'We'll keep it quiet from now on.'

'Want to be out catchin' murderers instead of hasslin' honest blokes,' the first man mumbled.

'What was that?' Woodend asked sharply.

'Nothin',' the man replied.

'I'll be back this way in ten minutes,' Woodend told him. 'Make sure you've gone by then.'

He walked on. He'd sounded just like a beat constable, he thought – which had probably been good practice for his future career. And the obnoxious drunk had been right – he should have been out catching murderers. The problem was, he had no idea where to look.

It took him five minutes to reach the park boundary. He turned around and retraced his tracks. He'd promised the drunks he'd return, and that was one promise – at any rate – that he should be able to keep.

The two men had left the bench, and were standing by the pond. He wondered at first why they were waving their arms in such a strange manner. Then he realized that what they were actually doing was throwing stones at the ducks.

He quickened his pace, but even as he narrowed the gap between himself and the two miscreants, he saw a third character arrive on the scene.

Dexter Bryant!

The drunks had stopped throwing stones, but only in order to give the Editor their full attention. He was by no means a small man, but they still towered over him menacingly.

Bryant waved his hands in angry remonstration. The drunks' aggressive stances stiffened. Woodend was now almost running.

One of the drunks placed his hand on Bryant's shoulder. The Editor brushed it angrily away, and the second drunk, taking that as a signal for the start of the hostilities, swung his fist at Bryant's face.

The fight – if it could be called a fight at all – was over in seconds. Bryant blocked the punch with his left arm and jabbed at his attacker's throat with the extended fingers of his right hand. The man collapsed in a heap. His partner was in no position to either assist him or continue with the assault, for, simultaneously with the jab, Bryant had run the heel of his right shoe down his shin, and now the drunk was hopping around on one leg in a desperate effort to reduce the pain.

The Editor flicked an imaginary speck of dust off the sleeve of his coat, and began to walk towards the exit to the park. It was only then that he saw Woodend.

'I can't stand cruelty to dumb animals,' he said furiously. 'It's so completely bloody pointless.' He paused. 'Or am I just making excuses for myself? Is the truth that I was looking for a fight as a way of alleviating a little of my misery?'

Woodend shook his head. 'You've no need to reproach yourself. You didn't start it – they did. They only got what was comin' to them.'

'Were you looking for me?' Bryant asked.

'No, I was just walkin' – hopin' it might help to clear my brain.'

'I was doing much the same thing. Or rather, I was searching.'

'For what?'

'For one small mitigating circumstance which might mean that I could blame myself just a little less for Constance's death.'

'You can't hold yourself responsible,' Woodend said.

'But I do,' Bryant replied fiercely. 'I should have seen the truth earlier. I should have stopped making excuses for LH, and recognized him as the real menace he is.'

'Wait a minute,' Woodend said. 'Are you tellin' me that you now think Richard Quinn *did* kill your wife?'

'Yes. And the other poor women, as well.' Tears began to run down Dexter Bryant's cheeks. 'I didn't want to consider the possibility, Mr Woodend, so I shut my eyes to it. But now that it's out in the open, it's obvious to me that something like this was almost bound to happen eventually.'

Monika Paniatowski gazed down at her vodka glass and tried to remember if this was her fifth or her sixth double. It didn't matter. Nothing mattered any more, now that everything was turning to shit.

She was so absorbed in her own thoughts – and her own misery – that she didn't even know Woodend had entered the bar until he sat down in the chair opposite hers.

'What are you doin' here, Monika?' the Chief Inspector asked.

'What does it look like?' Paniatowski replied, realizing for the first time just how drunk she was. 'I've taken the rest of the day off, and now I'm sitting here, all by myself, having one hell of a good time.'

'Has somethin' happened?'

'You might say that. Did you know that Bob's going to resign?'

'Yes, he told me.'

'And did he tell you why?'

'Yes.'

'I should have left him alone,' Paniatowski said morosely. 'There's plenty of fish in the sea. Why did he have to be the one I pulled out?'

'It was his choice as well as yours,' Woodend told her. 'Anyway, there's no point in dwelling on it now. What's done is done.'

'Did you find your one big clue down at the newspaper office – the one big clue that will ena ... enable you to crack the whole case wide open?' Paniatowski demanded. 'No, of course you didn't.'

'I think you should go home,' Woodend said. 'I'll drive you.'

'Did you know they'd got the results on the knife back from the lab?'

Bloody hell, that was quick! Woodend thought. They must really have pulled out the stops.

He imagined the look on Marlowe's face as he read the part of the report which stated that the boffins could find no connection between Quinn's knife and the one which had been used to commit the murders. Mere *evidence* probably wouldn't make the Chief Constable abandon his belief that Richard Quinn was the killer immediately, but even

298

as inflexible a man as he would eventually be forced to see that, without a forensic link, there was no case.

'It's ironic, isn't it?' Paniatowski slurred.

'What's ironic?'

'You've been right so many times in the past, but this time – when it really matters, when you've put your career on the line – you turn out to be completely bloody wrong.'

'What are you talking about?'

'The knife! Richard Quinn's knife! He'd tried to clean off the evidence, but he didn't make a very good job of it.'

'You're surely not trying to tell me...'

'I'm not *trying* to tell you anything. I *am* telling you. Richard Quinn really did kill those three women. The forensic evidence on the knife couldn't be more conclusive.'

Thirty-Seven

It was the mid-afternoon quiet period in the Kettledrum Cafe, and the only two customers were the big detective and the very intimidated-looking junior reporter.

'Tell me again what you an' Mrs Bryant talked about,' Woodend said. 'An' this time, I'd appreciate the truth.'

'It was the truth!' Jamie Clegg protested.

'No, it wasn't,' Woodend said emphatically. *It couldn't be.* Not after forensics had proved it was Richard Quinn's knife which had killed the three women!

'It was partly true,' Jamie Clegg said. 'She *did* tell me that she could see I was a lad who wanted to get on in life, and that she was prepared to give me some coaching.'

'But that wasn't the real reason she wanted to talk you, was it?'

'No.'

'So tell me what was.'

They sat opposite each other in the cafe. Mrs Bryant seemed very nervous. No, Jamie thought, that wasn't the right word at all. She seemed very driven.

'The trick to being a good reporter is to notice things,' she said.

'I know that.'

'No, you don't. You only think *you do. Close your eyes.'*

He closed his eyes.

'Describe the people on the next table,' she said.

'I can't.'

'I could have done.'

'I didn't know I was goin' to be tested.'

'You never do, but when you're a reporter, your whole life's a test. Open your eyes again.'

'Doesn't seem to be much wrong with that,' Woodend said. 'Sounds very sensible, as a matter of fact.'

'That was only the beginnin',' Jamie told him. 'The softenin' up.'

'What does my husband do?' Mrs Bryant asked.

'He's the Editor.'

Her laugh showed just the slightest edge of contempt. 'I know that. What I mean is, does he do anything unusual?'

'Like what?'

'You shouldn't have to ask that question. You should already have an answer.'

'I don't know what to say.'

'Does he ever leave the office unexpectedly, after – say – he's had an unexpected phone call?'

'I wouldn't know.'

She sighed. 'You're hopeless. You'll never make Fleet Street at this rate.'

'I'm sorry.'

'Don't apologize to me. It's your career we're talking about. Let's try again. Is there ever any occasion on which he seems worried when, as far as you can tell, there's nothing for him to be worried about?'

'You see what I'm sayin'?' Jamie Clegg asked.

'Yes,' Woodend said.

He was beginning to see a lot of things.

'You're not lost yet,' Mrs Bryant said brightly. 'You can still be trained. Shall I set you an exercise?'

'I suppose so.'

'For the next two weeks, I want you to watch my husband like a hawk. I want a concise report on everything he does. But here's the tricky bit – he must never suspect that you're watching him.'

'I'm not sure I'd be happy doin' that, Mrs Bryant.'

'Why ever not?'

'He's my boss.'

'As a matter of fact, he isn't. He's your Editor. I'm the one who owns the newspaper.'

'Even so—'

'He won't mind, I promise you.' She laughed again. 'How could he mind, when he wouldn't even know?'

Jamie felt sweat trickling down his arms. 'It's

not right.'

Constance Bryant's face was suddenly stern – almost vengeful. 'I'm not interested in employing reporters who won't even try to better themselves. If you can't complete even this simple task, then I think you'd better start looking for another job. And I wouldn't look in the newspaper industry, if I were you – because if you did, I'd feel obliged to inform anyone you might apply to that you're a no-hoper.'

Crude, Woodend thought. Very crude. Yet what other choice did the woman have? She was dying of cancer. She had neither the time nor the strength to develop a more subtle approach.

'Did you agree to do what she asked?' Woodend said.

Jamie Clegg nodded. 'Yes. I didn't see I had any option. She could have made up any number of reasons for her husband to sack me.' His youthful face turned a deep red. 'She might even have said that I made a pass at her.'

'How long was it before you told him all about it?'

Jamie Clegg's eyes widened with surprise. 'How did you know...?'

'A week?'

'Ten days.'

Jamie tapped nervously on Dexter Bryant's

door, and as he walked into the office, he realized that his heart was beating out a frenzied drum solo.

Bryant looked up at him and smiled. 'Yes, Jamie.'

'Mrs Bryant...'

'What about her?'

He had meant to say it smoothly – had rehearsed it that way. Instead, it all came out in a blurt. 'Mrs Bryant told me to watch what you do an' write a report on it.'

He didn't know quite what to expect. A verbal explosion, perhaps? Or maybe even worse? Bryant was still a powerful man. He could easily express his anger with his fists.

Instead, the Editor nodded, a little sadly. 'I see.'

'I didn't want to do it, sir. She made it seem like I had no choice.'

'You did quite right to agree to do what she wanted. And you did quite right to come to me. Take a seat, Jamie.'

Hardly able to comprehend the way in which events were turning, Jamie Clegg groped his way to a chair.

'Did you know my wife was ill?' Bryant asked softly.

'I thought she might be a bit under the weather.'

'I'm afraid it's much worse than that. She has cancer. She's dying.'

'I'm s ... sorry.'

'So am I, Jamie, so am I. What I've just told

you must never go beyond this room. Do you understand?'

'Yes, sir.'

'I've done some reading about the disease. It's such a big worry that women often develop other worries to take their minds off it. I think that's what Constance is doing. She's worried about me. And what, specifically, do you think she is worrying about, Jamie?'

Clegg could feel himself going red. 'I ... I don't know. I ... wouldn't like to say.'

'You can say it. I won't be offended.'

'Maybe she thinks you're seein' another woman?'

Bryant beamed with approval. 'I knew you were a smart boy, Jamie. You've got a great future ahead of you. Yes, that's what she thinks. That I'm having an affair. Do you think I am?'

'I ... I don't...'

'Perhaps that was an unfair question, so let me ask you another one. If I said I wasn't having an affair, would you believe me?'

'Yes, sir.'

'Then let me assure you that I'm not. But that doesn't solve our problem, does it? As long as my wife thinks I am, she'll be unhappy. And we don't want the poor woman to be unhappy. So what can we do about it?'

'I could do the report, just as she asked me,' Jamie Clegg suggested.

'How would that help?'

'If I said in the report that you were always in

305

the office – even when you weren't – she'd see that you had no time to be messin' about with another woman.'

'Very clever,' Bryant said, admiringly. *'Yes, that really would do the trick. And just to make sure it works, wouldn't our best plan be to have me write it, and you make a copy of it?'*

'Yes, sir.'

Poor bloody Constance, Woodend thought. She had been attempting to shine a light on the truth, and had done no more than give her husband an opportunity to throw up a smokescreen.

'When did this conversation take place?' he asked.

'It must have been about a month ago, now.'

Of course it was about a month. That would have given Bryant just the time he needed.

'Thank you, Jamie,' Woodend said.

'Is that all?'

'Yes.'

Woodend *could* have added that if the young reporter hadn't confided in his Editor, there was a good chance that Betty Stubbs, Lucy Tonge and Constance Bryant would still be alive. But he didn't. The lad had no idea what part he'd played in the scheme, and there was no point in upsetting him by telling him now.

Thirty-Eight

Woodend checked his watch. Richard Quinn had been under arrest for something over six hours. For the first two of those hours, the doctors wouldn't have let anyone near him, but after that DCS Newton had probably been able to persuade them that the suspect was fit to be questioned. All of which meant that – given the man's precarious emotional balance and grip on reality – he'd likely have confessed to any number of crimes he hadn't committed by now.

Which was, of course, just what the man who'd fitted him up would have been hoping for.

The Chief Inspector picked up the phone and dialled the number of a large house buried somewhere deep in the Home Counties.

'Yes?' said an unmistakable clipped military voice on the other end of the line.

'Reduced to answerin' your own phone these days, General?' Woodend asked. 'Talk about the decline of Old England, eh!'

'The servants are all out getting—' the

307

other man began. He paused. 'Who the devil is this?'

'It's—'

'Don't tell me! Let me think about it.' Another pause, then the General said delightedly, 'It's Staff Sergeant Charlie Woodend, isn't it? It has to be! No one else would have the *bloody nerve* to talk to me like that!'

Woodend smiled fondly. 'How are you, sir?'

'Getting older by the day, Charlie. But more importantly, how are *you*, you old reprobate? Haven't heard from you for years.'

'No, sir, you haven't. We don't really move much in the same circles any more.'

General Stockton chuckled. 'That's your fault rather than mine,' he said. 'If you'd taken the commission when I offered it to you, you could have been a full colonel by now.'

Unlikely, Woodend thought. Highly unlikely.

He might just have made captain, he supposed, but sooner or later he would have come up against the Army's equivalent of Chief Constable Henry Marlowe – and there his progress up the ladder would have come to a grinding halt.

'So what can I do for you, Charlie?' the general asked. 'Got a son who wants to join the regiment? If that's what you're after, consider it as good as done.'

'Thank you, sir, but the favour I want doin' is of a more clerical nature,' Woodend said, choosing his words carefully.

'Clerical nature? What's it to do with?'

'A man involved in my latest investigation. I'd like to know what's in his war record.'

'Well, good heavens, Charlie, why are bothering *me* about that? You're the police. No one's going to obstruct you. Just put your request in through the normal channels.'

'If I do that, I'll get *a* war record – but I'm not sure that it'll be the one I want.'

'Whatever do you mean, old chap?'

'I'm almost certain that if I went through the "normal channels", I'd be told that the man I'm interested in suffers from fallen arches. An' from the way I saw him movin' in the park this afternoon, I don't believe he does.'

'Not making a lot of sense, you know,' the general said. He fell silent for a second. 'Unless...' he continued, '...unless the man you're interested in had *two* war records. Is that the track your mind's running along?'

'Yes, sir.'

'One record to *account for* his time in the Army, the other to say what he actually *did*?'

'Exactly, sir.'

There was a longer silence this time, then

the general said, 'You're asking a hell of a lot of me, Charlie.'

'Yes, I am,' Woodend agreed.

'And at what point do you intend to mention a certain sticky situation which occurred during the Ardennes Offensive of 1944?'

'I believe that situation actually occurred in early '45,' Woodend said, 'but in answer to your question, I'm not planning to mention it at all.'

'Really? You're not trying to collect on an old debt, then?'

'There is no debt. I only did for you what you would have been equally prepared to do for me if our positions had been reversed. So it doesn't even count as a *favour*.'

'If you *had* tried to use the fact you'd saved my life to put pressure on me, I'd have hung up on you,' the general said.

'I know,' Woodend replied.

'So perhaps you're applying pressure by *not* applying pressure.'

'Perhaps I am.'

The general chuckled again. 'Nothing changes. You were *always* at least one step ahead of me.' His voice grew more serious. 'If this file contains what you seem to think it contains, it's for your eyes only.'

'Agreed.'

'You can't show it to any of your subordinates. You can't use it in court.'

'Fair enough.'

There was a third silence, then Stockton said, 'I'm not promising anything, but I'll do what I can for you, Charlie.'

'Much appreciated, sir,' Woodend said.

Dusk was falling as Woodend, armed with the information General Stockton had supplied, pulled his Wolseley up in front of the hotel where Elizabeth Driver was staying.

The arrest of Richard Quinn had come just in the nick of time for the children of White-bridge, the Chief Inspector thought.

That morning they would have awoken only too aware of the dark cloud hanging over them.

They couldn't go to the bonfire they'd been looking forward to for weeks, their parents would have told them – not while there was a killer on the loose.

But the killer only attacked women, the children would have argued.

That was true *so far*, the parents would have countered, but there was no guarantee that children would be immune in the future.

The arrest had changed all that. Although the *Courier* said no more than that a man was 'helping the police with their inquiries', they all knew that was merely code – that the murderer was safely under lock and key, and the festivities could go ahead as planned.

There had never been any *actual* threat to the children, Woodend reminded himself as he climbed out of the car. There would have been no point in the murderer killing children, because such killings did not fit into his careful scheme of things. And *careful* was the only word for it. In all his years on the Force, he had never come across a crime which had been so meticulously planned.

He entered the hotel and headed straight for the bar. Elizabeth Driver was sitting at one of the small tables, sipping at a gin and tonic. And why shouldn't she be? She had no need to go out chasing information. After her phone call to Marlowe that morning, the information would come to her.

When she noticed Woodend standing over her, a look of alarm came to her face.

'No worries, lass, I'm not lookin' for trouble,' Woodend said. Then, without waiting to be invited, he pulled up a chair and sat down. 'You've never been exactly scrupulous, Miss Driver,' he continued, 'but, I have to say, you seem to be gettin' worse by the day.'

'I don't know what you're talking about,' Elizabeth Driver replied.

'Still, if you were goin' to blackmail anybody, I think you were wise to choose Bob Rutter, rather than Monika Paniatowski. Bob's a bit of an old-fashioned sort when it comes to dealin' with women – but Monika would have knocked your front teeth out.'

'How dare you suggest I tried to blackmail your inspector?' Driver demanded.

'Come on, lass, there's no point in puttin' on a show when there's nobody but me here to appreciate it,' Woodend said. 'Besides, if we're goin' to be partners – even *temporary* partners – we should at least try to be honest with each other.'

'Partners?' Driver repeated, amazed.

'That's right,' Woodend said. 'For once I'm changin' the rules, an' I'm goin' to make you a special offer.'

'What kind of special offer?'

'I give you an exclusive on this case, an' in return you promise to forget everythin' you've ever found out about Bob an' Monika.'

Revenge was sweet, Elizabeth Driver thought, so very, very sweet.

'So you can be corrupted, after all,' she said.

'Like I told you, it's a one-time offer, an' though it sticks in my craw to make it, I'm doin' it to prevent three lives from bein' ruined.'

Elizabeth Driver took a long, slow sip of her drink – prolonging the moment, squeezing every drop of pleasure she could out of her victory.

'A few days ago, I might have been interested,' she said. 'More than interested.

313

Really excited. But I've moved on since then. I'm in the big league now.'

'Meanin' that you're gettin' your information straight from the horse's arse – the horse in this case bein' the Chief Constable.'

'A journalist never reveals her sources.'

'An' you still intend to run this story about Bob an' Monika, do you?'

'Not just now. I've got much bigger fish to fry at the moment. But when I hit my next quiet patch, I'll probably dig it up again.'

'You really don't care about the damage you'll do, do you?'

'They're the ones who couldn't keep their underwear on. I'm just reporting the facts.'

Woodend smiled, suddenly and disarmingly. 'I really don't know why I'm fussin',' he said. 'You won't be printin' the story of Bob and Monika in the *Globe*, because you won't be *workin*' for the *Globe* after tomorrow. An' who cares if you run it in your next paper – which will probably be the Back-of-Beyond *Weekly Advertiser*, if you're *lucky* – because only three men an' a dog will read it.'

Elizabeth Driver laughed. 'Is that the best you can do?' she asked. 'Some kind of veiled threat that I'd have to be an idiot to fall for? *Won't be working for the Globe after tomorrow!* I'll never have been in a stronger position than I'll be in tomorrow. I'll have an exclusive!'

'True,' Woodend agreed. 'But you'll have

the *wrong* exclusive.'

He sounded *so* confident that alarm bells started to ring in Elizabeth Driver's head. 'What do you mean – the *wrong* exclusive?' she asked.

'You'll be pinnin' the murders on an innocent man, while all the other newspapers – which I will have personally briefed – will be namin' the guilty one. On the other hand, if you do the deal with me, it could just as easily be the other way around.'

Thirty-Nine

In most of the houses in Whitebridge, food had been bolted down and favourite television programmes ignored for once.

Crowds had already started to gather at the dozen or more bonfire sites around the town. Small children, woollen hats pulled down tight over their ears and mittens fastened to their hands, gazed up in wonder at the large dark shape which was soon to be set afire purely for their pleasure. Slightly older kids held on tightly to the cardboard boxes which contained their precious hoards of fireworks. Parents issued last-minute instructions on safety and good behaviour.

Civic-minded adults and older teenagers began to pour petrol on the rags they would use to start the fires. It was cold – devilishly cold. But it would soon be as hot as hell. Guy Fawkes, the enemy who had lurked menacingly within the very centre of government, was about to be burned in effigy once more.

The curtains which were drawn across the front window of the house at the end of the cul-de-sac were made of thick velvet, but even so they could see that there was a light on inside.

'I'd be happier if we'd brought more men with us,' Bob Rutter said.

'No point in goin' in mob-handed,' Woodend told him. 'I want Bryant spooked – but I don't want him spooked *yet*!'

'What if he doesn't get spooked at all?' Paniatowski asked.

'He will.'

'I don't see how you can be so sure of that. So far, he's shown nerves of steel. And let's face it, sir, you haven't got enough evidence to get a rat convicted of being a rodent.'

'Ultimately, it won't boil down to clear-cut evidence,' Woodend assured his sergeant. 'That's not the kind of game he's in.'

'I hope you're right,' Paniatowski said.

'Do you think he'll have a gun?' Rutter asked.

I bloody *hope* he will, Woodend thought. If he doesn't, my whole plan will fall apart.

But aloud, he said, 'He won't be armed. He's too professional to run the risk of keepin' a weapon in the house.'

'How can you say that, considering all the risks he's run already?' Rutter persisted.

'That was different. The risks he ran before were *worthwhile* risks. At least, that's how they'll have seemed from his standpoint.'

'And having a gun *isn't* a worthwhile risk?'

'No,' Woodend lied. 'In Bryant's line of work, a gun's not much use – because by the time you feel the need of one, you're already finished.'

Rutter shook himself, more as a gesture of disbelief than because he was cold. 'Let's get on with it, then,' he said.

'You're stayin' outside,' Woodend told him.

'Why?'

'Because if we don't come out again within forty-five minutes, I'm goin' to need somebody to radio headquarters an' inform them of the fact.'

'If he's not armed – as you claim he isn't – why *shouldn't* you come out?'

Woodend sighed. 'Look, nothin's goin' to go wrong, but it's always wisest to keep somebody in reserve,' he said.

'Then keep Monika in reserve. Let me go in with you.'

'No.'

'Why not?'

Because things could go *very* wrong, and Rutter had a wife and child who depended on him, Woodend thought.

'I'm takin' Monika in because Bryant will feel less intimidated by a feller an' a woman than he would by two fellers,' he told Rutter.

'I don't believe you,' Rutter said.

'I don't give a bugger what you believe. You'll do as you're bloody well ordered,' Woodend snapped.

All over Whitebridge, the night sky began to redden as the fires caught hold. Now the fireworks started. Rockets escaped from the empty milk bottles in which they had been placed, flew through the air until they burnt up all their powder, then arced and hurtled back to the ground. Catherine wheels spun furiously on fences, roman candles flung up bright green stars and silver fountains.

In this wonderland, the children danced around the blaze in a frenzy of excitement. There were no big kids to get in their way or tell them to shove off. The big kids didn't consider it cool to arrive at the bonfire so early in the evening. Instead, they stood on street corners, throwing penny bangers at one another. To the uninitiated, it sounded rather like gunfire.

It took a single ring to bring Bryant to the

door. He ran his eyes over Woodend and Paniatowski, checked to see if they really were alone, then said, 'I'm surprised to see you here, Chief Inspector.'

'Are you, sir?' Woodend asked. 'I'm a little surprised that you're surprised. Would you mind if we came in?'

'What if that's not convenient?'

'Then we'll go away. An' you'll spend the rest of the night wonderin' what it was I'd been goin' to say. *Is it* inconvenient?'

Bryant favoured him with a thin smile. 'Not really,' he admitted. 'In fact, I'm glad of the company. It's better than being left alone with my own thoughts.'

'Aye, they can be very uncomfortable, can your own thoughts,' Woodend said.

Bryant led them into his open-plan living room, and gestured that they should sit down. 'Now what was it you wanted to say?'

'You're a clever man, Mr Bryant,' Woodend told him. 'Perhaps sometimes a little *too* clever.'

'Is it possible to be *too* clever?'

'Oh yes, I think so. Because cleverness often leads to complications. Take your idea of sendin' Jamie Clegg to cover the first murder at Mad Jack's Field. That was clever, but it also made him stand out in my mind – and he was the last bugger you needed to have me rememberin'.'

'I can't claim to understand anything of

what you've just said,' Bryant told him. 'Why was it clever of me to send Jamie Clegg?'

'Because you'd got the measure of him by then. Even if you didn't tell him to, you knew he'd do somethin' stupid like sneakin' on to the field an' tryin' to steal evidence.'

'And why ever should I have wanted him to do that?'

'Because not only did it give you a plausible reason for meetin' me, but it also allowed you to demonstrate what a nice feller you were to your employees – an' by extension, what a nice feller you were in general.'

'But why should I have *wanted* to meet you?'

'Because you believe in the old maxim that you should keep your friends close, an' your enemies closer. It was another nice touch, by the way, to arrange it so that the first person I talked to in the Dirty Duck was your wife. An' the way you managed to make sure that I got a glimpse – but only a glimpse – of your stepson, was nothin' short of masterful. Sort of like settin' the scene before the play had really begun.'

Bryant assumed the impassive carved face of an Indian warrior in a bad western. 'The marshal speak in heap big riddles,' he said. 'He want tell Tonto what whole bloody thing about?'

'Very amusing,' Woodend said dryly. 'Take

a note of it, Monika – I might want to use it at parties.' He turned his attention back to Bryant. 'Let's move on to somethin' else, shall we? Like your war record, for example.'

'My war record?'

'Most of the people I know who didn't see any action in the war like to keep quiet about it, even when it wasn't their fault,' Woodend said. 'But not you, Mr Bryant. You went out of your way to tell everybody – me included – that you worked in the Army Pay Corps. Now why is that?'

Bryant grinned. 'Because I'm more honest and open than most people you know?'

'No. Because it wasn't true. You *did* see active service. But you were told not to talk about it.'

Forty

The guys had long ago been totally consumed by flames, and though the children might tell themselves they wished Bonfire Night would last for ever, the thrill was already starting to pall a little. Rockets no longer elicited the 'ahs' which had been no more than their due half an hour earlier. Catherine wheels had lost a little of their magic. Even the bonfires themselves were past their zenith, and though true enthusiasts were searching for more material to keep them going, some of the children were already drifting away. Like everything else in their short lives, the actual event had not *quite* lived up to the anticipation.

Bob Rutter looked down at his watch. Woodend and Paniatowski had passed through Bryant's front door only fifteen minutes earlier, he calculated, so why did it feel as if they'd been gone for at least two hours?

He wished – he *really* wished – that he knew what Cloggin'-it Charlie was up to. Woodend had *said* he intended to get a confession out of Dexter Bryant, but if he was right in his theories about the man, there was no way that Bryant would be willing to spill the beans. Woodend had *said* that Bryant wouldn't be armed, but again, if he was the man that Charlie was convinced he must be, he'd be a fool not to have some kind of weapon on hand.

Rutter stamped his feet against the cold. He should never have let any of this happen. He should never have allowed Monika to go inside. If anything happened to her...

He had no claims over Monika Paniatowski, he reminded himself. She was not his to command. At the very best, she had lent herself to him. And should she die on this night, he must force himself to mourn her as a friend rather than grieve for her as a lover – for anything else would be yet another betrayal of wonderful, blameless Maria.

He looked at his watch and saw that a mere two minutes had ticked painfully by since the last time he had consulted it.

Woodend had been silently counting off the seconds which had passed since he mentioned Dexter Bryant's war record, and had reached a hundred and forty. Bryant himself had neither said anything nor shown, by the expression on his face, what he was thinking. But thoughts *were* speeding through his brain. Woodend was sure of that, because Bryant was one of the most intelligent and *calculating* men he had ever met.

A slight flicker of the Editor's eyes revealed that he had decided what to say next.

'You don't know anything about my war record. You're only *guessing* that I've seen active service.'

'Am I? I know that you speak both Russian and French...'

'It's true that I did study those languages during my time at Oxford, but so what?'

'You learned a lot more, but we'll come back to that later,' Woodend said. 'The people who were training you probably intended to drop you behind enemy lines in France – now that *is* a guess – but when

Hitler invaded the USSR in 1941, the Russian front became much more important.'

'This is beyond speculation,' Bryant said. 'It's pure fantasy. Who's writing your script for you, Chief Inspector? Walt Disney?'

'It'd save time if you'd just admit it, but I can give you dates an' places if that's what you want,' Woodend said.

'Anyone can name a few dates and places. That really doesn't prove a thing.'

Woodend sighed. 'In February 1942 you were flown to Egypt. From there you journeyed overland, through Turkey to Persia. You headed north, to the Caspian Sea, and crossed the Russian border at—'

'All right, so it wasn't speculation, and it wasn't bluff!' Bryant said, frowning. He examined Woodend closely, as if seeing him for the first time. 'You don't seem like the kind of man who'd have influence in intelligence circles.'

'You're right,' Woodend agreed. 'But I know a man who does.'

Bryant's frown turned to a smile. 'Let me guess. The man you're talking about – the man who *does* – is the captain you served under in the war.'

'He was a major, as a matter of fact.'

'And you – oh, this really is too clichéd for words – you saved his life, so that now he's willing to tell you anything you want to know.'

'It wasn't quite as easy as that,' Woodend said. 'I did save his life, but it still took a fair amount of arm-twistin' this afternoon to get him to look up your records.'

'But he *did* look them up in the end. So now you can prove that I was a hero after all. Do you want to arrest me for that?'

'No, not for that. But I do want to *arrest* you.'

'Do you think I had something to do with the Bonfire Murders?'

'Of course I do! An' you've *known* I do since the moment you saw me standin' on your doorstep.'

'Naturally, I deny it.'

'I'd have expected no less from you. But it won't do you any good. All the odd bits an' pieces of the puzzle have fallen right into place. I've got the whole picture now.'

'How interesting,' Bryant said. 'But nowhere near as interesting as the fact that instead of bursting in here with ten burly bobbies, the only person you chose to bring with you was Sergeant Paniatowski.'

'Don't be fooled by that,' Woodend said. 'Monika may not be built like a Russian weightlifter, but size isn't the only thing that matters – as you proved in the park this afternoon. You'd never have been able to deal with those two drunks in the way you did if you hadn't been *trained* to do it.'

'Yes, training is important,' Bryant agreed.

'And I'm sure the sergeant can handle herself if the need arises. But that's not the point, is it? You're not expecting to have to use force. You're here to offer me a deal.'

'Maybe.'

'And perhaps I might be interested in one. But before we deal, I need to know what it is you're selling. In other words, I'd like to be sure that when you say you have the whole picture, you're not just bluffing.'

'I'm not bluffin'.'

'Prove it.'

'Did you know when you married her that your wife was a spy?' Woodend asked.

'That isn't how this particular negotiation works,' Bryant said, shaking his finger at the Chief Inspector.

'What do you mean?'

'I want to know what *you* know, not what you think you can *find out* from me. So you don't ask me questions – you tell me things.'

'All right,' Woodend agreed. 'Yes, you did know that she was a spy. The people who run you had told you. That's the reason you married her.'

'Wrong!' Bryant said. 'Totally wrong! I loved her.'

'But there were things you loved more.'

'But there were things I loved more,' the Editor conceded.

'When did the KGB recruit you? Burgess, MacLean an' Philby all signed up while they were at Cambridge. Were the Russians runnin' a similar operation in Oxford?'

'When I was up at Oxford, it wasn't called the KGB. And I did no more than flirt with Communism while I was an undergraduate. If I had signed on – and I'm not saying that I did – it would have been later.'

'In Russia?'

Bryant smiled. 'You're really rather good at interrogation, aren't you? I tell you at the outset that I'm not answering any questions, and before I know what's happening I'm responding to half a dozen.'

'After the war, most of the covert communists joined the Foreign Office,' Woodend said. 'But not you. You went to work on Fleet Street.'

'You'd be surprised how many secrets are passed across the desks of national newspapers. We knew about the Profumo Scandal long before the government did. The problem was, we weren't allowed to run a lot of our best stories on security grounds. It seemed such a pity to waste them.'

'So you passed them on to the Russians?'

'If that's what you choose to believe, then by all means be my guest. I'm admitting nothing.'

'You married your wife partly through love, an' partly through loyalty to the Party. She didn't know that *you* knew she worked for British intelligence. It was a good arrangement. If her controller ever wondered about you, then all he wondered was if you had suspicions about *her*. It must never have occurred to him that you were workin' for the other side. She gave you the best cover you could ever hope for, plus the possibility to pick up snippets of intelligence from her when she let her guard down. Then Constance got sick an' wanted to move to Lancashire.'

'Isn't that where your argument breaks down?' Bryant asked. 'Surely, if I really were a spy as you claim, I would have resisted the move to Whitebridge. You don't get state secrets passed across the desk of the Mid Lancs *Courier*. To all intents and purposes, such a move would have meant the end of my useful life as an agent.'

'No, it wouldn't,' Woodend contradicted him. 'Half the British military aerospace industry is located in this county. Havin' spies around is no novelty to us, is it, Monika?'

'No novelty at all,' Paniatowski agreed. 'You can hardly open your front door without tripping over half a dozen of them.'

'In fact, I think it's more than likely that your controller was delighted that you'd got an excuse to relocate here,' Woodend said.

'So you're saying that this mythical controller, having supervised me while I ran one spy ring in London, now asked me to take charge of another one in Lancashire?'

'More or less.'

Bryant smiled. 'You really do have a knack for making wild speculation sound almost like deductive logic,' he said.

'If you hadn't been involved in espionage since you came to Whitebridge, your wife would never have started havin' her doubts about you,' Woodend told him.

'She had her doubts, did she?'

'You know she did. That's why she all-but blackmailed Jamie Clegg into watchin' you.'

'This is all news to me.'

'No, it isn't. Jamie had what you might call a crisis of conscience, an' told you all about it. Once you knew what Constance was doin', you also knew that she had to die. An' in a hurry! Because the longer she lived, the more chance she had of exposin' you an' your network. But how to kill her – that was the question. My guess is that your first thought was poison, but then you decided that would be too risky.'

'Risky?' Bryant repeated, with mock incredulity. 'I'm not a criminologist myself, but I've talked to a fair number of them in my time. And the general consensus is that poisoning is the safest of all methods. Think about it, Chief Inspector. In many cases, the authorities don't even realize there's *been* a murder. And even if they do, the murderer doesn't need an alibi, because no one can say exactly when the poison was administered. You can rest assured that if I *had* been thinking of killing my wife, poison would certainly have been my weapon of choice.'

'No, it wouldn't,' Woodend contradicted him. 'Constance's minders in London were still keepin' an eye on her. They knew roughly how long she had to live, an' if she'd had died any sooner – even of apparently natural causes – they'd have suspected foul play.'

'Whereas, the idea of foul play would never have occurred to them at all if she had her throat slit and was dumped under a bonfire? Come on, Chief Inspector, that makes no sense at all!'

'If you don't treat me like an idiot, I'll promise not to treat you like one,' Woodend said. 'If she'd been the only woman to be murdered, her ex-bosses *would* have been suspicious. But if she was just *one* of the victims – an' all the victims seemed to have somethin' in common – then London might reasonably suppose that her death had nothin' to do with her former life. An' the plan worked out beautifully. That's exactly what the bowler-hatted brigade from London *did* think. I know – because I talked to them.' He paused for a second. 'Didn't you feel any guilt about what you did?'

'Whoever the killer was, he gave Betty and Lucy a little happiness in the last few weeks of their miserable lives,' Bryant said. 'As for their deaths, they were quick, and far more merciful than allowing the cancers to run their course.'

'Why did you fit your stepson up for the murders?'

'If I had have been the killer, then I would probably have considered framing Richard to be a calculated gamble. I'd have told myself that he'd be no worse off in an asylum for the criminally insane than he was before, and that once the police had arrested him, they'd stop looking for anybody else.'

'So you tipped off some reporter in London about Richard's background, an' he, in turn, tipped off Elizabeth Driver?'

'The thing about nasty pieces of work like Miss Driver is that it's usually quite easy to guess what they'll do in any given situation. It should have come as no surprise to anybody when – purely for her own ends – she made immediate contact with the police.'

'It was a mistake to use Richard's knife for the killin's, you know,' Woodend said.

'Was it?'

'A *big* mistake. Though I'd never have believed that he was capable of carryin' out three such well-planned murders, I might well have assumed – without the knife – that he'd been fitted up for the crimes by someone else on the outside. The forensic report made that an impossibility. The only people

331

who had access to the knife were you an' him – an' if he wasn't the killer, then it had to be you. See what I mean about bein' *too* clever?'

'I'm beginning to,' Bryant admitted.

Forty-One

Most of the children under parental supervision had now gone home, and the bonfires had become largely the domain of the bigger kids. For some of them, slipping penny bangers into other kids' pockets had still not lost its novelty. For others, the collapsed bonfires presented the ideal opportunity to show off their bravery and athleticism, and after taking a long run up, they would leap over the still-glowing wood. Bottles of beer and cider – bought under false pretences from the off-licence – were being opened now that the adults had cleared off, and several couples had moved away from the bonfire for a spot of slap and tickle. It was all a sight that the pious, fanatical Guy Fawkes would neither have understood nor approved of.

Woodend did not dare to look at his watch for fear of spooking Bryant too much, but he

332

calculated that at least thirty minutes must have passed since he entered the living room.

'Why did you put your victims in the bonfires?' he asked.

'Ah, a trick question – but not a very subtle one!' Bryant said. 'If I were to tell you about the disposal of the bodies, I'd be as good as admitting that I was the killer. Since I'm not, I'll have to say that I have no idea where the idea of using the bonfires come into it.'

'Then let me tell you what I think,' Woodend suggested. 'You wanted everybody to believe that there was a reason for the murders, but not a *rational* one. That was one of the attractions of choosin' cancer sufferers. From then on, any little refinement you could add which suggested that a lunatic was behind the killings could only be to your advantage. I suppose you could have decapitated your victims, or covered them in yellow paint, but the bonfires were an even better idea. There's somethin' so fundamental an' primeval about fire, isn't there?'

'That's rather fancy thinking for a PC Plod, isn't it?' Bryant asked.

'You can tell you're gettin' close to the truth when the man who doesn't want to hear it starts to insult you,' Woodend said mildly. 'The other advantage of usin' bonfires, of course, was that you could blame the whole thing on Richard, if you felt the need to. The idea that he might have been committin' involuntary suttee had my boss jumpin' through hoops with delight.'

'But not you?'

'No. Again, it seemed just a little *too* clever. Like somethin' a crime novelist – or a crime *reporter* – might have come up with.' Woodend lit a cigarette. 'Well, I've said my piece, an' I rather think the next move's up to you.'

'Is that all you've got on me?' Bryant asked, sounding slightly surprised.

'Isn't it enough?' Woodend countered.

Bryant yawned ostentatiously. 'To arrest me? To put me on trial? You know it isn't.'

Woodend nodded. 'You're probably right,' he agreed. 'So you're just goin' to have to give me a written confession, aren't you?'

'Why on earth should I do that?'

'Because if you don't, I *won't* arrest you at all.'

'And how is *that* a threat?'

Woodend took a drag on his Capstan. 'Towards the end of the war, I was seconded to an intelligence unit. Not as an intelligence officer myself, you understand. I was just in charge of the guards an' the escorts. But I did get to see how the intelligence officers worked. An' a terrible process it was. They didn't just question a man, which is what I'd been expectin' – they dismantled his mind. It still makes me break into a sweat, even thinkin' about it. Given the choice, I'd rather have had a bayonet through the gut any day of the week.'

'I assume there's a point to this story,' Bryant said coolly.

'Oh yes. If you won't confess then I can't arrest you – but I can tell MI5 about you. The fellers who work there don't need the sort of evidence a jury would demand. A hint – a suspicion – is good enough for them. Can you even imagine what they'd put you through? It'd be dyin' by degrees!'

'So let me get this straight,' Bryant said, sounding genuinely intrigued. 'You think I'm a spy, but you'll only hand me over to MI5 if I refuse to confess to the murders. In other words, you're quite willing to put the interests of the criminal justice system ahead of the interests of national security. Don't you think that's a little parochial?'

'Maybe, but I don't think I have any choice,' Woodend replied. 'As you've already pointed out, I'm just a PC Plod – a simple bobby. It's my job to arrest criminals. It's some other bugger's job to worry about the Russians.'

'I'd almost be inclined to accept your deal if I thought it might work,' Bryant told him.

'Does that mean you admit to killin' Elizabeth Stubbs, Lucy Tonge an' Constance Bryant?' Woodend asked.

He was trying to say the words casually, but there was a certain tightness – a certain constriction – in his voice which made Paniatowski wonder what the hell was going on.

Bryant noticed the change of tone, too. 'You're very formal all of a sudden, aren't you?' he asked.

'Just answer the question, if you don't mind,' Woodend said, the tightness still there.

'Yes, I killed them. There's not much point in denying it now, is there? But what I wanted to talk about was the deal you've just offered me.'

'Then by all means talk about it,' Woodend said, his voice sounding more normal again.

'If it were a choice between a long prison sentence and being handed over to the interrogators, then of course I'd choose the prison sentence,' Bryant said. 'But it would not be as simple as that. MI5 might agree to let me stand trial, but they'd never consent to me going to prison. The moment sentence had been passed, they'd insist I was handed over to them, and that, as you so rightly pointed out, is death by degree. And now, I really think I need a drink.'

Bryant walked over to the drinks' cabinet and opened the door. When he turned around again, there was a pistol in his hand.

'The gun doesn't change anythin', you know,' Woodend said. 'You're caught up in too big a web to be able to shoot your way out.'

'I take it you've got men posted outside.'

'Aye, a dozen of them,' Woodend lied. 'Isn't that right, Monika?'

'No,' Paniatowski replied. 'There *were* a dozen of them. By now, there'll be twice as many.'

'In that case, when I leave here, I'll be taking Sergeant Paniatowski with me as a hostage,' Bryant said.

'I can't allow you to do that,' Woodend told him.

'You can't stop me.'

'I can try.'

'If you do, I'll shoot you.'

'What would be the point of that?' Woodend asked. 'You know you're not goin' to escape. An' anyway, you're not really the hardened revolutionary you seem to think you are.'

'Aren't I?' Bryant demanded, clearly stung.

'No, you're not. Because you've got an aversion to killin' needlessly.'

Bryant laughed. 'You truly are amazing, Chief Inspector. You know that I've slit three women's throats – including my wife's. How can you say I've an aversion to killing?'

'Because it *was* only three.'

'One of us is mad,' Bryant said. 'And I'd be willing to put my money on you.'

'Maybe we're *both* a bit mad,' Woodend said. 'But my point's still valid. You didn't want to kill your wife, but you *had* to in order to protect your cover. An' once you'd decided to do that, you realized you'd have to kill other women if you were to create the necessary smokescreen for your motives. But why only two? Why not three or four? That would have been even more convincin'.'

'The more I killed, the bigger the risk of getting caught.'

'Bollocks!' Woodend said. 'Your plannin' was so meticulous that there was very little chance of you bein' apprehended. The fact is, you'd rather not have killed any of them, but if you *had to* kill, you calculated that two was the minimum number you could get away with. Then there's the bobbies I left guardin' the bonfire. You could have killed them, too, but you didn't. You haven't got the stomach to be a truly effective member of the KGB. You can't even stand to see ducks gettin' stoned in the park!'

'There may be a grain of truth in what you say,' Bryant agreed, 'but, as you've already pointed out, I *will* kill if I have to.'

'Say you did kill a couple of my lads an' made your escape. What good would it do you? Where would you run to?'

'Russia.'

'An' do you really think you'd be welcome there?'

'Why not? Burgess, MacLean and Philby all were.'

'Ah, but you see, they didn't escape – they defected.'

'What's the difference?'

'You shouldn't have to ask me that. You *know* the way spies' minds work. The Russians would never believe you'd managed anythin' as dramatic as an escape. They'd think that we'd *let* you get away, because we'd turned you. An' by the time they were convinced otherwise, you wouldn't have enough of your brain left to stuff a turkey with. That's what I meant earlier, when I said you were caught in too big a web to shoot your way out. I wasn't just talkin' about the men surroundin' this house. I was talkin' about the others – the men who'll never stop watchin' you, an' will never trust you again, whatever you do!'

Bryant raised the pistol, so that now it was pointing directly at Woodend's forehead.

'You can put up a very convincing argument when you want to,' he said. 'That line about me not wanting to kill needlessly was very impressive. But saying I hadn't got the stomach for it was a bit of a gamble. Are you really as confident as you sound, I wonder?'

'Well, of course I'm bloody not,' Woodend said, as a drop of sweat fell from his brow and rolled slowly down his cheek.

The explosions had abated a little, but they

had not ceased, and every time a penny banger went off somewhere in the distance, Rutter felt himself jump slightly.

He checked his watch again. It was forty-two minutes since he'd last spoken to Woodend and Paniatowski, three minutes before he was supposed to radio through to the station to say that something had gone seriously wrong.

He wondered if he should have done something before now – if he should have already disobeyed Woodend's orders and gone into the house. He was almost certain that if Paniatowski had been in his place, that was exactly what she would have done.

Another minute ticked by, and Rutter came to a decision. He would *not* call in reenforcements from the station. He would go into the house alone – because if Woodend and Paniatowski were in trouble, he should be the one who got them out of it.

It was then that he heard another explosion. It was not a banger this time. It was too loud for that – too ominous and final.

He was only yards from the house, but he broke into a sprint anyway. He tried the front door, and was not surprised to find it locked.

The door, like the rest of the house, was good and solid, and it took three kicks before the lock groaned and the wood around it splintered. Panting for breath, Rutter entered the hallway. There had only been one shot – he was fairly sure about that – but the air was thick with the stink of cordite.

The lounge door lay ahead of him. The sensible course – the one he had been trained to follow – was to call for back-up and not to do anything until it arrived. Instead, he opened the door, fully expecting a bullet to slam into him at any moment.

It was Paniatowski he saw first. She was sitting on the sofa, hugging herself tightly. And then he saw the body lying on the floor, with half its brain spread over the expensive carpet. He felt a shooting pain in his stomach, and knew he was about to be sick.

As he doubled over, he heard a voice from somewhere to his left say, 'That's the trouble with you lads who were never in the war – a bit of blood an' guts an' you turn all girly on me.'

Forty-Two

Woodend and Rutter were sitting opposite each other in Woodend's office. The Chief Inspector was talking on the phone to his boss, the inspector was examining the glowing end of his cigarette as if he thought it held the meaning to life.

Woodend replaced the receiver on its cradle. 'I look forward to the day when we get a result that will actually please Mr Marlowe,' he said. 'I look forward to it – but I'm not holdin' my breath waitin' for it to arrive.'

'He shouldn't have been in such a hurry to arrest Richard Quinn,' Rutter said.

'He knows that – an' he knows that *we* know it – an' that only makes it worse. No organ grinder likes to admit it's really the monkey that's runnin' the show.' He paused. 'I'm not sure you deserve it, Bob, but I've got Elizabeth Driver off your back.'

'How did you do that?'

'Read tomorrow's *Globe*. The answer should be obvious.'

'You gave her an exclusive, didn't you?'

'Aye. While other newspapers are runnin' the story about Richard Quinn, the *Globe* will be leadin' with the real story – or at least, part of it.'

'I know how much that must have cost you,' Rutter said, feeling thoroughly ashamed of himself. 'I never meant to put you in that position, sir.'

'You *didn't* put me in it. I could have let you sink if I'd wanted to, but I *chose* to throw you a lifebelt instead.' Woodend lit up a Capstan. 'You'll be breakin' it off with Monika now, will you?'

'It's as good as done,' Rutter said, wondering if he really had the strength to see that particular promise through.

'An' have you told Maria about it?'

'Not yet.'

'Then don't! You've already been your own worst enemy. Don't turn yourself in to Maria's as well.'

'I want to be honest with her,' Rutter protested.

'What you mean is, you want to assuage your guilt by confessin' your sins.'

'Yes, there's that as well.'

Woodend clapped his inspector on the shoulder. 'Suffer for your sins, lad,' he advised. 'It's character buildin'.'

There was the sound of footsteps in the corridor, then the door swung open to reveal a dapper – and very angry – man with a silver moustache.

'I've been away from London far too long to remember how people behave down there,' Woodend said, 'but here in Lancashire it's considered polite to knock before you enter anybody's office.'

Perkins glared at him. 'I'd like a word with you in private.'

Rutter started to rise to his feet.

'Stay where you are, Bob,' Woodend told him. 'Anythin' you've got to say, Mr Perkins, you can say in front of my inspector.'

'It's about the matter we discussed the other night,' Perkins said, through clenched teeth.

'Aye, I thought it might be,' Woodend said, 'but you can still speak freely. Inspector Rutter knows all about Constance Bryant's double life.'

Perkins scowl widened into outrage. 'You said you'd keep that information strictly to yourself.'

'I know I did, but I had my fingers crossed when I was sayin' it.'

'This isn't a game!' Perkins exploded.

'Yes, it is,' Woodend told him. 'However you choose to see yourselves, the truth is that all you spies are nothin' more than big kids. What was it you wanted to ask me?'

'I want to know if it's true that Dexter Bryant was a Russian agent.'

'Yes, it is. He confessed as much himself,

just before he killed himself.'

'We should have been told.'

'I'm tellin' you now.'

'And what good is that – once he's dead?'

'I think you're contradictin' yourself a bit there,' Woodend replied. 'You told me that if the opposition knew Constance Bryant had been a spy, the KGB would be able to track down the others in her network easy enough. Well, surely, you're in the same position with Dexter. Now you know he was a spy, you should be able to start roundin' up all his little mates.'

'We'd rather have had *him*! Once you suspected him, you should have contacted us immediately.'

'I lost your telephone number,' Woodend said, making no attempt to sound convincing. 'As Bob here will tell you, I'm very careless with things like that.'

'This will reflect very badly on your record,' Perkins said. 'Very badly indeed.'

Then he swivelled on his heel and marched off furiously down the corridor.

They were sitting at their table in the Drum and Monkey. The waiter had just served them their drinks – a pint of bitter, a half of bitter and a double vodka – and now they were free to talk.

Yet Woodend didn't seem as willing as usual to open up, Paniatowski thought. It

345

was almost as if he had a burden on his mind which he was not quite ready to shed.

'I've just been on to the psychiatric ward of Whitebridge General,' she said, to fill in the silence. 'They're keeping Richard Quinn in for observation tonight, but they think he should be fit to be discharged in the morning.'

Rutter nodded. Woodend didn't even seem to have heard her.

'I've called Dr Shastri as well,' Paniatowski continued. 'She's cutting up what's left of Dexter Bryant's skull, as per regulations, but she's got a sneaking suspicion that it was the bullet which killed him.'

'I'm sorry I had to tell so many lies,' Woodend said, coming out of his semi-trance.

'Lies?' Rutter repeated. 'Who exactly did you lie *to*?'

'Pretty much everybody involved, starting with the pair of you,' Woodend said guiltily. 'I told you Bryant wouldn't have a gun, but I knew he would. I took you in there under false pretences, Monika.'

'It wouldn't have made any difference if I'd known the truth,' Paniatowski said. 'I'd have gone in with you, anyway.'

'An' I lied to Bryant. But maybe that doesn't count – because he *knew* I was lyin'.'

'What exactly did you lie to him about?' Rutter asked.

'I told him he'd be safe from MI5 if he

346

confessed to the murders. That wasn't true at all. They'd never have let him stand trial – or even be charged with the murders. He was too valuable to them for that.'

'Then what was the point of—?'

'Worse still, they'd have sacrificed somebody else in order to save Bryant for themselves.'

'Richard Quinn?'

'That's right. Richard would have been tried and convicted, while Bryant was quietly whisked off to an interrogation centre.'

'You think they'd actually have done that?'

'I'm certain they would.'

'But I don't see what MI5 would have got out of behaving in that way,' Rutter said.

'Don't you?' Woodend asked. 'Then I'll explain. As I see it, an espionage ring is no more than a piece of machinery – but it's a far more complex piece of machinery than the engine in my Wolseley. It takes years to build up, an' once you've tinkered with it – once you've altered the delicate balance – it'll be more years before it starts runnin' smoothly again. Are you startin' to get the point?'

'Not really,' Rutter confessed.

'If Bryant had been arrested, his controller would have been reluctant to dismantle the network, but he'd have done it anyway – because he would have thought he didn't have any choice. But what if Bryant *hadn't* been arrested? What if he'd only *disappeared*? Then his controller's facin' a real dilemma.'

'His training tells him to shut down the network as soon as possible,' Rutter said.

'But his survival instinct tells him there may be a perfectly harmless reason for Bryant's disappearance – and that if Bryant re-emerges a few days later to find he no longer has a network left to run, it's the controller's own neck which is going to be on the block,' Paniatowski added.

'Now you're gettin' it,' Woodend said. 'So for the moment, the controller does nothin'. And that's exactly what the security people want! By allowin' Richard to go on trial rather than his stepfather, MI5's buyin' itself time – time to find out what Bryant knows, time to organize a swoop on his network before it vanishes into thin air.'

'So even if you'd got a written confession out of Bryant, it wouldn't have made any difference,' Paniatowski said.

'That's right,' Woodend agreed. 'The paperwork would simply have disappeared. An' however much I ranted an' raved about it, the people who matter – includin' our beloved Chief Constable – would have denied that it ever existed.'

'But once Bryant was dead, he'd no longer be of any use to the security services, so there'd be no point in them denying he was responsible for the killings?' Rutter asked.

'Exactly. An' the moment that became true, then even a *verbal* confession would become quite valuable. Especially a verbal confession delivered by a man who knew he was on the point of death, an' so had nothin' to lose by telling the truth in front of two police witnesses.'

The implications of what Woodend had said were having a disturbing effect on Rutter. 'In other words, the only way Richard Quinn was ever going to avoid going down for the murders was through Bryant's death,' he said.

'That's how I saw it.'

'And so you persuaded him – you *cajoled* him – to kill himself!' Rutter said, outraged.

'Did I?' Woodend asked.

'That's certainly how it looks to me.'

Woodend turned to Paniatowski. 'Is that how *you* see it, Monika?'

'No sir, it isn't.'

'Then you don't really need to hear what I've got to say next, so you might as well go an' get another round of drinks.'

'The waiter can—'

'I'd prefer it if you did it,' Woodend said firmly.

Paniatowski nodded, stood up, and walked over to the bar.

'Do you remember the conversation we had at this table just yesterday?' Woodend asked Rutter. 'The conversation about you

349

an' Monika?'

'Yes, but what's that—?'

'I said you shouldn't go blamin' Elizabeth Driver for your troubles. I said that if you had a gun at your head, it was your own actions which had put it there.'

'I'm not sure it's exactly—'

'It *is* exactly the same. I'm no god. I'm not even an amateur puppet master. I didn't tell Dexter Bryant to become a spy. I didn't create the situation in which he couldn't win – whatever he did. He put the gun to his own head – an' he was the one who decided to pull the trigger.'